We the Oodles

We the Oodles

Atul Kumar

PRABHAT
PAPERBACKS

Published by
PRABHAT PAPERBACKS
4/19 Asaf Ali Road,
New Delhi-110 002 (INDIA)
e-mail: prabhatbooks@gmail.com

ISBN 978-93-90378-03-6
WE THE OODLES
by Shri Atul Kumar

Edition
First, 2020

Price
₹ 400.00 (Rupees Four Hundred only)

Printed at
R-Tech Offset Printers, Delhi

To my
Late Parents

Prologue

This book is not to tell the world that for decades, the International Cricket has been nothing but a continuous hoax on the unsuspecting masses, though that will get repeated through this book. That was done years ago through earlier books, press conferences by me. The issue has continuously been highlighted for years through similar and more painstaking efforts including the filing of a successful PIL (public interest litigation) in the Hon'ble Supreme Court of India. That has been a fait accompli now. If the world still remains largely unaware, it has to ask questions of itself or the media it has created and has been nurturing to keep itself informed. This book is to convey something much beyond, much deeper—and that something will sink into any intelligent reader by the time he finishes reading this book, hopefully even if one doesn't have much open mind to start with.

What is so openly happening in cricket and is well proven; in all probability should be happening more or less in football and other sports of the world also that are open to betting. The purpose of this book is to make us realise what we are in reality—deep down—under the façade of being just, righteous, cultured and civilised. That realisation should not come as a result of someone's word, someone saying so, but from the churning of facts—hard facts—in our conscious and subconscious mind, of our own volition. Those facts have been there all along for years, but unknown to the majority, or lying neglected by those who knew—discarded because these were unpalatable, neglected because their minds conditioned by vested interests failed to value these. It is being attempted to present those facts at a place now through this book, along with my commentary, for ready reference and critical examination of the public, the intelligentsia, and for posterity.

The realisation of the truth is the first prerequisite for us to make any honest efforts to raise ourselves up, from being just manipulated numbers; but it is not going to be easy, given our evolution, and given how difficult it is for a man to shed his conceit, and how near impossible it is for him not to be a hypocrite. Yet I have no option but to continue trying till I breathe and till my faculties work.

While this book brings out and documents the interactions with the Supreme Court of India, on the issue of on-going monumental fraud and crime through the game of cricket, the purpose is not to point fingers at the Hon'ble Court. As a matter of fact, the purpose is not to point fingers at individuals or even institutions, but to make us realise our collective shame. It is imperative that fingers will still get raised in the process, even though that is not the intent. When there is something fundamentally wrong with everything, pinpointing individuals or institutions becomes meaningless. In telling facts and in order to bring out the correct overall perspective, the individuals and the institutions do get blasted. The contents of this book need to be understood and appreciated in this context.

The documents incorporated in the book are to validate and confirm its contents, giving readers a first-hand knowledge of all that has transpired. Readers may find some of the essence of this book in the documents also even if pursued independently. There is also bound to be a lot of repetition in between various documents for obvious reasons. I had to go on writing repeatedly, all the authorities including India's top Court having decided to go under deep slumber!

Hope the book makes an interesting reading for all, not only for those interested in cricket. In fact, it is aimed to address all the educated and intellectuals of the world, whether interested or not interested in cricket. The book should markedly intrigue the Indian and Pakistani armed forces. It should excite tens of thousands of law enforcers in India and other cricket-playing nations. It should especially fascinate the students and practitioners of law since it chronicles how truth and conviction helped a common man overcome the strong judicial barriers (credit goes both ways!) and indeed force the mighty Supreme Court of India to unmask itself, even in pre-Corona days. Last but not the least, the medical fraternity and the authorities grappling with COVID-19 will have a lot to think about after going through this book.

As the erudite readers go through this book, I am sure they will appreciate that I get liberty from none other than Time and Truth to say whatever I have said in this copy.

Contents

Initiation to the Incredible

At a time when the dread of the pandemic COVID-19 has forced almost whole of the world to put on masks, cricket has been finding it hard to get appropriate masks for it. Still, it's not bothered, it has nothing to worry. Even unmasked, it has unfailing immunity to authorities' clutches and people's wrath. Cricket was first unmasked years ago, but remained cloaked in dreaming people's imagination. Most of these billions are still asleep, helped by the continuous doses of sleeping pills being given by the cricket experts and the media. The global media has seen to it that any attempts by anyone to wake people up from their slumber from time to time don't succeed.

Time has its own strange ways of settling scores. While all those in authority play with time, trying to use it to their own advantage, with the least regard to the Truth, Time continues acting unknown to them and as least expected by them. In this case, all those in authority in cricket and outside including establishments and the media let the time go by and let the hoax continue and prosper. They all were power-drunk, feeling like God, since all those who mattered were cohorts; but they forgot history, they all acted too moron to realise the ultimate power of Truth and Time. Today same Time—7 long years of inaction by all who mattered—has left them defenceless, because even any attempt by anyone to explain inaction for so long (when same for even a few days is inexplicable) would just be laughable! The authorities, both cricketing and law-enforcing, just can't absolve themselves through any explanations or excuses now for feigning blind and not acting at all for years on a repeatedly reported big-time crime even though confronted with a plethora of evidence to act upon. Same applies to the media—much more so than the concerned authorities. They all have hung themselves well and truly with the rope they went on giving to selves for seven long years.

Moreover, for more than last couple of years, the fact of cricket being 'institutionally fixed' has been too open, more so in recent times, through tens of tippers crowding various social media platforms like twitter, telegram channel, WhatsApp, YouTube, etc., and catching clients through amazingly correct tips at times, only to fool and rob them later on and beyond. These amazingly correct predictions are far too frequent—many times a day—to rule out any possibility of a coincidence. This has already been brought out in my various public posts and communications to the Hon'ble Supreme Court of India including the writ petition (PIL). The repeated amazingly correct such tips beforehand in social media day and night make the existence of large-scale continuous fixing in cricket so readily obvious that only ignorant or incorrigible buffoons can still have any doubts. Such continuous large-scale fixing in international cricket just cannot be possible if it was not institutionalised.

Why to go to betting tips even; one must comprehend when one sees a batsman of Pollard's caliber tapping the last ball of a T20 match for a single when a four was required to win, the conspicuous absence of even the effort tells it all! Again, one comes across such inexplicable efforts from the world-class cricketers—batsmen, bowlers, fielders alike—many a time in every match. Being blind-sided, one fails to grasp what was happening. A glimpse of this was also brought out years ago by the eminent journalist Shantanu Guha Ray through his article *'Arrested bookie Sanjeev Chawla to confess how spot-fixing works in international cricket'* dated 29/9/2016 published in Firstpost (website). Following is some relevant excerpt from that article:

> '...Chawla, whose case will be heard at the Westminster Magistrates' Court in London on 3 October, has told his interrogators that spot-fixing (which replaced match-fixing) was rampant with huge stakes of money at play.
>
> Last week, his interrogators conveyed to the Delhi Police how a top Indian bookie splurged ₹ 5 crores every day for a four-day gig at one of the biggest casinos in Las Vegas, home to gambling in the US. "The bookie, based in South India, organised cash through *hawala* and had a great time during his stay in Vegas," a top Delhi Police source said.
>
> Chawla, considered the biggest cog in the 'fixing wheel' by cops in Delhi and Mumbai, could be headed for India next month, requests for his extradition by the Ministry of External Affairs already accepted by the British government through its foreign office.
>
> "Chawla also named a top Indian cricketer, now retired but we will not be able to reveal the name," a top source in the Crime Branch of Delhi Police said in a brief interview. Investigators in London have agreed to share

crucial details they collected from Chawla with the help of Interpol and associates of the bookie.

Officers of the Crime Branch said they are in touch with their counterparts in Mumbai, Chennai and a few other cities high on the betting radar, and would be interrogating a large number of alleged bookies and former cricketers.

The interrogators of Chawla said the bookie also shed some light on the recent West Indies-Pakistan match at the Sheikh Zayed Stadium in Abu Dhabi and how the Caribbean batting in the third and final T20 was a total give-away of what Chawla described as 'institutionalised fixing of international cricket'.

Chawla explained the entire fixing operandi and how it worked in this particular match, Delhi Police officials who are in touch with his interrogators in London said. In the end overs, with decent wickets in hand, the hard-hitting Caribbean batsmen like Samuels and Pollard—known for hitting huge sixes—played dots and took singles, not even attempting to hit a boundary. "He (Chawla) explained how the team—a T20 World Cup winner few months ago—folded up at an abysmal low of 103/5 in 20 overs, failing miserably for the third consecutive time and how the matches looked fixed because nothing in cricket or in logic explained the way the West Indies batted in the three-match series." Chawla explained to his interrogators—who, in turn, explained the same to the counterparts in Delhi.

"Anyone betting on the Caribbean cricketers will expect the team to play its natural game and accelerate

> at least from 16 overs onwards with five wickets in hand and place bets accordingly. But, strangely, WI did just the opposite. They scored only 26 runs in the last four overs and 28 runs in the last five overs with five wickets still in hand. Nothing in cricket or in logic can explain West Indian batting," said Atul Kumar, an author and exponent of modern-day sports betting and cricket spot-fixing. Cops of Delhi Police say they will work on multiple leads when Chawla returns to India and that interrogations will happen in both the cases—the 2000 India-South Africa series and the 2013 IPL spot-fixing…'

There are a few things worth noting from the above. One that the journalists tend to use the term 'spot-fixing' as a fashion for fixing since while the heading of this article uses the term 'spot-fixing', the content is telling of 'institutionalised fixing' in international cricket, there being a vast material difference between the two terms. Secondly, the media at large remained totally hushed on such an explosive report and its content. It is the same media that would continue reporting on and discussing some petty local scam for days. A very substantial report highlighting that international cricket was institutionally fixed meant nothing to it. Yet we allow ourselves to be governed by such outrageously fake media. Thirdly, no one knows or is bothered to know as to what happened regarding follow-up by the concerned authorities of many important points brought out in this report. Last but not the least, no one sought to seek any answers from the ICC, from the cricket authorities. The institutionally fixed cricket continued insanely and merrily.

And, therefore, one fine day, on 8th June, 2020, when Sudhir Chaudhury on Zee TV in their programme 'DNA' talked about match-fixing in cricket consequent upon reported revelations a week ago by the same Sanjeev Chawla (the bookie) to Delhi Police that "no cricket match is fairly played" and "...all the cricket matches which people see are fixed", it was quite amusing hearing what he talked. Sanjeev Chawla had also pointed to the involvement of 'a very big syndicate/underworld mafia' that influences all cricket games that, according to him, were like 'movies which are already being directed by someone'. Credit to Zee for at least raising the issue in the main-line media talking of some of the very serious implications as well, since all or almost all electronic and print media that mattered had maintained a deafening silence till then, even after the sensational report in the Indian Express dated 30th May, 2020 for the first time.

Sudhir Chaudhury mentioned of the possible/suspected murder of Hansie Cronje and Bob Woolmer. But he didn't mention anything about Sunanda Pushkar. He didn't tell the millions of viewers what Sanjeev Chawla said about cricket had also been said by none other than Bishen Singh Bedi about IPL about a couple of years ago in different words. Sudhir Chaudhury like all his peers didn't tell viewers how many top cricketers and other insiders had been telling frequently and repeatedly that Cricket was fixed. The viewers were kept ignorant of many revelations over the years that had been in line with what Sanjeev Chawla had said, another sensational and all-revealing exposé by Al Jazeera about two years ago being one of those (it is detailed in my rejoinder to COA/BCCI's report documented in this book). Whether Sudhir Chaudhury did so out of his ignorance, out of journalistic incompetence, or whether he did it deliberately, he would know best.

While allegations by a bookie rated very highly with Sudhir Chaudhury, the same thing having been brought out successfully in a detailed petition to the Hon'ble Supreme Court of India, the highest platform for the country, by two responsible citizens of the country, giving plethora of evidence—in fact, a repository of it—didn't mean anything to him even now, not even worth mentioning. Leave alone what all had progressed or hadn't progressed consequent to that petition including meeting of petitioners with COA/BCCI, their report and my rejoinder. Zee is supposedly one of the biggest media houses of India.

Sudhir Chaudhary left his viewers, at least me, wondering what he wanted to convey and what his purpose was, when he abruptly ended his talk leaving a WhatsApp number and inviting public to tell anything anyone knew about match-fixing on that number or his or Zee's twitter handles. So, here was Zee Media telling the world that it was ignorant of the tens or hundreds of tippers openly telling about fixing of and fixing in various cricket matches day and night for more than a couple of years over various social media platforms. It was totally ignorant of the fact of a petition saying all cricket matches were fixed having successfully passed the scrutiny of even the Supreme Court of India years ago. This talk by Sudhir Chaudhary summed up Zee and the media as a whole.

While Zee News through their editor-in-chief Sudhir Chaudhary announced height of media's incompetence/complicity in crime to the world, on the other hand, the sports editor of the Statesman, a leading English daily of India, had this to say about the issue of match-fixing in cricket, media, and society, through his weekly column 'short point' a day before.

‘Back home, Chawla confirms cricket’s make-believe character

PULAKESH MUKHOPADHYAY

If the world weren’t ravaged by the novel coronavirus now and everyone virtually everywhere, masked or not, weren’t feeling so utterly helpless in the face of its apparently irresistible inroads, with talk of a second wave dominating social discourse in some horribly affected lands, Sanjeev Chawla’s backhome

comments, duly reported by the media, might have kicked off a few storms in the

argumentative Indian’s sporting teacup, at breakfast or later. Urban and semi-urban segments of the country might have debated their validity with their customary alacrity and their ability to move on to something else that makes for longer, fruitier conversations, online or offline, like the pregnancy of a controversial cricketer’s glamorous live-in friend or Virat Kohli’s lockdown hairstyle.

These, after all, happen to figure high among the subjects readers are sought to be lured with, though the practitioners of the craft of glossy trash don’t really disabuse us of the notion that they are up against it despite purportedly knowing the magic of the marketplace.

But given the way things are, it’s been as easy as ABC for pandemic-dominated India socially to distance itself from two nuggets of obviously interesting information supplied by Chawla, of match-fixing infamy and extradited after a lot of hurdle surmounting from Old Blighty.

"All cricket matches we see," goes part of his spiel, "are fixed."

Chawla has also been quoted as saying that those games are akin to movies plotted and filmed by a director whom we don't know, see or hear. Much the same, of course, has been said for years at a stretch by Atul Kumar, whose mathematical mind is at the core of the series of books he has written on cricket corruption, betting and allied subjects.

He has gone to the global authorities, our own control-oriented board and the court of law, but felt shaken off. Nothing came of it all. He has also aimed at greater public awareness of the phenomena—going about it with a crusading zeal—but his press conferences in Kolkata have foundered on the rock of journalistic incomprehension of his basically academic approach.

"What's the proof you've got?" has been the question he has come to be asked, and his answer wasn't the sort that made for instant copy and headlines.

One is left wondering how those sceptics, many of whom didn't even bother to write a line subsequently, reacted—if at all—once a confirmation of a researcher's proposition came from the other end of the spectrum: the man who pulls the string and gets things done and stashes the cash away

Chawla has reportedly spoken of his elaborative inability, considering a perceived

threat to his life from his presumably erstwhile accomplices.

Away from those who take only a superficial interest

in things like this, even the media might not really feel inclined to delve deeper into the subject as that could knock the bottom out of the archetypal hack's everyday chore, with his gloves on or without.

The virus, thus, has the run of the world of cricket, such as it is, and there is no vaccine to stop its incursions.'

The seasoned editor, the only one in the world from media to raise his voice so comprehensively and so eloquently against the fraud of cricket in its totality, repeatedly, has said a lot, in fact, whatever he could, in the above column which has been his own space.

After some deliberations in my mind, in response to invitation by Sudhir Chaudhury, I sent the following message after a few days to the given WhatsApp number:

"While credit is due to Zee News for raking up the issue when most of other media has still maintained a deadly silence, very strangely Zee News has shown its total ignorance to the world through talk by Sudhir Chaudhary, editor-in-chief, in prime-time show DNA on the evening of 8th June, 2020 on the subject of match-fixing in cricket, consequent to reported explosive revelations by Sanjeev Chawla. Many exposés on match-fixing which have been swept under the carpet by the media time and again over the last many years were not mentioned yet again.

But since you have asked people to come out with any information they have, please go through this write-up by the sports editor of the Statesman, published in this national daily on 7th June, 2020, a day before your above telecast:

'Back home, Chawla confirms cricket's make-believe character...' (the complete write-up as above was reproduced.)

I am Atul Kumar mentioned in the above article. An encyclopedia of evidence already exists in the public domain to show that what Sanjeev Chawla is reported to have told the Delhi Police is the stark reality. If you are interested in letting your viewers know the truth, you may kindly respond and contact me further.

Since now I am contacting you this way, you being a powerful Media House may please take the necessary action through the Government of India or the Courts to ensure my safety now onwards in view of what Sanjeev Chawla reportedly told about there being a threat to his life from the powerful mafia if he spilled the bins further.

Your response to this and your subsequent actions will establish your true intentions in the subject matter and your credibility as a responsible media house.

While you may again go to sleep in response to it or mislead the world as you along with other media have been doing for years, but I do hope that nothing untoward happens to me as a result of this message. Needless to say, the record of this message will be available to many people.

Thank you."

I also asked Zee media to acknowledge my above message. The message to the much publicised WhatsApp number went unanswered/unattended/ undelivered. Without my bringing this out here (an accidental happening), the world would probably never have known what jokes were being cracked by the big media on public. I didn't hear anything further on the issue on Zee or anywhere else. The whole media and all the journalists, without any exception, had again forgotten everything about cricket matches being fixed—in no time.

The above are chance developments having happened during the course of writing of this book. These, I hope, would make it a bit easier for the readers to grasp what this book proposed to convey anyway. The fact that when these explosive all telling revelations were coming out even recently in some part of media, media at large was still not only silent on these, but was continuing to talk about and promote cricket and cricketers as always; the world remaining as unconcerned as it has ever been—is in the backdrop of what this book is all about.

While this is not the purpose of this book to bring out the failings or inadequacies or disinclinations of the august institution of the Supreme Court of India per se, that is bound to happen through this book, being unavoidable. Since developments in the Supreme Court of India over the years are necessary for one to understand how humanity has been evolving and how we stand today as a people. The point is that the Supreme Court of India is the supreme institution created under the Constitution of India, by the people of India, to safeguard the interests of the masses when every other institution is failing or has failed. If the Supreme Court of India also falters so openly and as blatantly as one would see in this book, for reasons best known to them, we have to understand that we have failed collectively, in our evolution—through the institutions and systems created and developed by us. It has been and it would be suicidal for us to accept so with a resigned attitude and move on. As an extremely unfortunate occurrence, the tragedy of COVID-19 that befell the world during the course of drafting of this book confirmed so through making those in India and the world see how overall degradation in our systems in the course of our evolution made us suffer many times more than was necessary.

The objective of this book is to bring home our collective failure as a people—in addressing a massive international public fraud that has been continuing unabashedly. To bring home the fact of how falsehood and folly have been the twin foundations of our evolution, notwithstanding our pretensions and boastings otherwise. I doubt if anything else can establish that as indisputably as the contents of this book would. Though the recent pandemic of COVID-19 has belatedly made at least some of us realise this stark truth, it has been too evident all along. We all had just been closing our eyes till nature forced us to open the same. Once we realise our failings and accept them, corrections are bound to follow automatically. It is for this reason it becomes necessary for us all to know and appreciate the truth rather than to go on defeating self, indulging in self-deception.

I do hope that with the little awakening forced by nature through the recent global pandemic, still around, the intelligentsia of the society will at last wake up to the contents of this book to guide them. The readers' minds must be pure and open, devoid of any preconceived notions about any individual or any institution. For example, to assume that Tendulkar or Dravid or Kumble or Lara or Richards or Ponting or Vaughan (I can go on and on) or National Security Advisor (NSA) (of India) or the Supreme Court had to be and would be above board could be self-deceiving for one. One will have to forget the reputations and will have to go by hard facts on record, and try to apply an unconditioned mind to the facts and developments.

As mentioned in the beginning, what gets repeated through this book is the indisputable, unparalleled, and incredible fact of existence for more than a decade of a magnificent fraud and crime and it's still continuation, a big source of terror funding as well—so massive that readers may find it very difficult to comprehend (and yet it very much stares us all in the face 24 × 7)—through thoroughly fixed and scripted international and league cricket. Undoubtedly, it is a matter of great collective shame for us. The shame emanates from the existence of the fraud itself, and much more from the fact that it continues unbridled despite being exposed for the last long seven years repeatedly at all possible public and official forums and platforms. **The continuance of the unfettered fraud defies and mocks at all human religions, norms, rules, conventions, laws, sermons, and Constitutions that the mankind has lived by and lives by.** Better if one pauses, thinks, and visualises the import of these words before proceeding further. Because I doubt if words—all the evolved adjectives combined—can even remotely express the depth, vastness and reach of the fraud as it has been existing. One will have to think and use grey cells a bit to understand and comprehend it because it defies everything about society and governments we have grown up believing—through our conditioned minds. Things should become clearer as one proceeds and goes through the documents incorporated in this book, and knows about the unbelievable inaction of all the authorities one can think of, none excluded.

As mentioned above, more significant is the fact that such

a massive fraud continues unfettered even seven years after having been publicly exposed and having been mathematically proven, having been highlighted repeatedly since then—all the authorities in India including Prime Minister and President of India, the parliamentarians, BCCI and ICC, the Indian and international media, Mudgal and Lodha Commissions, and, most unfortunately, even the Supreme Court of India having chosen to act deaf, dumb, and blind or unconcerned, allowing the fraud to continue and prosper all the time.

To understand the above, let us consider this quote of Lewis Mumford: ***'Man's main purpose is the creation and preservation of values; that is what gives meaning to our civilisation, and the participation in this is what gives significance, ultimately, to the individual human life..!!'*** The continuation of a colossal fraud as mentioned above certainly is something opposite to the creation and preservation of values.

There are three main aspects:

1. The existence of a massive fraud
2. Large-scale ignorance of it (doing of the media)
3. Total apathy to it by the society to the extent people are aware and by all the authorities.

While the second aspect signifies failure of media in totality as an institution, it is the third aspect that is the most depressing and forces us to introspect a lot. The continuation of this colossal fraud is like thousands of rapes and murders taking place all around in the open and yet the rapists and the murderers being allowed to remain at large, continuing with the crimes. That is happening in a society that boasts of and poses as being highly cultured and civilised. And to my mind that renders all our literature meaningless and all talks of spirituality as height of hypocrisy, because, in reality, we are not only accepting and allowing to continue, but also are continuously celebrating a crime equivalent to thousands of rapes and murders. I give this comparison in another attempt to make the readers and the world gauge the magnitude of the crime and comprehend how hypocrisy and folly have been ruling us at least in the last decade, leading us to our waterloo.

It is not that I am the first to talk of these traits governing the humanity. This was highlighted in internationally much acclaimed books '*Animal Farm*' by George Orwell, and '*Catch-22*' by Joseph Heller decades ago. Those were iconic works of fiction. Through this book—a work of non-fiction—one would be amazed to see for sure how hypocrisy along with attendant foolishness has been governing the conceited humans.

Let us try to understand this with a very recent example (that came into being after the first completion of the manuscript by me). The unfortunate death of a young highly talented actor Sushant Singh Rajput in mysterious circumstances became a continuous topic for discussion for many days all over the Indian media. No complaints for that. Scripting and execution of cricket matches day and night like movies are directed is a much greater mystery, each match a crime much bigger, surely involving hundreds of celebrities hundred times more powerful than the suspected involvement of a few in Sushant's death. The whole thing is too intriguing. Yet, in total contrast, the same media doesn't consider it even worth a mention, or at best makes some stray mention once in a blue moon—to forget the next moment. We, the people, especially the intellectuals, think about or talk about anything only if the media does. Something akin to this has also been said by Yuval Noah Harari, the well-known and leading present day thinker in the world.

This is what Harari said in an interview to Times of India as reported in early September 2018 (https://timesofindia.indiatimes.com/home/sunday-times/all-that-matters/in-the-news-market-youre-not-the-customer-but-the-product-yuval-noah-harari/articleshow/65639339.cms):

> '....In every age, the problem of telling the difference between fiction and reality manifests itself in a different way. In past centuries, people suffered from a severe lack of information, which made it difficult to verify what's true. Today we suffer from too much information, so people are too distracted to investigate the truth. There are so many things competing for our attention that our attention itself becomes a scarce resource. The struggle to capture people's attention has resulted in a destructive model for the news industry: "exciting news that cost you nothing—in exchange for your attention". Our attention is captured by sensational headlines, and is then sold to advertisers and politicians. In this battle for attention, there is little incentive to safeguard the truth.
>
> You might think that you are nevertheless getting a good bargain here. You don't have to pay anything, and you are entertained with interesting stories. But, in fact, you are not the customer at all, you arc thc product. You are being sold. You are giving up your most valuable asset—your attention—and you allow powerful corporations and politicians to brainwash you. That's crazy.....'

The shocking death of Sushant Singh Rajput is just one recent example; one will find hundreds of such examples, much less significant, over last many years. We all feel sure that we have brains, but do we? Will anyone with slightest brain bother, worry and think about anything silly or not so silly, but will not care a damn about an all-embracing gigantic deceit and fraud just because media or authorities or leaders don't tell to do so? Exactly this has been happening for years. We, the intellectuals, across our professions, gender, age, or religion, have been heatedly deliberating in social media on mysterious death of SSR, and all other issues raised in the media over the years, but don't utter a word about all cricket matches being fixed just because media assiduously refrains from raising this issue. Doesn't it amply show that largely we go through life as puppets, more than being free spirits? It may hurt us deeply to realize so, it may hurt our ego no end; but if we are honest to ourselves, it should not be much difficult to grasp that indeed it is so. Yuval Noah Harari, after all, is no fool. More on this in later chapters.

By the time one finishes this book, one would feel like coming out of a fairy tale, hardly able to ingest and accept the starkest reality of modern times largely unknown till now. One would be left wondering about the inadequacy of even the Supreme Court of India and asking oneself: "How can the Supreme Court of India be so unconcerned/protective to such an immense ongoing public fraud and crime?" One would also be wondering for sure what Prime Minister Modi and his government in India meant by claiming zero tolerance against corruption since assuming power in 2014. Because more than anyone else, it was he and his government who let the crime continue unhindered even after the same was brought to their notice repeatedly for years. No one can deny full knowledge of the crime to the government after the copies of the petition and subsequent submissions to the Hon'ble Supreme Court of India were served to it, even if acknowledgements of various letters to top executives earlier in this regard weren't considered enough by anyone. The same applies to the BCCI (Board of Control for Cricket in India) and the ICC (International Cricket Council)—they having been made aware repeatedly earlier also.

The correct actions can follow only after honest realisation. We must understand what has become of us, the people. Which traits are leading our evolution? Then only any conscious efforts for course correction can start. The documentation is brought out because that is necessary to make the world aware of and understand beyond any doubt what reality is. Readers will judge by themselves whether and how the Hon'ble Supreme Court of India and judicial commissions appointed by it erred/failed in their responsibilities to the people of India. But the real criminals have been the ICC, BCCI, and the cricket world—continuing to commit a colossal crime in letter and spirit. And the Government of India, along with its various law-enforcing agencies, viz., the Police, CBI (Central Bureau of Investigation), ED (Enforcement Directorate), NSA (National Security Advisor), etc., has been in default in allowing the criminals to continue with the crime for years. The door of the Hon'ble Supreme Court of India had to be knocked at since all others were failing to address the issue, but sadly that august institution also failed to rise to the occasion. So much so that now a claim of ₹ one crore (₹ 10 million) compensation by me against it (that letter is documented in this book later on) is pending unattended even though lying registered by the Court for about a year. Other cricket-playing nations also can't escape the blame since the deceit in the name of cricket has been equally rampant in all such countries. That must force us for the much-needed introspection and reflection as a people, **beyond boundaries of institutions and beyond borders**.

It is no wonder that the world is full of many frauds, wrong-doings, and crimes continuing under one disguise or another, many not known publicly, some known but not proven. But, talking about cricket, here is an international fraud and crime of fantastic proportions, lying mathematically proved for seven years, and legally established (in the top Court of a country) for the last two years. Recently, a few months back, a key insider for many years has also spilled the beans. Yet, the elephantine international fraud and crime is not only continuing, but has been prospering all the time, even now; not a soul who matters being bothered. **That is incredible to the power of incredible.**

□

Deciphering the Design

There is an inexhaustible material and evidence already available in the public domain to show anyone willing to know that what Sanjeev Chawla is reported to have said is absolutely true. As a result of my efforts alone, other than my books and the petition on the subject, hundreds of my posts over the years on the Facebook page https://www.facebook.com/BettorsBeware/ have periodically and in parallel been exposing institutionalised fixing in cricket matches in various tournaments and formats everywhere over the last many years. These include even matches of the last ODI World Cup, 2019. Like my earlier books on cricket fixing and fraud, these posts give a rare insight into the correlation between the movement of betting odds and scripting of matches. These public posts also remain unchallenged and uncontested. The purpose of these posts has also been to periodically warn the bettors the world over about the existence of thoroughly scripted cricket for the benefit of the betting mafia and, thus, guard them against losing big. I am sure some bettors must have benefitted, but millions and millions of bettors must still be unaware, since the media won't help them in being aware and protecting themselves!

The posts being open to the public, in the initial days, some people had genuine questions, some reacted as if I was mad, and some tried to browbeat me (on their own or at the stance of someone else, I won't know). But, by and by, I could answer all the doubts/queries and could deal with them all. Anyway, with total fixing being so unabashedly open now, there is no scope left for anyone to question the posts on this page. These posts have also withstood the greatest test—the test of time.

It will be relevant to reproduce a few posts here for ready perusal of the readers to give them some idea of correlation between, and the intricacies of, betting and fixing.

Bettors Beware

Published by Atul Kumar—6 July, 2019

In his book 'Fixed! Cash and Corruption in Cricket', the awarded and highly acclaimed journalist and writer Shantanu Guha Ray has devoted a chapter to the findings of the Mudgal Committee. This chapter is titled 'The Mudgal Files' and brings out many interesting facts unknown to the public. It tells this about one Javed Chutani, an associate of Dawood Ibrahim: '...Chutani would routinely convey opening rates to key bookies in India, Pakistan, Singapore and Kuala Lumpur. He was sure about what would happen in a match and rates were fixed accordingly. No one dared argue with him...'

I don't know whether Mr. Ray understood the

meaning of this too explosive a finding by the Mudgal Committee, since he didn't dwell further on this in his book, or whether he kept quiet on purpose because the finding was too explosive. But why did the so high-placed offices of the caliber of Mudgal Committee and the Supreme Court of India act blind to the meaning of this and why have they, Modi Government and the men of caliber of Vinod Rai been acting blind since then? The book was published in 2016 and the report of the Mudgal Committee was submitted in February 2014.

I shall request readers to apply their own minds a bit to this finding before reading further on. This means the opening betting rates are not based on team strengths, pitch and weather conditions, past and recent performances of the teams, relative strengths and weaknesses of the teams, etc., as everyone has been made to believe and is made to believe even today; but were based on the outcome of the match and to be progress in it as known beforehand to those deciding on the opening rates/odds. Can anyone know what would happen in a match beforehand if matches were not to be played as per a pre-decided script or if fixing were not institutionalised? Could there be any scope for a few players here or there acting on their own and change that pre-known outcome of the match without team managements and coaches coming to know of their misdoings? Does it not then mean that periodic instances of spot-fixing by a few players detected by the cricket administration or law-enforcing agencies now and then and highlighted by the media are only meant to pull wool over our eyes so that we never understand the reality, and that those instances are, in fact, something else other than some players trying to fix matches?

If one were to go through a recent explosive book 'No Ball' by another journalist-cum-writer Chandramohan Puppala, it also conveys that there was something much more sinister than what met the eyes. And the same was conveyed in even more explosive Shantanu Guha Ray's book more than two years ago. The silence of the media even on these two books not only shows but proves its complicity in the colossal crime that cricket is.

Before we proceed further, let us try to understand what this finding means in the context of the recent India vs. Bangladesh match in ICC WC 2019 played on 2nd July, 2019. It is just one example among thousands of such examples available over the years. But it has added importance since it is from one of the matches of the much coveted ICC World Cup.

The opening rates for betting for this match after the toss were about 21-22 paise in favour of India, meaning thereby that one would have got profit of only 21 paise for one rupee risked if India won and profit of about ₹ 4.5 (1/.22 = 4.54) if Bangladesh won. Did the recent performance of Bangladesh and public claims by their senior players like Shakib that they had plans in place for India justify these opening rates from any objective analysis, especially when Bangladesh had won their last match and India had lost theirs? Bettors know it, but it should not be difficult even for non-bettors to visualise that most of the bets in such a scenario would be placed against India to start with, bettors/punters hoping to cut profit on both sides during the course of the match. It may not be wrong to say that the opening rates/odds were such as to force most of the bettors to place bets against India to start with.

Let us now see briefly how the match proceeded and how the odds moved during the match. In contrast to their last match, Indian batting started briskly, helped by a simple dropped catch of Rohit (part of the plan in place?☺☺), all necessarily part and parcel of the script, scoring 69 runs in 10 overs. The odds dropped down fast to 14 paise just after the first over, and to around 6 paise further during the course of the Indian innings, such that even when India inexplicably stuttered to 314/9 from 277/4 after 44 overs and 251/4 after 40 overs, with the legendary Dhoni batting during all these overs getting out only in the 50th over, the odds remained around 13 paise—below the starting odds. Could such odds have any objective justification on earth when Bangladesh was the only team having successfully chased 300-plus score in this World Cup? They had chased 321 against the potent WI attack with great ease only in the 42nd over, just a fortnight ago. It was the same strong WI attack that had skittled out strong Pakistan, the Champions Trophy winners, at 105 runs a few days ago.

Digressing a little here, the stutter by India towards the end served double purpose. One, the usual one. It made punters lose on the Indian innings score since most of the viewers and punters naturally expect acceleration towards the end of the innings, especially with the legends like Dhoni on the crease. In this case, it served another very big purpose. There was a lot of public and media outcry nationally and internationally on India going slow in the end overs against England to surrender the match. Similar slow scoring in the end overs even against Bangladesh was meant to be used to tell later on that Dhoni was suddenly past his prime and not able to score briskly now, and, thus, justify India's unexpected and shocking surrender to England.

Let us now see how Bangladesh went about their chase and how the odds moved throughout that chase. The chase started reasonably with Bangladesh scoring 16 runs in the first 3 overs. Even with the match appearing wide open to any cricket fan at that point, the odds remained around 17 paise only. What would any naïve punter do at such odds—and there are millions of them? He would start licking his lips and lay India (bet against India) at such tempting odds. And if Bangladesh batted even reasonably well, expected to compete well enough in this 'do or die' match for them, he would make good money. But that was not to be. (Have we ever thought why teams mostly fail even to compete in 'do or die' matches for them? Because punters would expect so and bet accordingly). Needing to win this match to stay alive in the tournament, for some strange reasons, Bangladesh slowed their scoring after 3 overs to be at disappointing 40/1 after 10 overs. They lost a wicket just before the end of the session. They did do some brisk scoring in the next session of five overs, but again lost a wicket, of Soumya Sarkar, soon after the session this time. Then again, there was a partnership and Bangladesh appeared well in contention at 121/2 in the 23rd over. The odds still remained around 22 paisa only. Before the odds could rise further to the advantage of the punters, Mushfiqur Rahim decided it was time for him to get out. No fruitful partnership built and odds never went beyond 25 paise (touching 25 paise only for moments). Some late surge came from Saifuddin only when the match was all over for Bangladesh bar the shouting.

Thus, there was no opportunity for punters to make profit in this match, most of them losing their money. This match, like many others, showed how those controlling the opening odds knew what would happen in the match. And it doesn't require special intelligence to understand that one could know what would happen in a match—that too in a game of glorious uncertainties like cricket—only and only if the match was pre-scripted or fixed.

Without thinking much, many would ask that if the syndicates set the starting odds of a match knowing what would happen in the match, how come West Indies started favourites in SL vs. WI match, but lost to Sri Lanka? Yes, there would have to be matches like that now and then, otherwise punters would continuously place money on the favourite team as per bookies and make money match after match. Sure, those controlling betting and betting odds can't allow that. So, there will be matches now and then where the bookies' favourite team at the start loses. Also punters are to be made to win once a while to keep their hopes alive and keep them addicted to betting 😊.

The correlation between odds, movement of odds, session scores on offer, and fancy bets on one hand and the puppet show in the ground on the other hand has continued for years to trap the bettors/punters and earn trillions of dollars for the underworld and D-company. It is to continue this way since World Media, the boasting

Modi government, all political leaders and political parties in India, and even the Supreme Court of India have decided to remain complicit in the crime through their acts of commission and omission.

Many times, we can see how a batsman was getting out on his own accord, if it were not for the accompanying commentary and commentators' explanation. The commentators were talking of wind, wind speed, pitch, ball bowled being slow or fast, swing, spin, etc., in this match also like in any other match, to keep fooling us, while the match was nothing but a staged drama as per a written script, like any other match. Mr. K.B. Vijaykrishnan very aptly said about the ongoing World Cup recently that 'Lagaan' (the film) was much better as acting there was far superior.

Can it be that commentators and cricket experts are unaware of the matches being scripted and fixed, when I and you know it. Ponder over it a little and you will know the answer. What about the cricket journalists the world over? Some of them may still be ignorant. But, if so, they are to blame themselves. This involvement of the whole cricketing world in the CRIME makes it all the more mind-boggling.

There is nothing new about cricket being scripted in what I have said above. All this and much more has been said in my books and press conferences and on various social forums including this page repeatedly for years, since much before the books by the two journalists, and in my petition to the Supreme Court of India in November 2017. That the colossal fraud and crime still continuing with gay abandon, and being celebrated the world over, should be a matter of great shame for the Supreme Court of India and the hypocrite media and the world. But, unfortunately, 'shame' has become an extinct emotion in the human world.

But my dear bettors/punters, you better beware because it is your money and you are the biggest victims of the colossal fraud and crime called Cricket.

Bettors Beware

Published by Atul Kumar—25 July, 2019

England, the World Champions, bowled out for 85 in the first innings of the only Test match against Ireland (who were not found capable even to compete for the World Cup).😃😃So what? Have not we been taught that cricket was a game of glorious uncertainties?😂Inherent capabilities/incapabilities of players can go for a toss anytime and surface anytime. 😃😂 What for then do we require commentators and cricket experts? Have you ever wondered?😃😃

Poor mother Earth has to bear the weight of billions of rank fools who celebrate the biggest proven fraud and consider themselves the wisest species. 😂😂😂😂

Footnote: With Ireland having taken 122 runs first innings lead, England are still favourites to win by far at odds of 1.35 only. Fixers alone know what will happen next. 😀😁

England went on to win this match by 143 runs. Haha....!!

Bettors Beware

Published by Atul Kumar—16 July, 2019

The Trillion Dollars Loot

'An Epic Final for Ages' screamed the Newspaper Headlines for the WC final between England and New Zealand played on 14th July, 2019 at Lords. The social media is abuzz with discussions on the stupidity or fairness of the rules that decided the World Cup winner. Probably, they all enjoyed the final between England and New Zealand with their minds totally shut. 😊 If it were not so, they all would be asking the real obvious question, and not bothering about the stupidity of the rules? Why was it that neither of the two teams was playing to win the prestigious World Cup?

Let us fast forward and go to the last over (the 100th over) of the match. England needed 15 runs with 2 wickets in hand and Stokes on the strike. First 2 balls played as dots, for Stokes to retain the strike. 15 runs required of 4 balls, the Cup was all New Zealand's for the taking. But, Boult chose that very moment to bowl a ball that could easily be hit for a Six by Stokes to bring England back into reckoning. Next ball, freakish 6 runs through an overthrow. Now the match and the Cup were England's for the taking, requiring only 3 runs off the last two balls. One run and a run-out off the next ball. 2 runs required off the last ball with Stokes on strike. He receives a ball he could have easily hammered to boundary, but he taps it for non-existent 2 runs. Result—one run and a run-out. A Tie—what a thrill! But sure the two teams were supposed not to be playing to thrill us, but to win the World Cup. No?

Many would jump to argue that freakish 6 runs of the 4th ball of that over couldn't be designed? Why not, considering the capabilities of the players involved/on the field? It is commentators who tell us that Ben Stokes inadvertently deflected the throw off his bat. But is it not Stokes alone in the world who would know whether his action was inadvertent or otherwise? It becomes difficult for people to see the truth again and again because they are made to see through the eyes of the commentators. Secondly, even if that attempt to freakish-looking 6 runs hadn't succeeded, a Tie could be achieved by scoring accordingly in the remaining 2 balls. Vice versa, if these 6 runs were indeed freakish and not designed, the scoring in the next 2 balls was adjusted accordingly to achieve a Tie.

Did the finish not remind the viewers of the finishes in some of the IPL/T20 league matches? Is it not strange that people believe matches in IPL/T20 leagues to be fixed, but expect that the same rogue players and the same rogue cricket administration become saints when it comes to international matches? Could it be possible that Boult and Stokes and other players were acting on their own at the behest of some bookies, and the cricket experts the world over couldn't see what anyone with an open mind and the minimum of common sense could see? And does fixed cricket take place in some vacuum with heroes and superheroes of cricket remaining not involved and cricket administration remaining unaware?

Let us now go to the super-over and fast forward to the last ball bowled by Archer with Martin Guptill on the strike. Now New Zealand needed 2 runs of it, the last ball of the tournament, to lift the much-coveted World Cup. This time Guptill played it for the existent 2 runs, but ran too lethargically, especially for the 2nd run, to get himself run-out by some margin. Anyone having doubts about it may see the recording and see how Guptill was running for the second run. Cricketers across the globe can easily visualise that 2 runs could be completed by good/hard running considering the speed of the ball and distance travelled by it before being fielded, and Martin Guptill is very agile otherwise.

Probably, the above doesn't constitute a proof of what is what (an encyclopedia of that exists otherwise), as the literate man understands proof or has been trained to understand the proof (what one can see is no proof? 🙂), but the above is sufficient for a man of common prudence to understand and realise the reality of international cricket if hc bothered to apply his mind a little. Applying mind to the last few balls of this Final for the ICC World Cup and asking oneself natural simple questions that emanate alone can make one understand the stark reality—without having to go through Cricket Insider's tweets; without having to know of session betting; without having to bother how application of the basic principles of probability to score books scientifically and beyond any doubts, beyond any ifs and buts, established the continuance of institutionally fixed cricket for over a decade; without having to apply mind to the explosive finding by the Indian Police that one Javed Chutani—an aide of Dawood Ibrahim—opened the odds for the matches as he knew what was going to happen in a match; without having to bother why a man of the stature of Vinod Rai acted so blatantly dishonest in dealing with me and our petition; without having to bother why Bishen Singh Bedi said that IPL was the biggest ever scam of India and people were blind not to see what was happening; without having to think why Shashank Manohars of the world made noise when out of the cricket administration and why they forgot everything as soon as they were at the helm of cricket administration; without having to apply mind to the explosive claims by Al Jazeera that were soon brushed under the carpet by the world media with Al Jazeera itself mysteriously going quiet; without having to think why even the Supreme Court of India chose to expose itself rather than to act purposefully in the matter; without having to bother why media had always been hiding the truth; without having to bother how and why none of the reports of match-fixing coming to light every now and then, and also disclosures by ex-cricketers on match-fixing from time to time, were ever acted upon by ICC and ever reached any conclusion for years; without having to bother about mysterious deaths of Bob Woolmer and Sunanda Pushkar in almost identical circumstances; without having to know that Sanjeev Chawla, the bookie involved in the match-fixing scandal of 2000 involving Hansie Cronje, had told the British police/law-enforcers a couple of years ago that international cricket was institutionally fixed—echoing one of my posts on this very page that time, and without wondering why the masses didn't know about this explosive fact and why did ICC do nothing about it, without having to think why the ex-Pakistani captain Aamer Sohail blurted on the Pakistani TV during the last Champions Trophy matches that external factors/forces had helped Pakistan reach the final and why did ICC not question him or investigate further, without having to bother why Mr. Sampath Kumar, IPS, was shunted out of probe and falsely charged (he got vindicated later on) when he had found Dhoni to be involved in wrong-doings, and Dhoni continued to captain India?

The last few balls of this much publicised WC Final forming the last act of the drama that ended in a Tied match and, thereafter, a tied super-over were sufficient for one to know and understand the stark nakedness of international cricket and, consequently, the modern world, if one opened one's eyes and applied common sense.

People around me feel, and rightly so, that I am obsessed with cricket fixing. But is it wrong to be obsessed with something so massive that if and when addressed has the potential of revolutionising the human machinations on earth? Am I to be blamed for my obsession or the world for continuing to be blind for years? Had the world woken up and acted as it should have, I would not have had to waste my precious years in pursuing the same issue.

The most conservative estimates based on available data tell us that through this open crime of institutionally fixed cricket, bettors/punters round the world have been looted of trillions of dollars over the years, and are being looted of more than a trillion of dollars every year.

And this money goes to the underworld and unknown part of it to fund the terrorist activities around the world.

To my mind, even more concerning than the above financial angle is the fact that this colossal loot/fraud is continuing as a result of collusion/nexus of the establishment, corporates, judiciary, political leaders, celebrities, and the cricket world. In short, it is a fraud and a crime being perpetrated by the world on itself to harm itself. The boastful Modi Government of India parading its zero tolerance to corruption from the house tops has been acting blind, deaf and dumb to this biggest proven manifestation of corruption for the last 5 years.

And even more concerning is the fact that the cricketing world—the Vikrant Guptas, the Boria Majumdars (cricket journalists), Brian Laras, Sachin Tendulkars, Gavaskars, Shastris, Flemings, Kallises, Bret Lees, David Lloyda, Nasser Hussains, Mccullumns, Pontings, Michael Clarks, Kohlis—the list is endless—continues to bluff and fool the world 24 × 7 with a straight face that competitive cricket matches were being played all around, even though the nakedness of cricket lied indisputably exposed for more than 5 years.

And, above all, the most concerning is the fact that the world—including men in the street, the illiterates, the literates, the students, the housewives, the unemployed, the artists, the writers, the activists, the office goers, the intelligent advocates and doctors, the IT professionals, the teachers, the entrepreneurs, the businessmen and women, the powerful bureaucrats, the top CEOs of the world, and millions of the punters who themselves are the victims—still continues to be fooled, taking pride in being fooled while celebrating the colossal crime.'

Bettors Beware

Published by Atul Kumar—7 December, 2018

There are hundreds of examples in cricket archives when just one ball in a match told loud and clear that the match was a scripted one, but, unfortunately, mankind has chosen to remain blind and foolish to the extreme.

Just now, another such manifestation took place in the 23rd match of the Mzansi Super League between Durban Heat and Jozi Stars.

Jozi Stars required 12 runs off the last two balls with only one wicket in hand and their number 9 batsman Z. Pongolo on strike. M. de Lange was the bowler in good bowling rhythm having bowled the first 4 balls of the last over for just 2 runs and taking a wicket. Suddenly, for no rhyme and reason, he bowls a high full toss—a 'no ball' that could easily be hit for a six even by a number 9 batsman—and was hit so. He repeats the doze in the next ball also, ensuring a loss for his team with 2 balls still to spare.

Nothing in cricket and no cricketer can explain bowling of such balls as above if it was not on purpose 😊😀. If Mr. Lange's indiscretion was his own, and not a result of any script dictated to him, he should not be playing cricket anymore. But, in the past, players guilty of such indiscretions have continued to play uninterrupted, (and sure enough, Mr. Lange also would continue to play 😊), thus signifying institutional fixing of cricket.'

Bettors Beware

Published by Atul Kumar—30 December, 2016

TEST CRICKET

There are many who find it difficult to believe or even think that Test Cricket was also fixed. Probably, the example of 1st Test concluded today between SA and SL helps them understand or at least they will start thinking. SL had beaten Australia 3-0 not long ago in Sri Lanka, and Zimbabwe 2-0 in Zimbabwe very recently. SA had lost their last Test against Australia having won earlier two matches against them.

Against this background, the bookies fixed the odds in the first Test at less than 1.3, i.e., additional return of only 30 paise against one rupee waged on SA win, SL win and Draw being the other two possibilities. Such odds (low return) are very uncommon for a Test Match and are fixed when the two teams are class apart. Did the form and the performance of the two teams justify such odds?

The bookies know how a match would progress; they fix and manipulate the betting odds accordingly. That implies continuous institutionalised fixing of cricket and not stray fixing at the behest of some outside forces as people are deceived to believe by ICC and international media.

There was peculiar manipulation of the betting odds by the bookies in this match. Batting first, even when SA lost 10 wickets within 200 runs (104/0 to 286/10), the betting odds moved in a very narrow range of 1.2 to 1.28 or so. With SL having bounced back strongly, bookies appeared to be sure what would happen further in the match. And they were proved to be on the money. Responding to 286 by SA, SL sure enough lost top 3 wickets for a meager 22 runs, and never came back in the match. Even when SL appeared to be competing at times, the odds never went beyond 1.2 for SA. SA did win comfortably in the end in what turned out to be a one-sided contest. Exactly as the bookies had envisaged before the start and continued believing throughout the match.

Some could say SL team didn't have the potential to compete with SA and the bookies were smart enough to decipher so. Maybe initially (though, as explained above, the recent team performances didn't at all indicate so), but how could they know for sure as they did that SL would capitulate from positions of strength during the match. Sccondly, SL did have potential to compete as they showed through their bowling in the first innings and batting in the second innings (they were 80 plus/0 and 190 plus/3). Had SL batted in the first innings as they did in the second, the bookies would have been proven wrong. But that was not to be.

One, especially if a cricketer or a cricket journalist must be an utter imbecile to think that sudden, complete capitulation by Pakistan against New Zealand or by England against India in the last Test matches between the two teams in the end overs when a draw looked inevitable had anything to do with cricket. The matches are turned on their head now and then when no one would be expecting so, especially towards the end, to leave a big majority of bettors high and dry.

The 2nd Test between Australia and Pakistan that also concluded today is another point in case. Pakistan had scored 400-plus runs in the first innings and Australia scored freely in thc first session today against a potent Pakistani bowling attack. Thus, there were no demons in the pitch. Yet Pakistan lost 10 wickets well within two sessions to hand over the match to Australia on a platter. The shot Misbah played to lose his wicket tells all.

T20 leagues are taking place around the globe all the time. Right now, Big Bash T20 is underway in Australia.

A few days back, Bangladesh Premier League concluded. The international players of repute participate in these leagues. In every match, there are many balls bowled or shots played by reputed players that clearly show that no cricket but only acting out of scripted dramas was taking place. Expecting the same players to play competitive cricket in Test matches will be foolhardy.'

These are just a few out of hundreds of posts on this page to give a glimpse. If one went through only some of these posts alone, one won't have to look anywhere else to know what an all-encompassing fraud cricket was. **It is another matter that the dense global media still continues to pretend, and the clever continue to be tricked.**

□

Foes or Allies?

There is no dearth of intellectuals, super intellectuals, and geniuses who think that cricket matches being fixed is no big deal. They don't know or understand the extant of fixing that exists. Most of them are not even interested in knowing. Consequently, they remain ignorant of what it means. It is not some innocuous or petty cheating taking place in sports. It involves so many big and powerful people in cricket and outside cricket that it becomes an expression of our self-defeating degradation hitherto unknown. Not only that, the money involved at around a trillion dollars is many times more than the monetary estimation of all other scams and frauds known to man till date combined! Yet we feel happy in talking and discussing all those relatively petty issues, but want to remain blissfully oblivious of this all-embracing crime and fraud.

Even above too big implications would pale into insignificance in comparison to a very peculiar implication of cricket being fixed the way it is. The skirmishes and the animosity between two neighbouring countries India and Pakistan govern the psyche of the masses in these two countries more than anything else. That becomes the reason for many arms deals/purchases by these two countries. It is a perennial subject of discussion at many international forums and among world leaders. What if one was to suddenly realise and know that this much-publicised animosity was fake rather than real? Indians and Pakistanis will find it almost impossible to comprehend.

Howsoever hard it may be for them to comprehend, it is so. The continuation of fixed cricket matches between the two countries at world stage for over a decade does tell us so. Cricket in both countries has been administered by top political leaders or with their blessings. So, it just can't be that cricket matches between India and Pakistan have been fixed and scripted without their political leadership being aware. Or can it be so? No one from amongst my acquaintances or from the media in my press conferences, or from authorities in response to my letters or in the Supreme Court did ever say that it could be so. The matches between the two countries have always been a matter of great national pride and, hence, of deep passion among their citizens. How the winning country erupts in euphoria and the losing country goes into depression with breaking of TV screens is a matter of common knowledge in these countries. Therefore, the extent of Indians and Pakistanis being fooled and emotionally tortured as a result of fixed India Pakistan matches is probably unimaginable. Would the intellectuals, super intellectuals, and geniuses still like to say, 'So what if cricket is corrupted and fixed?' I don't know. They may because they are intellectuals, super intellectuals, and geniuses, not a commoner like me. They have their own common sense, own priorities and their own sense of proportion.

What does or would or should it mean to the armed forces of the two countries? It must mean a lot more. Because it is they who have to bear the brunt of this fake animosity through periodical martyrdom from among their ranks—to keep the facade going. Surely, rank and file of the armed forces must be totally ignorant. But how aware or how ignorant are the top commanders of this fake enmity? It's anybody's guess, only they would know.

As already indicated, I am not talking of this only now. It has been highlighted over the years at various forums, through press conferences and letters—to the media and the authorities. But, probably, it has been something too big for some to grasp and for others to respond to.

Global fight against terrorism is another enormous sham that gets exposed. That Dawood Ibrahim is a global terrorist and that he has or had been running betting syndicates has been said by the authorities. Here has been a big source of terror funding through fixed cricket and the consequent bonanza to the betting mafia (as per the official accounts) becoming more and more potent each passing day, yet the Indian and the World leadership have been unconcerned, have never bothered in the least. The same leaders never miss any opportunity of talking about terrorism, its menace and all out efforts to combat it at national and international forums, the public and the masses remaining fooled. What a joke and what outright hypocrisy! At the cost of the common man!

It will be relevant here for one to peruse the following blog post, dated 17th December, 2014 and titled ***'Drugs, terror, PM and cricket'*** by the renowned journalist and cartoonist late Rajinder Puri:

> *'Prime Minister Mr. Narendra Modi in his latest radio broadcast series "Mann kee baat" dwelt on the menace of drugs. Urging youth to shun drugs Mr. Modi*

said that apart from their debilitating effect on health and addiction the strongest argument against drugs arose from the risk that money generated by the narcotics trade was used for funding terrorism. Mr. Modi asked youth: "Have you ever thought that the money you spend on drugs might be going to terrorists who buy bullets to kill our soldiers? You also love Mother India. How can you help terrorists?" That is a good question. There is just one troubling aspect. Is the Prime Minister's deep concern expressed over funding of terrorism genuine?

These doubts arise from Mr. Modi's inexplicable response to the IPL cricket scam involving Dawood Ibrahim's betting syndicate. Very few people appreciate the extent of the IPL cricket betting and match fixing scam. To get some perspective of this one needs to read the two books on cricket match fixing, Bettors Beware and Inside the Boundary Line, written by former Railway Ministry official, anti-corruption crusader and author Mr. Atul Kumar. It is not just a stray player who is guilty. The IPL scam is a huge organized mega operation involving players, team owners, officials and politicians. It is a criminal industry. What is most sinister is the fact that the mastermind controlling the betting syndicates is Dawood Ibrahim who according to police investigations most likely uses funds generated by the scam to finance terrorists.

The Supreme Court (SC) panel headed by Chief Justice Mukul Mudgal inquiring into the IPL scam criticized the police for negligence in following up the terrorist angle. The Judges said: "Mumbai police admitted that protection by the underworld is essential to run the organized betting syndicate in Mumbai. The police failed to inform the panel as to which gang gives this protection to the betting operation....There is therefore cause for a distinct impression that for reasons not satisfactorily explained, the Mumbai police was not willing to investigate the involvement of Dawood Ibrahim in the betting racket." What could be the cause of the police reluctance to pursue the probe against Dawood Ibrahim as the SC has indicated?

Could it not be the fact that the BCCI management board that oversaw the affairs of the IPL consisted of India's top politicians and therefore the reluctance? During the height of the revelations about Dawood's involvement the board members included among others Mr. Narendra Mod and Mr. Arun Jaitley. The media is obsessed with the fate of BCCI President Mr. Srinivasan. That is a minor issue. Even the mysterious death of Sunanda Pushkar, late wife of Mr. Shashi Tharoor, immediately after she threatened to spill the beans about the murky details of the IPL scam to the media, was just a sub-plot. The main issue is the terror funding enabled by the IPL scam. Mr. Modi is worried about drugs funding terror. What about IPL match fixing?'

That was more than five long years ago. Even today, as this book is getting written and published, holding of IPL-2020—a well-known fraud—is conspicuously one of the priorities of a government unsuccessfully battling the Corona crisis!

India has always been complaining of being hit by terrorism emanating from the Pakistani soil. Dawood Ibrahim, believed to be settled in Pakistan and under the protection of the Pakistani Government, is the most wanted criminal for India. He is believed to have been the mastermind behind the infamous 1993 Bombay Blasts or Bombings in which 257 innocent citizens of India were killed. He was declared a terrorist by India and USA years ago in 2003. By Indian official accounts only, he was also the kingpin of cricket betting and match-fixing, earning big money from these activities. Thus, the link between match-fixing in cricket and terror funding becomes as obvious and as clear as daylight. Yet, in India, we have been having governments that have been protecting institutionally scripted and fixed cricket—a big source of terror funding and a big source of income to India's most wanted criminal—being sheltered by an adversary country. Everyone is happy about it; the successive governments, the Indian media, and the great Indian intellectuals and activists—they all lamenting the killing of their civilians and uniformed men through terrorism year after year! **Can there be any bigger manifestation of collective hypocrisy and duplicity of a nation?**

What does all this mean further for the global scene? India-Pakistan relations play a significant role in international politics. If the world were to follow this obvious lead to know the camaraderie between these two countries, won't the international politics become topsy-turvy? Throwing any light on the evident would have jeopardised many an arm-deal over the last few decades. How will poor tax payers' money from these third-world countries going to the Super Powers through million/billion dollar arms deals be justified then?

The following brief Press Release by me in February 2019 at Press Club, Kolkata, in the aftermath of the infamous Pulwama terrorist attack, summing up the above, has remained a cry in the wilderness.

PRESS RELEASE

(28/02/2019)

Subject: Pulwama Attack, Terror Funding, and Cricket

It is with a sense of great pain that I communicate the following to the nation in general and present Government in particular:

"At present there is acute grief in the country over martyrdom of 40 CRPF jawans in recent terrorist attack in Pulwama, and a lot of clamour to avenge it. Also a big public debate is going on whether India should now play against Pakistan or not in the upcoming Cricket World Cup.

Surprisingly a key issue leading to Pulwama attack still continues to be conveniently ignored by the government and all the authorities. That is terror funding – the lifeline of terrorism. Lakhs of crores of rupees per year earned by betting syndicates as a result of thoroughly scripted cricket matches globally – the major portion of this amount emanating from India and going from pockets of Indians – has been one of the big sources of terror funding for years. It still continues to be so, increasing everyday through mushrooming T – 20 leagues.

While the clamour for action/war against Pakistan rages, a very puzzling question haunts ever more. If Pakistan is an enemy country, how come we have been playing fixed cricket matches with them, even losing to them in the last Champions Trophy final in one such fixed match?

I say above with some authority on the strength

of success of my writ petition (Civil) 1163/2017 in the Supreme Court of India that had brought the above out.

The agonizing hypocrisy of the authorities is best exemplified by COA of BCCI headed by Sh. Vinod Rai announcing financial assistance to families of the martyrs from savings out of cancelled opening ceremony of IPL-2019, since they themselves become primarily responsible for continuing terror funding through fixed cricket and thus having assisted in Pulwama attack. Undoubtedly, IPL-2019 will contribute further to terror funding in a big way.

Pained by the dastardly killing of innocent jawans, I once again urge our government, the political leaders, and the concerned authorities to take immediate action at least now to stop scripted and fake cricket in order to strike a body blow to terror funding and terrorism.

As I give finishing touches to this book, killing of 8 policemen by one gangster Vikas Dubey at Kanpur and his arrest have been the talk of the town for the last few days (latest on this is his death in encounter even before producing him in any court), because the issue is being continuously talked about in electronic media and is making headlines in print media. In overall perspective, the issue is not even a peanut compared to terror funding through cricket and betting mafia, and the consequent killing of hundreds of civilians and uniformed men by terrorists perennially. It is further nothing compared to exposed fake enmity between India and Pakistan. But no one talks about these or bothers about these, because media doesn't talk about these or bothers about these.

□

Exposing the Exposed

I am sure, more than anything else, this book will leave one totally shattered about journalists and media. That is very necessary to understand and grasp the root cause of our deprivation today. Despite understanding how compromising and untruthful the present-day media is (this realisation has dawned on people of late), one still believes that media does and will act as a check on the lawlessness of the authorities and highhandedness of the governments. One still expects media to highlight any fraud or crime coming to its notice. One still expects the media to be largely on the side of the general public and raise its voice to protect the public interest. But now, one would discover how the media itself had been facilitating an unbelievably massive fraud and crime for years, hand in glove with the criminals and the establishment. It was fooling the public by coming up with only superficial stories every now and then, making false noises, while brushing the real thing under the carpet all the time.

Over the years, there have been innumerable sundry exposes and revelations about match fixing in cricket involving local league players as well as international cricketers of repute. It is meaningless to go into those involving individual players when we know that cricket has been totally scripted and fixed.

But were there any revelations indicating large scale fixing or any exposes about fixing of key matches; and, if so, what happened to such exposes? How did the cricket administration or law enforcing agencies and other authorities act or not act to reach a logical conclusion when such revelations surfaced and resurfaced? How did the media pursue or not pursue these? Let us see.

1. Rashid Latif, the ex-Pakistani wicket-keeper batsman and, later on, also the captain, revealed the correlation between session betting and fixing in an article dated 24/7/2010 titled *'How cricket matches are scripted'* published on the website espncricinfo.com.
2. Years ago, in November 2011 and years after the match, Vinod Kambli, a famous cricketer and a member of the Indian team, alleged through media that the 1996 World Cup semi-final between India and Sri Lanka was fixed.
3. In 2012, a book 'Bookie Gambler Fixer Spy' by the award-winning British sports journalist E.D. Hawkins got published. The back cover of the book says, *'...An Indian bookie sends Hawkins texts of a 'script' for an alleged fix during the 2011 World Cup that even he finds too astonishing for words; he watches—along with an estimated television audience of one billion—as the match unfolds according to the script and decides it is time to expose the inner workings of match fixing....'* The mentioned match was the semi-final between India and Pakistan.
4. On 27/1/2013, an interview of one Atul Kumar by the cricket journalist Bipin Dani was published in reputed

English dailies of India 'Deccan Chronicle' and 'Asian Age' following the publication of his reality fiction 'Inside the Boundary Line'. Atul Kumar was a retired (voluntarily) senior Railways officer and a national-level awardee for his crusade against corruption while in service. Through this interview, it was unambiguously announced to the world for the first time that international cricket was thoroughly and institutionally fixed. The book published in late 2012 had answered or attempted to answer all the questions that arose out of such an extraordinary and explosive deduction. A press-meet was held by Atul Kumar at Kolkata the next day on 28/1/2013 to share this seemingly world-shaking discovery with the world.

5. The concept of mathematical/scientific proof of thorough fixing in cricket by applying the basic principles of the theory of probability to session betting was brought out in brief through an article titled *'Cricket in Massive Fix?'* published in the Statesman, another highly reputed English daily of India, dated 10/07/2013 quoting same Atul Kumar.

6. Times of India news report dated 27/7/2013 and titled *'IPL betting rates set by Dawood, says chargesheet'* had this to tell, '...Delhi Police's chargesheet, likely to be filed the next week, is expected to explain how Dawood was not above pulling a fast one even on bookies who trusted D-company's 'tip offs', pointing to the treacherous world of illegal betting controlled by the don.

   "Small and middle-level bookies trusted the winning team information announced by D-company as this mostly turns out to be true. But, sometimes, the information was faked. A wrong winning team would be named. So, while some bookies knew where to place money, others who took the D-company information at face value lost. Both ways, D company benefitted," said a senior police officer...'

7. A news item published in The Statesman on 13th August, 2013 told this: '*Former Australian captain Steve Waugh was yesterday quoted as saying that bracket-fixing was the latest threat to cricket, along with spot-fixing, and that bookmakers were making a lot of money out of it. "With bracket-fixing, a segment of a 50-over game or a Twenty 20 contest is manipulated," said Waugh in an interview to news.com.au. According to Waugh, "In a five-over period, for example, the corrupt players ensure a certain amount of runs are scored, and if a captain is involved, the whole process can be achieved discreetly and effectively... opportunities to put such schemes into action are widespread, especially in second-tier tournaments, such as domestic Twenty20 competitions and other events away from the prying eyes of the global media and more stringent match officials." The former player said that these matters, apart from wider areas of corruption, had been discussed when Waugh, a member of the Marylebone Cricket Club's world cricket committee, met in Perth in 2010. Around the turn of the century, after some prominent players, including Test captains, were found guilty of corruption, a number of national cricket boards chose not to have certain leads fully investigated, for fear*

that more star players might be implicated, he said. The danger now lurks as Twenty20 leagues sprout up all over the cricket world.'

8. As per TNN news report dated 12/2/2014, match number 61 of IPL 6 (IPL-2013) between CSK and RR was under probe and raised many eyebrows. From a very healthy 83/0 in the 12th over, CSK in spite of having a very strong batting line-up ended at meagre 141/4 in 20 overs. G. Sampath Kumar, the IPS officer, investigating it that time said he had been a cricketer himself and by seeing the match, one could easily know that it was fixed.
9. Vindu Dara Singh, considered to be an insider in IPL-2013 spot-fixing scam, told that IPL was 100% fixed as brought out in a Zee News report dated 25/2/2014.
10. The following coverage was made by PTI consequent to the publication of Atul Kumar's book 'Bettors Beware' and his press meet in New Delhi in end February 2014 to introduce the book and its contents to the world.

'Almost All International Cricket Matches Are Fixed, Alleges Whistleblower

Updated: March 02, 2014, 06:21 IST | PTI |

A former Railways employee-turned-whistleblower sought to turn the heat on the cricket fraternity by alleging that almost all international matches are 'fixed'.

New Delhi: A former Railways employee-turned-whistleblower on Friday sought to turn the heat on the cricket fraternity by alleging that almost all international matches are 'fixed'.

Atul Kumar has published a book in December last year, 'Bettors Beware', in which he has claimed that 'fixing' was not just confined to the Indian Premier League or other domestic tournaments, but was very much prevalent in Twenty20 Internationals, One-dayers and Test cricket also.

Introducing his book to the media, Atul said he has analysed mathematically and proved that 'session betting' has been taking place in 'almost all international matches'.

"Not that only IPL is fixed, all or almost all international matches between any two countries are fixed," Atul claimed at a press conference in New Delhi.

"In fact, not just players, even the commentators are involved in fixing.

"Session betting has to be taken into consideration. I have worked on mathematically on a number of matches. From scoring patterns and analysing those mathematically, I could see how the matches were fixed," Atul, who had earlier written another book—'Inside the Boundary Line'—in November 2012, said.

The writer also said that he had analysed all the matches of the 2007 Twenty20 World Cup in South Africa and found that those were 'fixed'.

A chapter in the book is also dedicated to the 2007 T20 World Cup. "I have done some analysis to see how scoring progressed during the betting sessions in all the matches of Twenty20 World Cup held in 2007," asserted Atul.

Asked if he has evidence to prove his claims, Atul said the mathematical analysis of the matches could work as 'circumstantial evidence'.

On being asked why he hadn't filed a PIL in court on the basis of his allegations, Atul said, "I hope someone else files a PIL in court and I can mathematically prove that the matches were fixed."

Apart from 2007 T20 World Cup matches, Atul has analysed a number of IPL games and some Test matches in his latest book on match fixing.'

11. A review of the book 'Bettors Beware' by the sports editor of the Statesman, Mr. Pulakesh Mukhopadhyay, was published in The Statesman dated 27/04/2014. The same is self-explanatory. As per this review, the mathematical proof of continuous fixing in cricket given in the book was got examined by the reviewer by more than one person and was found to be satisfactory. This is what the review says in this regard:

    "And even if the chapter titled 'Wonders of Mathematics' isn't exactly as easy as ABC, and the prose isn't always crystal clear, several people familiar with both cricket and arithmetical complications, consulted on this, endorse it as quite all right. "Wow!" was the consensual judgement, delivered separately in miles-apart places."

12. In December 2014, Atul Kumar got another book titled '**Cricket: The Massive Fraud**' published. This book meant to ask the world why the massive public fraud through Cricket was continuing unabated

despite having been mathematically proved, ICC being well informed, and doors of the Supreme Court of India also having been knocked at through a comprehensive letter. The book was translated in Hindi and a few regional languages also.

13. The book **'Fixed! Cash and Corruption in Cricket'** by award-winning eminent journalist Shantanu Guha Ray was published in 2016. This book brought out many instances of fixing and malpractices over the years that had remained uninvestigated both by cricket administration and law-enforcing agencies. These included a report on the script of semi-final between India and Pakistan in ICC World Cup 2011 becoming a common knowledge amongst the media persons before the match. It was the same match that made E.D. Hawkins write a book. Among other things, the book brought out that Justice Mudgal's report (Justice Mudgal headed the Supreme Court-appointed probe into the 2013 IPL spot-fixing scandal) included this:

    "...Chutani would routinely convey opening rates to key bookies in India, Pakistan, Singapore, and Kuala Lumpur. He was sure about what would happen in a match and rates were fixed accordingly. No one dared argue with him...."

    Javed Chutani has been mentioned to be one of the close aides of Dawood Ibrahim, maintaining direct contact with the underworld lord. (Chutani, or any one, could not be sure about what would happen in a match until and unless matches were prescripted, something impossible without fixing being institutionalised).

14. In 2016, Atul Kumar got yet another book 'Underworld Cup T20 (Media, Modis, Mudgals, Mamatas all dial Dawood)' published. This book detailed how even the matches of the T20 World Cup 2016 were all scripted and fixed for the benefit of the betting mafia and the underworld.

15. On 10th May, 2017, three men, bookies/businessmen, were arrested from a Kanpur Hotel after the 50th match of IPL 10 between Gujarat Lions and Delhi Daredevils. They were staying on the same floor/ hotel as the two teams. One of the arrested men, Ramesh Nayan Shah, is reported to have spilled the beans telling that the match was fixed. In this regard, Indiatimes report dated 12/5/2017 mentioned that 'A dated WhatsApp message on his phone revealed that Gujarat Lions would lose the match despite scoring nearly 200 runs. And that is what exactly happened.'

16. It was reported in the media and was all over social media that a twitter handle under the name of Cricket Insider (@theDcricket) had made some peculiar predictions about the final of IPL 10 held on 21/5/2017, 8 out of 9 being bang-on target. The nature of predictions was such that it could be nothing, but script of the match being leaked beforehand. There cannot be any other rational explanation. There were predictions as specific and peculiar as Mumbai will bat first and make 120 to 130 runs and will win, Parthiv Patel will hit under 10, Pollard will hit 1 six.

None of such predictions could be a guess work that somehow came true. Other predictions were also similarly peculiar.

17. Close on the heels of cricket insider proving to the world that cricket was fixed, the ex-Pakistani cricketer and captain Aamir Sohail blurted out on a Pakistani TV channel after Pakistan had reached the final of CT 2017,

    "Sarfraz needs to be told that you have not done anything great. Someone has helped you win the game. There is no reason for you (Sarfraz) to be so happy. We all know what happens behind the scenes. Don't wish to get into the details on who won them the games. If asked, I will say that the prayers of the fans and God have won them the games. They have been brought to the final due to external factors and not based on on-field performance. The boys now need to be level-headed and focus on playing good cricket...".

18. A detailed writ petition (Civil) was filed in the Supreme Court of India by two petitioners, Atul Kumar and Shantanu Guha Ray in November 2017, establishing existence of institutionalised fixing in international and league cricket giving a plethora of evidence including mathematical and logical evidence, and requesting the Hon'ble Court to act by ordering necessary investigations and to do the needful to put a stop to the massive public fraud. It was brought out that the petition had been necessitated since all the authorities including the President of India had failed to act.

19. First hearing took place on 2/2/2018 and final order was passed by the Hon'ble Supreme Court of India on 7/5/2018. As a follow-up, the petitioners had a meeting with the Committee of Administrators for BCCI headed by Vinod Rai at New Delhi on 17/7/2018.

20. In October 2018, Al Jazeera Investigative Unit's latest documentary, *Cricket's Match-Fixers: The Munawar Files,* contained recordings of an Indian match-fixer phoning in details of spot-fixes in 15 international matches to a notorious bookmaker.

    The match-fixer gave a total of 26 predictions, of which all but one turned out to be accurate.

    The spot-fixes were all session fixes, predicting what would happen in a specific session of six, eight or 10 overs.

21. The Committee of Administrators for BCCI filed its report on 23rd October, 2018 in terms of an order by the Supreme Court on the petition, and a detailed rejoinder dated 14/11/2018 was submitted by Atul Kumar.

22. In November 2018, the 72-year-old ex-ace Indian bowler and captain Bishen Singh Bedi had this to say publicly about IPL (Indian Premier League), *"I have a lot of experience in cricket, you can tell what is happening in what match. If we stay blind even while seeing, then it's our choice."*

23. On 30th May, Indian Express, a leading Indian English daily had this to report: *"In his disclosure statement to the Delhi Police, Sanjeev Chawla, the prime accused in the 2000 Hansie Cronje match-fixing case, has said that*

'no cricket match is fairly played' and '...all the cricket matches which people see are fixed'." He also pointed to the involvement of 'a very big syndicate/underworld mafia' that influences all cricket games that, according to him, were like 'movies which are already being directed by someone'.

In the statement, which is part of a supplementary chargesheet submitted to the court, but doesn't have the accused's signature, Chawla revealed before the police that the syndicate had on its target the case's investigation officer DCP (Crime Branch) Dr. G. Ram Gopal Naik and that his life was under threat.

The New Delhi-born and London-based alleged bookmaker, while confessing that he was involved in match-fixing for many years, said he could not give more details since "a very big syndicate/underworld mafia is involved in this matter and they are dangerous people and if he says anything they will get him killed".

24. On 18th June, 2020, NDTV in India reported that "Sri Lanka 'sold' the 2011 World Cup final to India, the country's former sports minister said on Thursday, reviving one of cricket's most explosive match-fixing controversies. Mahindananda Aluthgamage, who was sports minister at the time, is the second senior figure to allege the final was fixed, after the 1996 World Cup-winning skipper Arjuna Ranatunga. 'I tell you today that we sold the 2011 World Cup finals,'" Aluthgamage told Sirasa TV. 'Even when I was sports minister I believed this'." (Subsequently dropping of probe soon after it began by the Sri Lankan Government makes whole thing only more laughable).

As I mentioned earlier, there have been many other pertinent exposes and revelations about fixing and corruption in cricket. I have mentioned a few that readily came to mind and have mentioned those as media would have seen. The list itself answers the questions we asked before listing the above. There have been a large number of such exposes over the years (any professional cricket journalist worth his salt should know more than me), each of which either indicates institutional fixing in cricket, or application of mind to or investigation to a logical conclusion of which was necessary, or which warranted media to ask a lot of questions of the authorities. Nothing like that ever happened. Authorities never acted to any logical conclusion, and media never pursued any of these or asked questions of the authorities.

A number of videos available on social media clearly depict treachery in cricket, but no journalist has bothered to go to the bottom. Manipulation of the toss results by international cricketers of high repute, and inexplicable actions by/involvement of Umpires are too evident through such videos. Out of such videos, the video of Rishabh Pant, the young Indian cricketer, telling that 4 will be scored off the next ball in an IPL match and a 4 was scored, takes the cake (https://sports.ndtv.com/ipl-2019/rishabh-pant-caught-on-stump-mic-making-bizarre-prediction-fans-cry-foul-2015474).

The above incidents and instances are not listed to prove anything since nothing needs to be proved today. When a murder is openly taking place in front of all and sundry, nothing remains to be proved to anyone. But the above should make the readers ask themselves a few questions. "How much of the above do they know, and if not much, why?" "For the game of cricket as a competitive sport, is cricket being fixed *ab initio* more important or are instances of ball tampering or sledging or corruption in cricket boards or subject of players' associations, etc.?" "Should we expect our media to tell us the reality about matches hundreds of millions give their hearts to or should the media be keeping us in the dark and go on selling fake cricket to us, eulogising the heroes of fake cricket as real cricket heroes?" "What is the purpose of media; is it to bring the truth to the masses or is it to keep on sweeping truth under the carpet and go on selling falsehood?" "Has it not been absurdity at its worst when the media has been reporting on and about various cricket matches as competitive ones, day after day for decades, when, in fact, these have been nothing but scripted shows in cricket fields?" **And these questions need be asked in allusion to global media, not only Indian media.**

Try to think about these questions and try to answer these. You would surely realise that 'Presstitutes' is a bit exalting epitaph given to the media because what global media has been doing by continuously concealing a monumental international crime amounts to protecting and facilitating an act of serial killing for years on, the killers having been on the rampage almost every day. Not only that, they have been glorifying the killers, and, even today, are projecting them to the masses as super heroes.

Was it not imperative on the authorities, both cricketing and law-enforcing, to go to the bottom of the matter years ago and tell the world what had been happening? Since the authorities kept on making a mockery of themselves for years at a stretch, was it not imperative on the world media to ask questions of them and take them to task? What happened to checks and balances we don't tire talking about? Is anything more required for one to know and understand how we are rotting, when the authorities and the media are so openly hand-in-glove in a mammoth crime? And what to say when one finds that the top judiciary also is watching silently?

Is it not a matter of fact that in India issues of large public interest coming up before the Supreme Court of India often make breaking news headlines both in print and on air, now-a-days almost on a daily basis? Not only that, debates and discussions take place about these in media even when the issues are subjudice. Yet almost total black-out in the Indian media about a petition bringing out the world-shattering fact of international cricket being a massive public fraud for more than a decade should make one understand not only utmost degradation of the Indian media, but also the invincibility of the contents of the petition if one applies a little mind. That too when initially not knowing what it was all about, a lot of media persons from print and electronic media had taken my interviews and recorded my bytes in the premises and the lawns of the Supreme Court of India on 2/2/2018, the day of the first hearing of our petition. Surely, they were looking for some superficial gossip they could play with. Coming to know how explosive and how sure it was, they kept largely quiet.

I am aware of only two reports of some substance by some journalists on their own (they had never come in contact with me and I don't know them till date). One, in the Hindi newspaper 'Hindustan' published from New Delhi the next day. The report in a few columns brought out that a petition had been filed in the Supreme Court of India stating cricket was a massive deceit, beyond comprehension of normal minds. Second, in the English daily 'The Telegraph', the report mentioning addresses of the petitioners also and that Dawood controlled fixing and betting as per petition, among other things. Was this to scare the petitioners or their families? Did the newspaper aim so? We never know, the newspaper group has been a co-owner of one of the IPL teams. After that, the media decided to forget all about the petition and to continue concentrating on selling fake cricket alone—something it has always excelled in, even after the PTI report of early 2014 and reported explosion by Sanjeev Chawla in mid-2020.

Many could argue that the petition and its contents were so frivolous that media didn't cover it. That would have made sense from the media's perspective if that were so and/or the Hon'ble Court had declared so. But that was not so and was not to be so, as has already been seen and would further be confirmed in the subsequent chapters. Something mathematically proved years ago and remaining unquestioned can't be frivolous. Or can it be? Yet the media totally blacked out even a somewhat potent order by the Hon'ble Court (at the face of it then). The media didn't bother about subsequent extraordinary developments in and actions by the Hon'ble Supreme Court. When the Committee of Administrators of BCCI decided to hold a meeting with the petitioners, a first time such act in the history of BCCI, it didn't matter to the media. COA's report and my rejoinder didn't bother the media.

Why did the Indian media choose to be deaf, dumb, and blind? Because it had no other option if it meant to conceal and keep the masses ignorant. There can't be any other explanation for the unprecedented silence of the media—not about a historical and unparalleled fight and crusade by someone against a very big public fraud and crime, but silence about the grotesque crime itself. Any mention or discussion about our petition in the media the same way as it normally covers even much less significant cases and thousands of other very petty issues (almost all the tens of thousands of issues covered by the media since 2013 with banner headlines would pale in comparison to this all-involving crime and fraud called international cricket) would have made the public aware of the stark reality. And that would have cooked the goose of the mafia and the betting syndicates. Why should have the media not liked it if its intentions are as it pretends all the time? Any relevant and truthful coverage by the media would have made the masses aware of the fact of cricket being institutionally fixed and made the millions of the bettors the world over much wiser. That would have dented the earnings of betting mafia—a big source of terror funding as well—a big way! The masses would have known that all the performances in the field were nothing but play-acting where the batsmen, the bowlers, and the fielders, all were acting in coordination as per the whims of some unknown directors. They would have known that cricket heroes were also like theatre actors only who acted through cricket. It was all decided beforehand who would score a century or who would score a duck. Which bowler would get a hat trick and who would get thrashed? The media ensured that didn't happen. That the masses didn't know. Why? Why did the media keep largely quiet or didn't follow the issue of continuing massive crime all these years despite being reminded through my press conferences and emails now and then including those to Press Council of India? Ask yourself these questions with a detached mind and true character of media as a whole and of all the acclaimed and illustrious journalists and editors will unveil before you shocking you beyond words. Probably, inaction by the Supreme Court won't have mattered much if the media had done its duty. Rather, there would not have been any need to go to the Supreme Court at all.

While on media, it will be quite relevant to relate one

particular instance here. In February 2014, after publication of my book 'Bettors Beware', when I was trying to contact media to make it aware of the reality about cricket, Mr. Rishabh Sharma, sports editor of Zee News at that time, responded and also sent a team of two to my residence at Kolkata to record my bytes for telecast that evening. Bytes were recorded, but never telecasted. It transpired to me later that they wanted me/were expecting me to say something against Dhoni/Raina (about that time some dispute between them was on), but had no intention to bring out the truth about cricket as a whole to the masses. That made me wiser that whatever people say on media is what suits the media. There was nothing objective about the functioning of the media. **The media brings out only half truths or gossips that it could twist anytime anyway to serve its own or others' vested interests. The complete truth is anathema to it. The above was too evident through Sudhir Chaudhury on Zee TV, in their programme DNA on 8th June, 2020, as enumerated in the previous chapter.**

It is the same media that more than a decade ago never bothered about the issue of leakage of more than ₹ 5,000 crores (1 crore = 10 million) of public money per year in the Indian Railways procurement through systemic corruption/ inadequacies. The leakage continued, much increased, and forgetting it, the Indian media continued bothering about leakages worth a few crores or a few hundred crores of rupees here and there, that too, generally to be quickly forgotten. As if existing material in the public domain bringing out above character of the media was not sufficient enough, explosive revelations by an ex-employee of India Today, Rakesh Krishnan Simha, expose the famed Living Media Group in a big way (https://kreately.in/ex-employee-exposes-india-today/ dated

29/8/2020, titled 'Ex Employee Exposes India Today And Rajdeep Sardesai'). The contents of his tweets as reported, another chance development, reconfirm what has been stated above.

Special mention is necessary here of journalists who are known for their anti-establishment stance and such reporting round the clock. They appear to be searching for the shortcomings of the establishment all the time. They get exposed the most by feigning ignorance of such a marvellous crime and fraud being committed for years under the protection of the same establishment. What is the relevance of their existence, other than pursuing some self-serving agenda just like others in their trade whom they are always criticising? Just to give an example, name of Mr Ravish Kumar of NDTV India comes to mind. The same applies to some known activists also in the same genre. Not surprisingly, gullible millions are taken in by such journalists and activists. These millions include a large number of the intellectuals of the society.

Let us see what the cricket journalists were doing all these years. There must be hundreds of them in India, and thousands of them in the world. What did their professional existence mean for the last decade or so? Without naming anyone, all these thousands of journalists had been talking or writing nothing but bunkum and nonsense while commenting on cricket or cricket matches all these years, day after day, hour after hour! Because no competitive cricket was existing at all as implied in all their gibberish. The same would apply to hundreds of cricket commentators and cricket experts. These morons or rogues had been holding the world to ransom within their capacity. **Once institutionalized fixing in cricket was exposed 7 years ago, it was for each and every journalist**

worth his/her salt to go to the bottom of the matter, appreciate what was happening and unearth the truth for the masses rather than going through the motions, feigning to be blind and deaf.

Even after the recent reported revelations by Sanjeev Chawla, a person of quite an interest to media all these years, these incompetent, shameless, depraved, and abominable cricket journalists are not in the least interested to see and tell the truth to the people, but are busy worrying about staging of IPL-2020, and T20 World Cup—about furtherance of the deceit, the fraud, and the crime. What despicable professionals they are!

Icing on the cake was that a Chinese company being sponsors for IPL-2020 was made an issue in the Indian media and became an issue for the billion plus Indians, but Cricket and IPL being totally fake was not yet an issue even remotely for anyone.

Now here is the real tragedy or comedy of the world of media, whatever way you like to call it, and, hence, of the human world. Mr. Pulakesh Mukhopadhyay, the sports editor of the Statesman, also writes a weekly column titled 'Short Point' in the Statesman as mentioned earlier. He has repeatedly been telling through this column for years how thoroughly corrupt cricket has been continuing, a recent sample having been reproduced earlier in this book. And yet, the same newspaper 'The Statesman' also, along with all other media, has been reporting on cricket in several columns all these years on a daily basis as if competitive matches had been taking place and would be taking place all around, and continues so even after the write-up dated 7/6/2020 reproduced earlier. **Could there be a better example of the absurdity of human practices?**

Could the same cricket be thoroughly scripted as well as competitive, both at the same time? Didn't the world need to be told by the media and/or the authorities that the cricket being so madly cherished was an unimaginably big fraud rather than leaving it for me to continue breaking my head?

Probably, it is right to say 'absurdity of human practices', since it will be unfair to single out media for such behaviour. I have come across many who one moment bemoan a match being fixed, and the very next moment in the same breath laud the performance of a player or players in the same very match forgetting that the performance being lauded was a result of some scripting. (A six was hit of a loose ball or a bowler got a wicket because the batsman played a bad or wrong shot!) If we look around, we very often find similar behaviour outside cricket also, though on a somewhat lesser note. For example, in the same breath, we talk about a leader being highly corrupt and being a great leader, both. Probably, humans are not rational beings after all!

Why should Atul Kumars be made to waste precious years of their lives because the world chooses to remain as base and banal as ever? With their competence, couldn't Atul Kumars achieve much more for the mankind if the world so encouraged them and valued their competence, time and energy? I do mean Atul Kumars here; because I am sure the world makes many like me waste their energies and life trying to improve its lot. Many crusaders and fighters are known even to have lost their lives, but our decadence has gone on increasing. Many will retort and say this is how the world is; I say I don't accept, let us correct ourselves for our own collective benefit, since no aliens will come to do that for us. The world is the way it is because collectively as humans, we have accepted so.

I have never been interested in individuals being punished, but all along have endeavoured in systemic corrections. But from the perspective of the authorities, all the fraudsters, scammers, and criminals must be punished, must be put behind bars. If it doesn't happen, the media shouts itself hoarse. Here in cricket, there are hundreds of criminals, most of them big celebrities, some heading or manning cricket bodies and organisations at state, national and international levels, on the loose, continuing to commit more crimes. The authorities are not acting. The media that makes so much noise, even if a petty criminal is not acted against, has not only been not demanding these criminals to be put behind bars, but is still presenting and projecting them as heroes and superheroes to the public. Why? Does or can the world media have any explanation?

In short, whatever media has accused anyone ever of, viz. being irresponsible, crook, shameless, idiot, arrogant, hypocrite, fool, rogue, liar, etc., applies to it first and foremost, applies to most of its editors and journalists. Something no one would ever tell you or make you aware of, no one would ever dare say because we get all our inputs from this '*Ravana*' of modern world known as 'media'. I say so not because of any grudge against anyone, but because this lies established beyond any doubt—as a matter of fact and records. I know it is very hard to assimilate this stark reality, but past many years have brought this out, leaving nothing to doubt. I am not talking about Indian media alone, though naturally most of my narrations relate to Indian media. Cricket is not a local Indian sport and is not being played by Indians alone. It is a popular international sport. Concealing its real character continues to be the doing and responsibility of the global media.

The purpose of above is to make the readers realise the

reality of journalists, editors, and media and how they control the human mind for the worse, feeding it with motivated propaganda and falsehood; notwithstanding all the good work being done by them. We don't realize, or rather are unable to realize, how our thinking process gets conditioned by the inputs we are stuffed with by the media. This realization is a key to understand the substance of this book.

□

The Excruciating Saga

Now, I try to give a brief account of how cricket continues unmasked and exposed for more than seven years. Almost all of it is already incorporated in the books and documents in the public domain; most of the key documents are now reproduced in this book or links are given for ready access/ reference. That is done **especially for the vast intelligentsia (that plays an important role in directing our collective destiny)**, to know and assimilate the unbelievable and untold reality not only of cricket, but of the human world. They are also welcome to ask any questions if still lingering after going through all the available documents.

More than a decade ago, with my information about betting, especially session betting, in cricket, and with application of mind/common sense, I realised for sure, to my great dismay, amazement, and astonishment that international cricket was institutionally scripted and fixed, with involvement of all concerned. It just couldn't be that only some sporadic fixing took place now and then by some players at the behest of some bookies or someone else, the game by large remaining clean and competitive—as has popularly been believed—the world being misled/brainwashed by the media and the establishment on purpose till date to believe so. It did sound unbelievable, but as I said it just was not possible that it could be any other way. I had no option but to believe my own common sense and logic, even though it totally defied what I and the world around me had been tutored to believe till then.

So, what could I do? What could I do to stop this fraud/crime or at least to make the world aware? It was not an ordinary/routine case of a very big corruption/fraud/crime that surfaces now and then and makes big breaking news headlines for days. It was something much bigger. I was just a common middle class man having no support or protection, and on the other side was the combined might of almost half the world. And the fraud was so big—giving rise to so many questions and counter questions, that it wasn't easy to explain it when the world was totally ignorant of it and won't even listen about such a possibility, leave alone believing about it. Everyone was bound to consider me super crazy, but I just couldn't ignore or disbelieve something that was certain to be, there not being any other possibility. Many, and there are hundreds of millions of them even today—unaware of all the developments in last 7-8 years, especially in the last 2-3 years, as a result of my efforts and/or otherwise, having a fixed mind duly conditioned (it may be wrong to find any fault with them)—would naturally retort how all could be involved in a fraud. The answer to this retort was rather simple: what is on display (obvious joke and drama in name of cricket) just couldn't be possible and couldn't be going on unfettered if all were not involved. A little application of common sense by one—clearing mind of the camouflage being created all around—**should and would easily make one realise this unbelievable, but rather easy to understand truth**.

Would a batsman ever tap the ball innocuously for a single

or two when necessarily requiring a six or four of it to win the game, if he were not being dictated by some script? Will the set batsmen fail to take advantage of 'free hits' more often than not in limited-overs cricket? Will acclaimed international players miss run-out opportunities or get themselves run-out so often displaying the basic mistakes even schoolboys won't be allowed to make? One can go on and on if one opens one's mind and eyes a little. I mention these here just to help readers realise rather easily and readily what is happening, not as a proof. Despite all its superficiality, the Amazon Prime TV Show 'Inside Edge' does help one see and understand how silly mistakes and brilliant plays can take place in the field as a result of fixing. The people remain largely ignorant of the stark reality—the same remaining concealed from them—even today because their ignorance, and consequently continuance of the colossal fraud, suits the media and the establishment in keeping the masses occupied and fooled.

Howsoever unbelievable or a fairy tale it may appear, the hard indisputable fact—now too open (as one would know after having gone through this book) though still unknown to the masses—is that Laras, Pontings, Tendulkars, Dravids, Kumbles, Gangulys, Cooks, Smiths, DeVilliers, one can go on and on, all have been part and parcel of continuing institutionally fixed cricket for at least more than a decade—mere actors in cricket grounds. All the talk about cricket day in and day out—in newspapers, in magazines, on TV, on the Internet, in social media, in private discussions—has been an exercise in utter foolishness or ignorance, or an exercise in most unashamedly indulged in fraudulent and treacherous behaviour, depending on one's awareness.

Today, one would readily know that someone is not talking

in the air, or indulging in social gossip, or having nightmares, or being paranoid because the above facts were also brought out to the knowledge of the Hon'ble Supreme Court of India through a detailed formal writ petition more than two years ago (details of it and developments since are mentioned/documented in this book) and no one could or did utter a word against the contents of the petition then and there. That renders above a matter of indisputable record now. **So, now anyone doubting the authenticity of what is said above will have no realistic ground whatsoever to do so, not even the Supreme Court of India or any of its esteemed judges. The opportunity for the BCCI and the Government of India as respondents, or the Supreme Court of India itself to question the contents of the petition was there in the presence of the petitioner/s when the petition was before the Supreme Court and before it was disposed of by it.** No one uttered a word against the contents then. Time for the same has gone for anyone; the petition has stood the test. The petitioner/s could be non-existent now for all practical purposes and validity of the contents of the petition can't be questioned behind their backs after disposal of the petition. Most of the world is still unaware of what is being brought out in this book. People today need not go through my earlier books or apply their minds to the available mathematical proof. They should and would know for sure, just from the facts and records brought out in this book that whatever is being said is absolutely true, howsoever unbelievable that might appear to be.

When the petition detailing a continuing massive public fraud came before it, all the Hon'ble Supreme Court of India was required to do was either to tell the petitioners and the world how, if so, the contents of the petition were misplaced; or to act and issue the necessary directives to the concerned authorities in order to stem the rot. **They didn't do the former and they did the latter.** And then the concerned authorities acted as irresponsibly as they could and everyone including the Court conveniently forgot everything. **The colossal international public fraud resulting in hundreds of billions of dollars of profit for the betting syndicates at the cost of the hundreds of millions of addicted bettors worldwide has been continuing unabated as a result. The question looms, "What made the Indian top Court forget its own Order?"**

Every one of my acquaintances tried to dissuade me from going to the Court, since without knowing much, most of them knew that I had no proof for the Courts, and, secondly, they didn't have much faith in the Indian judicial system. But I still took all the pain of going to the Supreme Court of India with a firm belief that it won't be possible for anyone to counter the contents of the petition and **that the Hon'ble Supreme Court of India won't be able to dismiss the petition whatever be its compulsions to do so**. By the grace of God, my well-founded confidence got vindicated.

When the revelations by Sanjeev Chawla to the Delhi Police were first reported by the Indian Express on 30/6/2020 that "no cricket match is fairly played" and "...all the cricket matches which people see are fixed", also pointing to the involvement of "a very big syndicate/underworld mafia" that influences all cricket games that, according to him, were like "movies which are already being directed by someone"; many thought and said that it was vindication of what I had been saying for last seven years. They were wrong in their appreciation or surmise. What I had been saying lied vindicated since 2013 through the mathematical and, hence, scientific proof presented in the public domain that was never contested by the ICC or any other authority. No Court or no Sanjeev Chawla was required to vindicate me. **The fact of institutionally fixed and scripted cricket, well vindicated, simply lied glossed over with utmost shamelessness and brazenness by ICC and all the other authorities, to allow continuance of the fraud and the crime, the rest of the world enjoying the big shame**. The reported revelations by Chawla didn't amount to any proof but did cause people take note of what was said. It was a pleasant surprise for me also since exactly what I had been asserting was endorsed by a key insider for the first time. As usual, everything was to be soon forgotten and media was to continue with its reports as if cricket was a competitive sport.

The world is well aware of the existence of the drug mafia: how the young generation throughout the world is made addicted to drugs and then drugs are supplied to them at exorbitant costs to generate large profits for the mafia. But, interestingly and unfortunately, the world is largely unaware of the existence of the cricket mafia—I am not calling it the betting mafia but the cricket mafia since whole of the cricketing world is a part and parcel of this mafia. This mafia has been addicting the world across age groups, religions, territories and professions to cricket betting. The institutionalised fixed cricket matches are scripted not only to rob these addicted bettors, but also to keep them addicted while attracting more and more people to betting. That is done by throwing in matches in between as lollipops where majority of bettors easily win. Now masses are being addicted openly through fantasy games like Dream 11, 11 Wickets, My 11 Circle, etc., with open support of the establishment and the media. The amount of money being robbed of the addicted bettors—tens of millions of them across countries—is anybody's guess, but it can safely be estimated to be in the range nearing a trillion of dollars.

Millions and trillions are just small words, their meaning and import has to be visualised. Near about one-third to half the population of the world is being fooled together round the clock through scripted and fixed cricket being sold as competitive cricket to them. A big part of this population has been made addicted to cricket betting through many tricks of the trade, and is being robbed through such matches to the tune of such sums as would be sufficient to sustain the human population on earth continuously. One has to pause a bit to grasp this fact.

Coming back to what could I do, I took pains to write a fiction (scared at the back of my mind since I was taking on a highly and vastly organised crime by about half the might of the world). It took me about three years (because I was in service then and was not a writer) in completing the draft of the book. To find a good publisher for the book turned out to be much more difficult. It took about a year or so further, along with spending money, in getting the book published with the title '**Inside the Boundary Line**' by Leadstart Publishing Pvt. Ltd. under the genre '*reality fiction*'. I hoped this book, published in November 2012, would make the world aware, and that would cause the desired and necessary corrections to set in, but nothing of the sort happened; even though my interview regarding this book was published in Deccan Chronicle and Asian Age on 27/1/2013, courtesy the unique cricket journalist Shri Bipin Dani (whom I searched and contacted through twitter), and I held a Press Conference in this regard in Kolkata on the 28th of that month. The cricket and the world continued with their merry way.

The year 2013 turned out to be a very significant milestone in exposing the massive fraud known as international cricket. My non-fiction work ***'Bettors Beware'*** got published this year by Diamond Books. It was republished under the title ***'All Cricket Matches Are Fixed'*** in 2016. While compiling this book, I also succeeded in mathematically and, hence, scientifically proving beyond any ifs and buts that international cricket across formats and popular league cricket like IPL and BBL were nothing but massive international public frauds. The mathematical proof was brought to knowledge of the world through an article ***'Cricket in Massive Fix?'*** published in the national English daily 'The Statesman' in July 2013, even before publication of the book. The publication of the book 'Bettors Beware' in November 2013 was followed up by me through a Press Conference in Press Club, New Delhi in end February 2014. This was covered by PTI as well and through PTI, the existence of mathematical proof of massive institutionalised fixing in cricket was further vastly conveyed to the world. The world including ICC and BCCI still continued to look the other way, since there was no one to question them. There has been no one to question them despite many explosive exposes including some by very senior and highly reputed cricketers over the years, in addition to my efforts. The international media, including the Indian media, strangely, has been acting as a keep of ICC and the cricket mafia.

This mathematical proof based on scoring patterns/ score books (the betting syndicates make killing in session or bracket betting by manipulating runs scored in a set of overs, session after session, match after match—and such continuous manipulated/controlled scoring is just not possible without involvement of all concerned) **has withstood the**

greatest test—the test of time—so much so that it remains unchallenged till date despite ICC being aware of it for years—I myself having sent a number of mails to ACSU of ICC. **Having all the mathematicians of the world at their back and call with the money and resources they have, the cricketing world has failed to utter a word against it even after being confronted with it as a result of my petition in the Supreme Court later on in 2017.** That alone should be sufficient enough for one to know that cricket being institutionally fixed and, hence, being a mammoth crime is an indisputable fact. Not only the cricket world could never even attempt to counter the scientific/mathematical proof; on the other hand, the sports editor of The Statesman got it ratified by a few mathematicians known to him when he consulted them about it—as recorded in the published review in the Statesman of the book 'Bettors Beware' by him in April 2014.

So, what could I do further? I continued thereafter writing books, holding press conferences, and writing to/approaching all the authorities I could think of including PM, Home Minister, and the President of India. I did write to a number of members of the parliament across parties and across states sending them copies of my book '***cricket sabse bada fraud aur moorkh bante log***'—Hindi translation of my book **'Cricket the Massive Fraud'** written after Bettors Beware, and published in end 2014. This book brought out the documentary evidence of inaction by the BCCI, ICC and other authorities.

I did write to the much-acclaimed NSA, Mr. Ajit Doval, since undoubtedly the issue involved terror funding in a very big way. There was no reason why he or his office should have not felt concerned. But no response from him/his office conveyed to me that despite all his reputation, sadly he also lacked comprehension, to say the least.

Not chronologically, but in the interim, I contacted the known crusaders and activists like Prashant Bhushan, Yogendra Yadav, Chetan Bhagat, and Arvind Kejriwal. Mr Prashant Bhushan bothered only half-heartedly, others didn't bother at all. It made me realize that no one was much interested in larger issues; mostly everyone was just a self-serving individual, whatever be the pretentions. No one was keen for the Truth; only half-truths and tending to superficial leaves (of trees) made people relevant and served them. I tweeted to a number of celebrities who publicly talked big, to learn that they all were also nothing but self-serving hypocrites or just superficial men and women of the world like anyone else.

I met Mr Prashant Bhushan a few times in 2014-15 for filing a PIL to bring the on-going cricket fraud to a halt. I had occasion to meet him and be in touch with him earlier also. He was kind enough to entertain me. He is a well-known advocate and activist in India who is known for filing PIL's to fight corruption and for having taken on Supreme Court of India for its failings over the years. So much so that even at the time of penning these lines, a much publicised and talked about Contempt case against him was under consideration of the Supreme Court of India. I contacted him towards end of 2014 since I was pretty sure that a very effective PIL could be filed even then on the basis of the contents of my book 'Bettors Beware.' I had a few meetings with him and the matter remained under his consideration for some time. Then once he advised me to contact Mr Rahul Mehra, the advocate, who was with him in the Indian political party AAP (Aam Aadmi Party) and was supposed to know about cricket much more than Mr Bhushan. I met Mr Mehra and could see that he was not even remotely interested in any PIL of the sort I was keen on. After that Mr Bhushan also didn't take much interest. Not much later, it came to light that Mr Rahul Mehra had some personal interest in IPL/IPL teams.

It is to the credit of Mr Bhushan that he gave me opportunity to speak on the subject of cricket fixing and its implications in the National Convention on Anti Corruption held in New Delhi on the 27th and 28th February, 2016. A Citizens Whistleblower Forum was formed with much fanfare. I requested and expected it to take the issue forward, but nothing happened. And nothing was heard of the Forum afterwards. All my emails thereafter to Mr Bhushan remained unanswered. He showed himself to be a half-hearted warrior earlier as far as the cricket crime was concerned. Later on he was not interested at all even though I kept him informed of the PIL filed and subsequent failings of the Hon'ble Supreme Court of India. Everyone has own priorities and sense of proportions.

Pleasantly, I came across some exceptions also. Mr Bipin Dani, the cricket journalist, who interviewed me first on the subject in 2013, was the first of them. I contacted and met Late Rajinder Puri, highly acclaimed Indian journalist and cartoonist, who did give the necessary support to the cause within his limitations, but, unfortunately, he didn't live long enough and passed away in 2015. Mr. Pulakesh Mukhopadhyay, the sports editor of the Statesman, himself a crusader against corruption in sports in his own way, did entertain me sufficiently within his limitations. Diamond Books and its erstwhile editor, Shri G.K. Santosh/Santosh Kumar did give me all the support. Kudos to the publication for being bold enough to publish my books that exposed the very establishment it was a part of. Sh. N.K. Verma, the owner of the publication was also always quite cooperative and courteous. From media, pleasantly surprising to me, I got total unflinching support to the cause from Shri Suresh Tripathi—the editor of Rail Samachar—known to me as a result of my crusade against systemic large scale corruption in Railway procurement during my service in the Indian Railways. And it was through him that I could finally contact Mr. K.B. Upadhyay, the advocate, who assisted me in my efforts with the Supreme Court of India, not demanding any fees. Later on, when the Indian media decided to go deadly silent on the PIL even after the Hon'ble Court's curious orders, it was Mr. Suresh Tripathi who acted beyond his normal call of duty. He came out with my elaborate interview to tell the world what was happening. That interview titled 'Cricket Clean Bowled by Railway Officer' is available on the website of Rail Samachar under the link https://railsamachar.com/english/?p=924 .

My books, my public posts in the social media on the massive fraud called cricket, and even the offshoots of PIL, brought me in contact with some people in India, who were totally unknown to me. They had understood the reality through my efforts. And they were the people, unknown to me, who truly appreciated my efforts. They asked me the right questions. One asked me what made me take on this fraud, which was never area of my work. My answer was that because I thought that no one else in the world could do what I had set to do. Someone else wondered what it would have required to believe in self in those initial days against beliefs of the whole world. He was right; probably that was the toughest part of it all. Then someone from as far away as Kerala came into contact with me after coming to know about the PIL and supported me as he could. But such people are very few in number, to be counted on fingertips. The very vast majority remains of those driven by nothing but parochial self-interest, ego, conceit, and petty mindedness etc. Most of the people are unable to take on or are not interested in taking on big ticket wrong-doings because mired in own petty wrong doings and weighed down by same, rightly or wrongly.

I met Mr. Bishen Singh Bedi, Mr. Surinder Khanna, and reputed cricket journalists including Kishore Bhimani and Pradeep Magazine. They didn't take much interest or were not interested in calling the bluff of something that was or had been their bread and butter. Mr. Surinder Khanna was honest enough to tell me so in so many words when I met him first and the only time years ago and presented him with the book 'Bettors Beware'. He said that no one would do anything since cricket made the fire burn in too many households. Precisely, that has been happening.

I met Mr. Bishen Singh Bedi, an ace international cricketer of his times, in Press Club of India through pre-appointment, soon after the publication of the book 'Bettors Beware'. As luck would have it, he was there on some cricket-related purpose (I am forgetting exactly what it was) and was to address the assembled cricket journalists. I felt happy to be introduced to them and to be able to distribute copies of my book 'Bettors Beware' to them. Funnily enough, there was never any response either from Mr. Bedi or from any of the assembled journalists ever, Mr. Pradeep Magazine being one of them—to the mathematically proven and thoroughly exposed fact of cricket being institutionally fixed, and many other very interesting and explosive revelations through that book.

It was to be only years later that Mr. Bishen Singh Bedi was to say at Sahitya Aaj Tak in November 2018 that there was no bigger scam than IPL in India. He went on to say, "***I have a lot of***

experience in cricket, you can tell what is happening in what match. If we stay blind even while seeing, then it's our choice." I don't know what led him to say so after so many years when the scam and fraud had been continuing for a decade, but such explosive statements by none other than Mr. Bedi were easily taken in its stride by the Indian media and brushed under the carpet with the same alacrity as it had been doing with many such or greater exposes in cricket over the years. The same way as they brushed under the carpet the massive outburst by Al Jazeera in 2018 in listing number of international matches including test matches alleged to having been spot-fixed (a sham phrase used by ignorant or rogue journalists or media for fixing) or sudden blurt by Aamer Sohail on Pak TV in 2017 saying Pakistan had won the ICC World Cup for reasons extraneous to cricketing abilities. It was the same media that marvelled in making big news out of some dog barking somewhere. The millions of intelligentsia, who crib about and discuss petty or non-petty cases of fraud, scam, and crime in social media for days on end, continued to celebrate the biggest known and proven scam and fraud saying cheers. The historical Sreesanth episode of match-fixing happened during IPL-6 in 2013. There was a lot of hue and cry in the print and electronic media. But everyone chose to remain busy only with superficial/sham news/exposes/investigations and making noises just for the sake. **The society, including investigators and judges, fooled by cricket experts and cricket journalists, betrayed total lack of common sense by believing that a bowler alone could fix and manipulate number of runs in an over.** The masses including great intellectuals across professions remain so fooled even today, such a portrayal even in 'Inside Edge', the recent somewhat popular fictional TV show on match-fixing in cricket further contributing to the camouflage. A small chapter titled *'Large Scale Fixing Gets Established but All Look the Other Way'* in the book 'Bettors Beware' as long back as 2013 brought out the sure existence of a much bigger scandal based on the facts of Sreesanth episode alone, compared to only one or two players being involved as masses were fooled into believing then, but as conveyed in the title of the chapter, everyone has continued to look the other way even till date. I approached many media channels, including all the leading ones, and celebrated journalists like Rajdeep Sardesai, Arnab Goswami, Marya Shakeel, Ravish Kumar, Rahul Kanwal, Navika Kumar, etc., that time or afterwards through emails or tweets in an effort to make the truth reach the masses, but no one was remotely interested in truth or rather in masses knowing the truth—contrary to the big claims and pretentions otherwise all the time by them all. That is the true character of the highly acclaimed and celebrated journalists, whether you like it or not—they are nothing more than paid servants of their masters, men/women totally devoid of minimum common sense. Vindu Dara Singh, the insider those days, was reported of having said then, years ago, that IPL was 100% fixed. But, as usual, every one continued to look the other way.

I did contact media in some of the cricket-playing advanced countries like Australia, South Africa, and England also through emails more than once without getting any response. I emailed to English-language media in Pakistan also a few months ago, but again didn't get any response from any quarter. I did email to editors' guild and Press Council of India, Law Commission, Bar Council of India, RSS—in short, any institution I could think of—but apparently no one was interested in looking beyond one's own nose. That is how we are—hypocrites to the core, whatever we may pretend all our lives.

This is the 21st-century human world for you and me—where the self-righteous journalists, editors, celebrities, leaders, preachers, and activists et al don't tire of giving sermons on any issue day in and day out, don't tire of quoting religious scriptures, don't tire of talking big, and the same very people close their eyes and minds to a colossal crime openly taking place, conveniently forgetting all their sayings and sermons. It is a world where any petty happening in any corner becomes a matter of discussion and pastime for millions of the wise on social media and thousands in media, and yet the same people feel totally unconcerned of a massive public fraud and crime taking place around them round the clock—fooling them, making a mockery of all their intelligence and consciousness, and looting tens of millions of their fellow beings. I do wonder what self-respect these people have. That being fooled so openly round the clock doesn't bother them. A world waiting for Nature to bring it on the right path?

I did approach Subramanyam Swamy also, especially since at a point of time, he was publicly making noise about a connection in IPL/Cricket and Sunanda Pushkar murder/death indicating involvement of many top politicians. The noise made by him also turned out to be another case of shoot and scoot—everything/everyone from Lalit Modi to Robert Vadra to Vijay Mallya in India has been nothing but a case of shoot and scoot by great Indian journalists and politicians. The public and the intelligentsia, remote-controlled by the media, don't tire of discussing such things/people for years, unconcerned of the fact that hardly anything ever reached a logical conclusion. Mr. Swamy, just like any other activist/journalist/celebrity/politician/law-enforcer didn't find a colossal on-going public fraud amounting to hundreds of millions of dollars per year—contributing to terror funding in a big way—cheating tens of millions of people round the clock across religions and countries—worth his attention. I made aware almost all those who mattered, officially or otherwise (whether themselves culprits or not), like Amitabh Bachchans and Sachin Tendulkars through tweets/emails/letters/personal contact, but with no result.

Consequent to Sreesanth episode, Mudgal and Lodha Commissions happened along the way. I took pains to approach them, sending my books to them with clear acknowledgements. By turning a blind eye/through inaction, they also proved themselves to be the culprits for the posterity. I wrote a detailed letter to the Supreme Court of India in April 2014, enclosing the necessary documents and copies of my books requesting it to take suo motu action against total/institutionalised fixing in Cricket followed by a reminder in end May 2014. Again to no avail.

I came up with another book titled '***Underworld Cup T20 (Media, Modis, Mudgals, Mamatas All Dial Dawood)***' in 2016. The title of the book itself said all. The book along with other aspects of ongoing colossal fraud analysed matches of the 2016 T20 World Cup to reveal that these were all pre-scripted and fixed. The purpose was to remind the world that in cricket, there was nothing sacrosanct even about World Cups—the tournaments considered to be a matter of big prestige for nations. Everything got controlled by the mafia and the bottom line remained maximising ever-increasing profits/gains for the betting industry/syndicates by continuously fooling hundreds of millions across the globe through fixed cricket matches. This book also like my previous books couldn't achieve much and the fraud went on unbridled, even though the books had answered or attempted to answer any question that could arise in any mind with regards to this human fraud and brought out the existence of the fraud with vivid details.

Still the cricket and the world moved on with absolutely no difference. Some very important questions still remained, answers to which had to be found out. Now there was no other option left but to knock at the judiciary and file a PIL in a High Court or Supreme Court of India.

□

Intriguing Questions

'To know that we know what we know, and to know that we do not know what we do not know, that is true knowledge.'

—Nicolaus Copernicus

It is true that I couldn't answer a few questions, answers to which can easily be found out by any genuine official investigator or the authorities, most of these being readily known to hundreds of cricketers, cricket experts, and should be known to at least some of those in cricket administration. These questions would be:

(a) What is the modus-operandi for execution of ball-by-ball script? How the scripted outcome of each ball is known to players on the field or gets conveyed to them before the ball is bowled? Since more than one player have to combine to ensure the scripted outcome of any ball.

(b) A lot of action takes place in the field, even other than the net result of every ball. Is that also directed, partially directed, or left to the experience of players, especially the senior ones?

(c) At times, the outcome or net result of any ball may not

be as intended or as per the script, given the inherent randomness and given that there can't be any retakes. How is that dealt with? (Though it has to be corrected in subsequent plays, but there will be many fine points of interest).

(d) What keeps so many perpetrators of the fraud glued together? Why doesn't anyone spill the beans about existence of the all-involving fraud even though some of them get taken up now or then like Shakib-Al-Hasan of Bangladesh, Nasir Jamshed of Pakistan, Sreesanth and some other league players of India? Punishment about a decade back to Mohammad Amir, Mohammad Asif, and Salman Butt, the three leading players of Pakistan in a spot-fixing case is well known. Are they duly compensated surreptitiously while being taken up now and then to keep the world fooled through camouflage? (The bigger the fraud, the bigger the camouflage!)

(e) Who writes the scripts for various matches/series/ tournaments? Some ex-cricketers? Are script writers being assigned for each series/tournament?

(f) Who or what body calls the shots and controls/manages this magnificent international fraud involving almost half of the world?

(g) How do the mafia and the authorities ensure that those in the know-how of the script can't misuse their knowledge for making money through their agents through betting?

(h) On what basis or how is it decided in advance which country/team would be winning which tournament? Is it through consensus among the participating teams or do they simply carry the orders?

(i) Which commentators/experts know the script in

advance and are assigned the role to mislead/befool the viewers/listeners, and, thus, the bettors?

(j) How and why Umpires and others give in to the mafia? How are Umpires briefed about/conveyed the decisions they have to take on the field?

(k) How the millions and trillions of dollars of loot money are distributed among various forces participating in the loot? Does majority of those involved like players work on fees basis?

And there may be some more similar questions. It would be real interesting for all of us to know answers to these questions, even though the answers would be too explosive. The answers will shock us beyond imagination when we shall know how openly and continuously we were being fooled all these years, for life time for many of us. There shouldn't be any doubt that these all are real questions, answers to which exist and are readily known to hundreds in the cricketing world. It is amazing that those, especially so-called intellectuals, who become very curious to know answers to questions even while watching or reading fiction, to get rid of suspense, don't feel much curiosity to find and know answers to these very absorbing real-life questions.

Any meaningful investigation will easily find answers to these fascinating questions. It will also mean hundreds of celebrities, especially in India, being put in the dock. These celebrities will include a number of superheroes, 'padmashris', 'padmabhushans', 'padmavibhushans', and even 'Bharat Ratnas' (titles of the Indian civilian awards). We shall know comedy of our evolved systems through which criminals had been receiving top national honours.

It is necessary to keep in mind here that the fraudsters/

criminals belong to all the cricket-playing nations, some of which being first-world countries like Australia, New Zealand, or United Kingdom. The cricketers and cricket administrators in all these countries had to be involved. India could take solace that it was not the only or main country corrupting cricket as was generally believed or as ICC tried to give impression from time to time. Something being thoroughly corrupt means all the participants are equally the culprits.

Till now, I have been forgetting the culpability of big corporate companies, media houses, etc., as owners of IPL teams. Similar culpability will be there in other countries where leagues on the pattern of IPL take place. In India, one of the IPL teams is owned by the topmost corporate of the country, its MD and major shareholder being one of the richest men in the world. Jobs and/or lives of many who would be reading this book or would have tried to associate with its publication could be under his control directly or indirectly, or of others who are party to this mega scam. Other teams are also owned by big corporate/media houses/top celebrities. One can expect governments, despite all their pretentions, not to be able to take on them, since it is an open secret that democratic governments are controlled by the corporate. Corporate companies are involved not only as team owners, but also as organizers or in organization of league cricket in various countries. The fraud also connects with Bollywood, the famous and influential Hindi Film Industry, a top Bollywood star and others from the industry even owning IPL teams.

There are many associated grave offences that would mean a lot of work for all the law-enforcing agencies. For India alone, the loot money through fixing and betting would be in the tune of scores of billions of dollars per year. All of it would be black money, betting being illegal in the country. As per the Law Commission of India itself, the amounts involved gave rise to parallel economy. That was years back. No one still bothered. The trail of the inter-connected crimes could seemingly be unending, with a large number of leaders and celebrities getting implicated and the amounts involved. At present, son of India's Home Minister is the Secretary of BCCI. There were intriguing cricketing questions and even more intriguing questions regarding criminality of hundreds of luminaries. Even today, these questions need answers.

Therefore, the judiciary became very important for upholding the much hailed checks and balances in our evolved systems. It remained the only hope for an individual—who had set out to take on the larger evils, on the combined might of the media, the corporate, the celebrities, and the establishment—learning on the way that he was all alone in his mission. So, in an attempt to bring a halt to the on-going public fraud and crime through cricket, and also to find answers to the above intriguing questions, I decided to knock at the doors of the Supreme Court of India.

That was the purpose; not to send anyone to the gallows, since I could foresee that many of who's who of India would be implicated and to take action against them would be too prolonged a process and any result a near impossibility in a country where leaders and VIP's hardly ever have to pay for their accumulated sins. **But the crime and fraud involving loot of hundreds of billions of dollars from tens of millions, and fooling of other hundreds of millions had to stop. The masses had to know.**

Many still greater shocks awaited me.

□

Big Betrayal

Finally having exhausted all avenues including a number of press releases through press conferences and published interviews over the years—everything costing me time, efforts and money (most of the times)—I successfully filed a detailed formal petition along with Mr. Shantanu Guha Ray, the award-winning journalist, in early November 2017, in the Hon'ble Supreme Court of India.

I felt that successfully filing the Writ Petition (Civil) no. 1163/2017 was my ultimate achievement since now there was an official record, duly supported by documents, of the continuing mind-boggling sins being committed by the world, by very those who don't tire talking of religion and rights or wrongs, who sit in judgement over everything, who hold high offices, by those who project themselves and are considered as pillars of righteousness, by those who are our celebrities and brand ambassadors! **I did believe that I had done my job and now it was for the world to act in its own interest.**

As mentioned earlier, Shantanu Guha Ray, the internationally acclaimed and awarded journalist, agreed to be my co-petitioner. I had traced and contacted him after I came to know of the book '**Fixed! Cash and Corruption in Cricket**' written by him and published by Harper Collins India in

2016. The book was quite explosive, but still no one bothered about what was going on and what this book brought out. This book remains the best journalistic work on continuous fraud and crime through cricket till date—far better than any other such work in contents—even though another journalist Chandramohan Puppala was to come up with another book on the subject titled '**No Ball**' much later in 2019 published by Pan Macmillan India. Strangely enough, neither the writer nor the publishers appeared to be aware that any mention about fixing in cricket not taking into account the contents of the PIL—WP (C) 1163/2017—on the subject filed in the Supreme Court of India was not much relevant at that point of time and was an exercise in utter ignorance. However, still the book 'No Ball' brought out and emphasised on the link between match-fixing in cricket and Dawood Ibrahim—officially considered the mastermind behind many terrorist attacks in India, especially Mumbai blasts of 1993. Shantanu Guha Ray did regret while writing forward to my book 'Underworld Cup' that he was not aware of my earlier books on the subject while writing his book 'Fixed! Cash and Corruption in Cricket'. I am not aware if awareness level of Mr. Puppala is any better even today.

How come even journalists interested in the subject have not been aware of my books or PIL in the Supreme Court of India, not to talk of common man or the masses? Has it been my fault or has it been the achievement of the media (in succeeding in suppressing what matters a lot if not the most)—of the news channels and the newspapers that don't tire of vying with each other and claiming to be the number one? To my mind, nothing exposes the media more and shatters its credibility more—to the smithereens. The media understands very well that the day masses become aware of the reality about cricket, all its business and big earnings from cricket and cricket-related activities will crash. And its masters in governments and in mafia will also get hit similarly.

So, after a lot of leg work, some failed attempts, and overcoming all the obstacles—the biggest being to find a suitable advocate at nominal cost to help file the PIL—I could finally successfully file the petition in the Supreme Court of India in early November 2017. Even though the world has failed to take note yet, I knew and know what a big and miraculous achievement it was. Because now there was an official record of the existence and continuance of the biggest fraud or one of the biggest known frauds on earth being perpetrated by the combined might of almost half the world. A few who had the opportunity to go through the contents of the petition then understood how indisputable these were. The petition brought out not only the existence of the colossal fraud, but also the documentary evidence of how all the authorities including Judicial Commissions and the President of India had failed to act and had shunned their responsibilities.

The petition being voluminous is not documented in this book, but some subsequent key communications with the Supreme Court of India are documented in the following chapters to give the readers first-hand knowledge and a very fair idea of how inadequate/evasive Supreme Court of India has been in meeting the common expectations. Though the petition is not documented in the book, the link https://drive.google.com/drive/folders/1XKSxqjTLlUEeZUaWyZs_5UHRs41DY99D?usp=sharing can be accessed by the readers for going through the same. This link not only gives the full petition along with all the annexures (as a part of the IA 81233/18 filed by me in BCCI main case 4235/14), it also gives the additional documents that were filed in the writ petition, and the I.A. (impleadment application) itself. Out of these all, I reproduce the relevant text of the additional documents (paras 3 to 28) filed on 25/1/2018, at the end of this chapter for ready perusal of the discerning readers. Also, the synopsis of the petition is reproduced in my open letter to Supreme Court judges; the letter is documented in the chapter 'The Deaf Statesmen'.

Let us now briefly see how the Hon'ble Supreme Court of India—the institution we all look up to and most of us still tend to hold in esteem—has acted in the matter till now.

Our petition to the Supreme Court was not about any legal or judicial issue or matter. It simply was to request it to direct the authorities to act suitably and do the needful in the matter of an established and scientifically proven ongoing colossal public fraud. When the matter came up for hearing first on 2nd February, 2018, I, appearing as party in person, just told the Hon'ble Court, the bench comprising the Hon'ble CJI, Deepak Mishra, and the Hon'ble Justices A.M. Khanwilkar and D.Y. Chandrachud that we had been compelled to file this petition and bother the Hon'ble Supreme Court due to inaction by all the concerned authorities despite repeated requests to them over the years. No further discussion took place and the Hon'ble Court passed the following order: '*Let a copy of this petition be served on the Central Agency so that it can make arrangements for the counsel for the Union of India to assist the Court. List on 16th February, 2018.*' The necessary service was done as per orders of the Hon'ble Court. However, I couldn't appear on 16th and sent a request letter for adjournment due to the sad demise of my mother in the early hours of 13th February, 2018. The Hon'ble Court passed the following orders on 16th February: '*List the matter after two weeks.*'

I came to know through the counsels of the BCCI, M/s Cyril Amarchand Mangaldas that they had filed a caveat and wanted copies of the petition/submissions made. The same were duly served. And, thereafter, it became a job to get the matter listed further. In all probability, now the respondents and the media had come to know of the explosive contents of the petition, and all the forces joined hands to push the matter under the carpet. The petition that had progressed smoothly till then in routine had suddenly lost all significance after its contents were known to the Hon'ble Bench and the media. I had to fight tooth and nail to get the matter listed again. Correspondence in that regard is a matter of record. However, I reproduce below the final communication in the chain—a very short email by me dated 1/5/2018—that will give readers a glimpse of working of the Supreme Court of India—an institution held in much awe and esteem:

> Dear Sir,
>
> Ref: Your mail dated 20/4/2018
>
> I had submitted a written reply dated 24/4/2018 to the above.
>
> Further, on 25th April, 2018, your website showed the tentative date of listing as 7/5/2018 for the subject case. The very next day, it was being shown as 28/9/2018. Again the next day, i.e., on 27/4/2018, the date was shown as 4/5/2018 and is still being shown as that, cause list for 4/5/2018 having not been issued yet.

To a petitioner like me, it is very puzzling and unnerving.

You may kindly like to look into it and do the needful at your end.

Regards

Atul Kumar

By God's grace, the matter was finally listed on 7th May, 2018 when the same bench as on 2/2/2018 passed the following order and disposed of the case without any discussion/deliberations: '***Heard Mr. Atul Kumar, the petitioner No. 1 appearing in-person and Mr. Parag P. Tripathi, learned senior counsel appearing for the Committee of Administrators. In our considered opinion, the Committee of Administrators may take a decision with regard to the grievance made in this writ petition and submit a report, which shall be considered in the main proceedings that relates to BCCI. The petitioners are at liberty to assist in the main case. With the aforesaid liberty and direction, the writ petition stands disposed of. There shall be no order as to costs. The interlocutory applications, if any, stand disposed of.***'

It took me quite a few days to realize that the above order meant that I had been given a walkover in the Hon'ble Supreme Court of India. I had been fighting the case myself, as party-in-person, and had been quite apprehensive, not knowing much about fine points of judicial working or of courts. Naturally I had been quite nervous representing in awesome top Court of India. And still I was given a walkover; no questions asked of me by anyone! Why? Simply because any debate in the Court would have meant opening a Pandora's box or a can of worms; it would have become very difficult to hide the reality from the world. The powers couldn't bargain for that.

This was an order that kept the hope and the door open, but was highly inadequate or evasive considering the contents of the petition. Was not use of the word 'grievance' by Court no. 1 for the contents of the petition a bit out of place? Was it some personal grievance of the petitioners? Does bringing out an unprecedented colossal public fraud with big implications for terror activities amount to 'grievance'? Maybe the right term legally! Anyway, **I rightfully expected to get standing ovation from the Hon'ble Court for making it aware of such a big international fraud, having been able to file such a petition against combined might of almost half the world, having done an unprecedented great public service,** but disappointingly it acted quite inadequately in passing the final order as it did. Still, as said above, all was not lost. Though the developments since then have confirmed that it was an evasive order only, the Supreme Court of India never meant to rise to the occasion, even though implicitly their own order confirmed that the contents of the petition were relevant and were in order. More than 2 years have passed since then, about 2 years have passed since the COA submitted its report as per the Court's orders—**a report that miserably failed to address the contents of the petition and was a big sham**—and I submitted a rejoinder showing with documentary evidence how bogus a report that was, the dishonesty of the COA in dealing with the issues standing exposed (nothing was ever heard by me in response to my rejoinder), but the Hon'ble Supreme Court of India seems to have forgotten all about the petition and the liberty given by it to the petitioners to assist it in the main case related to BCCI. It must be a unique case when the Supreme Court of India has miserably floundered to take cognizance of its own order. **And we are talking of the Supreme Court of India, not of any tom, dick or harry.**

That itself shows the power of those who are running and controlling the monstrous fraud and crime called Cricket as Sanjeev Chawla was later to mention as reported. The COA for BCCI appear to have acted as their puppets, even at the cost of losing all their credibility. What about the Hon'ble Supreme Court of India? Better to leave it to the imagination of the readers. ICC being their puppet is already a foregone conclusion. At the same time, all the developments have gone to show the power of Truth, whether man recognises or not, whether man remembers or not. Armed with that power alone, by God's grace, I was able to call the bluff of the world around me years ago, could succeed in exposing all the mighty institutions despite their awesome power, and got vindicated in my own life time. So much so that even the Hon'ble Supreme Court of India had no option left, but to unmask itself while in effect assisting and protecting the fraudsters through its inactions.

The Supreme Court of India is an institution that quite often directs the destiny of the country through its orders. We are talking of an institution at whose mercy the governments in the country fall or continue at times. We are talking of an institution that decides what is wrong or right in vastly varied matters of law, Constitution, and national life that govern and have governed the destiny of the country and billions of its inhabitants. And when on top of all other institutions constituted by man, such a mighty institution also starts acting indifferent and fails to answer public concern for an ongoing enormous public fraud and crime, the human evolution itself lies exposed as being founded mainly on Falsehood.

This is how a recently retired judge from the Supreme

Court of India, Justice Madan Lokur publicly commented on handling of a PIL by the Supreme Court of India on the plight of migrant labourers as a result of enforced Lockdown in India in April-May 2020. (source: https://thewire.in/law/after-humanitarian-law-died-a-million-deaths-the-supreme-court-has-finally-stirred-itself)

> '*What could the court have done? Public interest litigation is all about public interest. Well-meaning persons approach the Supreme Court for the enforcement of constitutional and statutory rights of those who have no access to justice. This is precisely what the petitioner (and others) did. The Supreme Court was approached on behalf of migrant labourers on the road for a do-something direction. Sadly, the court let them down, badly. The court could have asked pointed questions to the state. It could have asked if the Central government had a plan of action for the "unforeseen development" (an expression used in the status report); it could have asked for the steps taken and proposed to be taken to mitigate the hardships that the migrants faced; it could have asked if the state governments were geared up for the massive influx of migrants whose presence "would aggravate the problem of spread of the virus". Issues of socio-economic justice and constitutional rights are vital and raise a whole host of questions, but not one was asked in a public interest litigation, and the issue buried ten fathoms deep. If any event ever shook the collective conscience of the nation, the travails of the migrant labourers did.*'

Though it might have not stirred the conscience of Justice Lokur and rest of the country because of their ignorance, the PIL on shamelessly open colossal public fraud through Cricket was no less well meaning, and the failure of the Supreme Court as pointed out by Justice Lokur in the above para was no less pronounced and shattering in dealing with our petition, given its contents.

The arrogance of ex-CJI Ranjan Gogoi, evident through his interviews to the media in March 2020 after taking oath as a member of the Rajya Sabha, appeared quite misplaced. He appeared to convey that the Supreme Court was supreme irrespective of what it did, and couldn't be questioned. Yes, but then, it also became all the more imperative on the Supreme Court to properly discharge its responsibilities and duties upholding public interest and the larger good as supreme. The interviewer Navika Kumar of Times Now could pinpoint contradictions in his short interview itself to him. Shri Ranjan Gogoi himself failed to give any heed knowingly or unknowingly to a very important letter dated 16/5/19 addressed to him by me when he was the Hon'ble Chief Justice of India. That letter is now documented in this book. The Supreme Court of India is a public institution answerable to public. For the world or for India—for the coached minds—the Supreme Court of India may be supreme. But in the larger perspective, Truth is supreme.

After all the authorities one could think of had failed, the Supreme Court of India remained the only hope. But, most unfortunately, it has also gone the way of the rest of the world. The way the Hon'ble Court has slept over the issues arising out of a gigantic ongoing public fraud and its explosive and far-reaching implications (that include continuation of terror funding in a big way and looting of hundreds of billions of dollars per year from the hapless cricket bettors by the betting syndicates and mafia) for seeming eternity, it should shame even a low-rung irresponsible bureaucrat of any local office. Not that I am saying anything behind anybody's backs, I have said it all repeatedly, in sterner words, in direct communications to the CJIs. The documents in this book are presented for ready perusal of the readers as are necessary for one to be able to appreciate the above.

Given below is the extract of paras 3 to 28 of additional documents filed on 25/1/2018 in the WP (C) 1163/2017 in the Supreme Court of India, as mentioned earlier:

1. That Petitioner no. 1 made a complaint to the cyber cell of the Mumbai Police on 1/11/2017 through email bringing out the above, after having filed the writ petition. He did so with full awareness that such an action involved the risk of taking the all-powerful betting mafia head on. Undoubtedly, almost identical fate (being silenced) of the well-known names, Bob Woolmer (the cricket coach) and Sunanda Pushkar when there was real threat from them of exposing the mafia activities in cricket was also at the back of his mind to add to the fear. Still he went ahead as he has gone ahead with the writ petition, in single-minded pursuit of an extraordinary mission, i.e., taking on a fraud being committed by the combined might of hundreds of super-celebrities, big industrialists, powerful politicians, and media moguls. Fortunately, for him, he has survived, probably because he was considered as a man of no consequence (and rightly so) by the mafia and those drunk with power in comparison to their combined might. That perception of such a threat is not imaginary, but real is borne out by a news article dated 21/10/2017 in the Hindustan

Times highlighting threat by betting mafia to an ex-Pakistani Cricketer Sarfraz Nawaz. A true copy of the news article dated 21/10/2017 in the Hindustan Times is annexed herewith and marked as ANNEXURE A/42.

2. That as no response to that email to cyber cell of the Mumbai Police was received by him, Petitioner No. 1 sent a written complaint dated 4/11/2017 to that office. The copy of the complaint was also marked to PMO, MHA, Minister for Sports and Youth Affairs, BCCI and some prominent editors in the print and electronic media. A true copy of the complaint dated 4/11/2017 by Petitioner No. 1 to the Mumbai Police along with a copy of the complaint through email mentioned therein is annexed herewith and marked as ANNEXURE A/43.

3. That Petitioner no. 1 did receive a phone call from someone in the Mumbai Police (Phone no. 022-22625028) a couple of days later asking whether he had sent this complaint and to which email id the complaint had earlier been sent. Due reply to the queries made was given by him. Subsequently, a copy of letter dated 14/11/2017 was received by him whereby the Jt. Commissioner of Police, Economic Offences Wing, Mumbai had referred the matter to the Dy. Commissioner of Police, Cyber Crime Mumbai. A true copy of the letter dated 14/11/2017 from the Jt. Commissioner of Police, Economic Offences Wing, Mumbai to Dy. Commissioner of Police, Cyber Crime, Mumbai is annexed herewith and marked as ANNEXURE A/44.

4. That this appears to have been the end of the action taken by the Mumbai Police in the matter since the Petitioner No. 1 hasn't heard anything further and the twitter handle @theDcricketOffi has been continuing with business as usual, bragging more and more by each passing day. Through his latest tweets, he has been showing how Big Bash League being held in Australia was fixed. In support, some of the tweets by him subsequent to the aforementioned complaint are annexed herewith. True copies of such tweets and a few more significant tweets by @theDcricketOffi are annexed herewith and marked as ANNEXURE A/45.
5. That a study of the continuing tweets by @ theDcricketOffi vis-à-vis progress/play in the matches tweeted about for the last many months now readily goes to show any open mind beyond doubt that T20 leagues the world over and international matches alike are fixed and that the script is known to him beforehand. He does slip in wrong tips now and then to befool his clients and followers and to ensure that they have to keep guessing all the time. What stands out here through these tweets is that of late, for some reasons, mafia itself is interested in exposing total corruption in cricket through @theDcricketOffi. One objective of making the bettors know that matches were fixed with script being known to mafia and then befooling them by tipping with the false script at times is too obvious.
6. That more shocking than anything else is the fact that even in the face of such a written complaint on brazen prowling by betting mafia, with cricket being

scripted and fixed becoming a foregone conclusion, there has been absolutely no reaction or response from BCCI or any Ministry or big names of media, except for a response from the Statesman, and the @theDcricketOffi continues with his tweets and WhatsApp messages least bothered since there is no one to question him. The Statesman came out with a meaningful though relatively obscure coverage (given the gravity of the issue) on the subject complaint. A true copy of the news coverage in the Statesman dated 15/11/2017 is annexed herewith and marked as ANNEXURE A/46.

7. That the Statesman is a very responsible and prestigious newspaper of the country, known for its impeccable integrity. Giving prompt cognizance by it to the complaint does mean that the complaint had at least some substance and wasn't trash. And yet, all others have maintained a deafening silence on such an enormous matter. That reconfirms the culpability of media and media editors at large in this ongoing massive fraud.

8. That a very pertinent question that also arises is why the cricket world comprising cricket journalists, cricket players, cricket experts, cricket managers and team owners, and cricket board officials is silent in the face of tweets for months by @theDcricketOffi clearly showing fixed cricket matches across the globe, match after match, and earlier tweets regarding IPL 10 final as brought out in the writ petition? Even if one cricket match involving star players and shown to be fixed remains uninvestigated and unexplained, it implies

something grossly wrong in cricket. We have been confronted with many such matches not only as a result of the tweets by @theDcricketOffi, but also as a result of various media reports over the years that remain unexplained.

9. That a big crime is not being committed by the players, coaches and administrators alone, but also by those who commentate on the totally fixed matches and write articles on and discuss about those in newspapers columns, cricket magazines, and TV channels as if competitive matches were being played. They become an essential part of this massive fraud. The following excerpts from the book 'Underworld Cup (Media, Modis, Mudgals, Mamatas All Dial Dawood)' are quite relevant. "*The way fixed cricket continues internationally continues getting clapped by thousands in the grounds the world over, and continues being analysed and discussed 24x7 as a competitive sport over internet, in hundreds of sports magazines, in hundreds of sports channels, in hundreds of news channels, and in sports pages of thousands of newspapers, in homes, in offices, in journeys, and in public places, even years after lying totally exposed, Indians can take solace in the fact that Om Prakash Aditya's poem didn't apply to India alone. The whole world is proving to be nothing but an ocean of the dumb.*" The poem referred to is the famous poem '*idhar bhi gadhe hain, udhar bhi gadhe hain......*'

10. The book 'Underworld Cup (Media, Modis, Mudgals, Mamatas All Dial Dawood)' brings out a lot of insight into the institutionalised fixing of cricket, especially

through study of matches in the last T20 World Cup 2016. A copy of the book 'Underworld Cup (Media, Modis, Mudgals, Mamatas All Dial Dawood)' by Petitioner No. 1 is annexed herewith and marked as ANNEXURE A/47.

11. That the above fact of total inaction/insufficient action by the authorities and media alike on a specific complaint bringing out open prowling by the betting mafia against a background of fixed cricket further confirms the whole substance of the subject petition howsoever unbelievable that may appear to one, salient points being:

    1. A massive public fraud through fixed cricket has been merrily going on for years.
    2. Cricket is not fixed as a result of cheating by odd players at the behest of odd bookies as is popularly believed and made to be believed, but fixing has been total and institutionalised with matches being thoroughly scripted as to how many runs are scored of each over/ball or when a wicket is to fall, etc. The scripting is done to ensure the maximum possible gain to the betting syndicates, teams winning and losing and performances of individual players being just by-products. The batsmen play shots, bowlers bowl balls, and fielders field as per the dictates of the scripts already in place.
    3. The establishment and the media at large have been too happy in allowing and facilitating the fraud to continue and prosper.

12. That another book 'Cricket: The Massive Fraud' by Petitioner No. 1 also brings out a lot of insight into the institutionalised fixing of cricket and fact of inaction by/complicity of various authorities/institutions to allow the massive fraud continue. A copy of the book 'Cricket: The Massive Fraud' by Petitioner No. 1 is annexed herewith and marked as ANNEXURE A/48.
13. That it becomes relevant here to draw kind attention of the Hon'ble Court to a news article titled 'IPL rot deeper, but no hard evidence: Cops' published in the Asian Age dated 18th May, 2013 that is self-explanatory. A true copy of the news article titled 'IPL rot deeper, but no hard evidence: Cops' published in the Asian Age dated 18th May, 2013 along with a true typed copy is annexed herewith and marked as ANNEXURE A/49.
14. That the above news article brings out that the Delhi Police were at least quite aware and sure of spot-fixing (a name given to fixing by media and establishment to purposefully dilute the public perception about it) being rampant in many matches of IPL that season as well as the previous season, i.e., IPL-6 and IPL-5, and involvement of a number of players, and yet they couldn't do anything since they didn't have the necessary evidence. They had a very strong evidence against 3 players, namely S. Sreesanth, Ankit Chavan, and Ajit Chandila, and proceeded against them (it is known now that they have failed to obtain conviction in Court even against these 3 players). There were many news reports those days of many matches in the past having been fixed. But not a single incident

of reported/suspected fixing was ever explained by cricket authorities or cricket journalists/experts to cleanse the air. When the police were quite aware of a continuing public fraud, was it not their responsibility and duty to ensure that the fraud discontinued? Was it not imperative on them to get to the bottom of the matter and get the necessary evidence against a fraud so rampant by their own admission? Instead, they failed to even move a finger when the Petitioner no. 1 contacted them to help them get to the bottom of the fraud they were aware of, as brought out in para 45 of the writ petition. As a result, the fraud has been continuing with great damage to the society as has been brought out and seen. And the present case of the Mumbai Police as brought out above in this submission further confirms that it is nothing but inaction, lack of will, and in all probability, complicity (as brought out in some journalistic reports from time to time) on the part of the Indian Police that has ensured that the massive open fraud through fixed cricket has been continuing unbridled. Evidence doesn't grow on trees. It is the job of the law-enforcing agencies to exert themselves to obtain and get the necessary evidence and to stop a rampant crime they are aware of. And it isn't something very difficult. Asking the right people the right questions and proper application of mind would have helped a lot in achieving the goal and bringing the culprits to the book. What was required was only the necessary will. Petitioner No. 1 could have helped them and can help them a lot in going to the bottom of the matter if the police so desired.

15. That while talking of evidence, it may not be out of place to reproduce here following extract from Petitioner No. 1's book 'Inside the Boundary Line' for kind consideration of the Court, "*...Was it that 'evidence' and 'knowledge of truth' were two different things? Was it that realisation of truth didn't have to depend on evidence? Was knowledge something much superior to evidence? Was too much dependence on evidence a man's folly? Or was it done so on purpose as evidence could be manoeuvred or manipulated by the powerful ones or could be interpreted or misinterpreted as per their command? Dhiren's experience told him that the answer to all these questions was in the affirmative. It was so mainly because evidence had any meaning only if a set of facts were examined and analysed by people having an absolutely open mind, fair intent, and similar common sense. And that was hardly ever the case, especially when the powerful got involved in a matter...*" By evidence, the author probably meant what is talked about as 'direct evidence' as in the Asian Age news article mentioned above. A question arises as to what is meant by evidence? Can there be anything above logic and common sense to arrive at truth? Isn't evolvement of science and of human civilisation based on common sense and logic? Isn't the very existence of various laws and Courts a result of application of logic and reason? Isn't acceptance or non-acceptance of the so-called evidence itself a logical action? Isn't it that logic and common sense are at work while the Hon'ble Court is examining the subject petition and this submission? All that has been produced for consideration of the Hon'ble

Court through the writ petition should leave no doubt in any open and logical mind regarding the existence of institutionalised fixing of cricket matches. And there is a maxim that 'people may lie but circumstances don't'. The existence of session and bracket betting proves continuous total institutionalised fixing of cricket beyond any doubt. One only needs to know about such betting and apply mind a bit.

16. And it is the natural tendency of human mind to go by logic that is exploited by the fixers and script writers. While millions of bettors across the world would be betting as per some logic or the other for competitive cricket, such scripts get unravelled in the field match after match that defy all such logic from a bettor's perspective, to stun the bettors, all under the garb of uncertainties of the game. That, and that alone, explains what people have come to see and term as shock/inexplicable performance of teams or players, or shock turnarounds/results so frequent in cricket. Set batsmen playing dots in slog overs, batsmen getting themselves run out rather than being run out, bowlers bowling wides and no balls at crucial moments—and many more such inexplicable and suicidal plays day in and day out—exemplify the above. A number of such illustrations from cricket matches the world over involving almost all teams and all star players have been chronicled in the Facebook page of 'Bettors Beware' by Petitioner No. 1.

17. That while the fraud through fixed cricket is massive beyond normal comprehension, its evidence is abundantly available before the eyes of cricket

viewers as brought out in the above para and paras 24, 25, and 28 of the writ petition. They aren't able to see it because they aren't looking for it and because it lies camouflaged by cricket experts and cricket commentators. Teams are supposed to be playing to win. Plays by batsmen/bowlers/fielders of different teams stare us in the face day in and day out that defy will/effort to win on their part. For example, when a boundary is required to win off the last ball and a batsman like Kieron Pollard simply taps the ball straight to a fielder with no attempt to hit a boundary without any reprimand from any quarter, the institutionalised fixing of cricket becomes clear with a little application of mind. Many such examples have been publicly given by the petitioners in their various writings.

18. That, in self-deception, one may tend to brush aside such evidence, though as clear as day light, as subjective and may tend to attach ifs and buts with it. But there can't be any sensible rebuttal of or ifs and buts attached to the objective and scientific evidence based on principles of probability and existence of session betting as detailed in the book 'Bettors Beware' and briefly enumerated in the writ petition. Even a billion of testimonies or a million of arguments otherwise can't defy or defeat the evidence of institutionalised fixing of cricket resulting from the application of the basic principles of probability to the score books. That is the importance and significance of scientific proof. Then there is easily understandable and equally irrefutable evidence resulting from the prophetic

tweets of one Cricket Insider about final of IPL 10 as brought out in para 54 of the writ petition. Many of the subsequent tweets by the same or another Cricket Insider as brought out reconfirm the continuance of scripted cricket. Thus, more than sufficient evidence about continuous institutionalised fixing in cricket is readily available, if one doesn't choose to be blind and devoid of human intelligence. No judge needs to wait 10 to 5 for even a day, leave alone years, to get evidence in this regard. The police citing non-availability of evidence for their inaction lie totally exposed.

19. A lot more direct evidence (as the world is accustomed to) for institutionalised fixing of cricket of the magnitude as evident would easily emerge when the hundreds of perpetrators involved are asked the right questions honestly and transparently and made to answer those. Many of them being young boys in their teens or early twenties would easily break down and sing as they can't be hardened criminals as yet. As brought out earlier, significant such direct evidence does have come up and continues coming up now and then, but lies ignored, buried and not acted upon.

20. That three recent significant media reports have surfaced, two of those after filing of the writ petition, that are self-explanatory and even these superficial media reports show how deep the rot in cricket has been and has been growing. As usual, the world has taken these also into its stride and the fraud continues unbridled and unabated.

21. That one of the reports dated 11/10/2017 published by 'The Guardian' feared women's cricket to be a

target for corruption. A true copy of the report dated 11/10/2017 published by 'The Guardian' is annexed herewith and marked as ANNEXURE A/50.

22. That another report dated 14/12/2017 published by 'The Sun' brought out that through a sting operation, two Indian fixers revealed prospective spot-fixing in Ashes (considered to be onc of the most prestigious competitions in Test Cricket). A true copy of the report dated 14/12/2017 published by the Sun is annexed herewith and marked as ANNEXURE A/51.

23. That another report dated 15/12/2017 published by 'The Sydney Morning Herald' brought out that a former player Dirk Nannes had revealed fixing in Bangladesh Premier League when he was participating in it, with even team-owners being involved. A true copy of the report dated 15/12/2017 published by 'The Sydney Morning Herald' is annexed herewith and marked as ANNEXURE A/52.

24. That the facts brought out in the writ petition and this submission raise several very serious and pertinent questions that needed to be addressed by all the four pillars of democracy in India. Since all the pillars including judiciary have failed till date, the onus has now come on the Hon'ble Supreme Court of India through the subject petition to apply itself and do the needful.

    (a) Has the Constitution of India miserably failed the people of India such that an open massive fraud goes on unbridled for years after having been detected, laid bare publicly, and proven scientifically? Does the failure of all the institutions created under the Constitution without any exception not mean failure of the Constitution itself? Is it time now for review and overhaul of the Constitution of India?

(b) Do members of the Indian Parliament have no responsibility to act when a massive ongoing public fraud is brought to their personal notice?

(c) Do we all accept such a deplorable condition of the country and simply keep quiet?

(d) Does an ordinary responsible and intelligent citizen have no worth and does all the worth lie only in those in authority and in power?

(e) What does a citizen do when all the institutions of the country under the Constitution fail him and his fellow citizens in the process?

(f) Is there absolutely no accountability of the police in India? Can nothing be done when the police openly aids/protects mafia and the criminals, allowing an open fraud to continue, taking shelter behind excuses? Is it alright for police and other law-enforcing agencies not to make any efforts to get the necessary evidence, to ignore the evidence when it is presented to them, and continue to allow a public crime to continue citing non-availability of evidence as an excuse for not doing anything in the matter?

(g) Does a big-time open massive public crime become legitimate simply because it is committed collectively by the super-celebrities and superheroes of the society, and has the blessings of the powerful industrialists (many of them own the league teams indulging in fake and fraudulent cricket) and politicians? Is it alright for judiciary also to be a mute spectator just for that reason (inaction by Mudgal and Lodha Commissions on repeated requests and appeals of Petitioner no. 1 and keeping secret the suspected/implicated 13 names submitted by Mudgal Commission to it by the Hon'ble Supreme Court itself refer)? Recently, the former BCCI President, Anurag Thakur also publicly mentioned that the Hon'ble Supreme Court should have disclosed those 13 names (interesting though that he mentioned so only months after and not when he himself was the BCCI President). A true copy of the news report dated 22/11/2017 published by 'The Times of India' in this regard is annexed herewith and marked as ANNEXURE P/13.

(h) Is there no accountability for the media in India? Is it alright for it to be the sweet will of media whether it will inform the public of an ongoing public fraud affecting millions of people or not? Can nothing be done for acts of omission by the media? Can nothing be done when the media chooses to highlight petty issues and non-issues, but sweeps the gravest of the issues under the carpet because of its own complicity in the wrong-doings or because the super-celebrities and the super-powerful ones are involved?

(i) Can nothing be done when, for years, the media

knowingly continues to spread falsehood by reporting about a sport as if it were a competitive one, even though it being fake and a fraud had been publicly exposed and brought to its knowledge repeatedly? Should there not be a system in place to prosecute media moguls and journalists for propagating frauds and scams? It is cricket journalists, like Vikrant Gupta and Boria Mazumdar, to name a few, that have been propagating the massive scam through fixed cricket the most in India.

(j) Does a big crime that financially strengthens the anti-social forces in a big way and is also a source of terror funding become legitimate just because it entertains the ignorant masses and is hailed by them? Undoubtedly, aiding terror funding means aiding killing of innocent citizens and army men over the years.

(k) Is it alright for mankind to continue with self-denial and self-deception in treating an out-and-out fake sport as a competitive and great sport? Have various institutions not been created to oversee and ensure overall well-being of the mankind and guard it against all-pervasive frauds?

(l) If those indulging in a massive fraud are allowed to earn enormous amounts through fraudulent acts and treated as heroes and super heroes, shouldn't all those jailed for petty thefts/crimes be set free straightaway? Can law also have double/multiple standards?

(m) Do all sermons and moral talk by the government, editors and journalists, political leaders, or even judiciary on any issue not become meaningless since one acting blind to and allowing continuance of a massive open public fraud loses all moral authority and credibility?

(n) Is it alright for the intellectuals of a country (judges of the highest court included) to bother about procedural wrongs and petty or grave improprieties within their institutions/spheres, but to remain immune to a massive scam/fraud encompassing all the institutions?

(o) Can two countries—India and Pakistan—playing fixed cricket matches with each other for years—really be enemies as made out by the media and the government? How will masses be informed of this hoax that has been used for years to befool them by diverting their attention from the real basic issues?

(p) Does the above not have big military, and international political implications? How will those be addressed?

(q) And, if the massive fraud called Cricket is to continue as it is and if the country and its Constitution have to remain a mute spectators to it as has been the case for the last many years, shouldn't children in schools be taught that there was no virtue in fair play and truth and that falsehood ruled India and the modern world so that they don't grow up as frustrated adult citizens?

25. That it may not be out of place to mention that these are the times when the faith of people lies shattered in law-enforcing agencies and legal and judicial systems in the country in the wake of the recent verdict in the well-known 2G case. Not very long ago, there was another case of Sahara-Birla Diaries/papers involving the current Prime Minister of India and many other leading politicians across political parties when the Hon'ble Supreme Court of India didn't allow even a probe, though to a common man prima-facie enough evidence existed to warrant at least such a probe. Probably, it is because of the resulting demoralisation and public perception that many seasoned citizens of the country have expressed their apprehension to the petitioners that rot is so deep and widespread that nothing may come out of this writ petition and the rot will go on. But the petitioners have gone ahead with the writ petition having faith in the power of truth and knowing that '*satyameva jayayte*' is the guiding beacon for the Hon'ble Court. Nothing is supreme but truth and truth alone.
26. That, above all, the scam brought to the kind notice of the Hon'ble Court through the writ petition is not a one-time scam that can be buried by the media and those in power for all times to come. This is a continuing scam that is bound to stare everyone in the face sooner than later. It will acquire much more significance after cricket betting becomes legal in India, process for which is on in full swing, Law Commission of India having recommended so as per media reports. Therefore, it will be most prudent

to deal with this massive ongoing fraud/scam of institutionally fixed cricket fairly and squarely now.

A question arises that should disturb and worry us all to our bones; **'Is it that only the Supreme Court of India betrayed the petitioners and hence the people by allowing a public fraud and crime symbolizing deep degeneration of the society to continue unabashedly, or the whole system stood abused, or did the developments signify serious flaws in our evolution?'**

□

Zero Governance

After the contents of our petition were vindicated in the Supreme Court, I wrote another letter in early July 2018 to PM Narendra Modi with copies to other concerned officials/ authorities. I was writing for the nth time to a Prime Minister who never tires of boasting of resolve of his government for zero tolerance against corruption. The letter met the same fate of being volleyed between home and sports ministries at a low official level with no action, as my earlier attempts over the past years.

That made me wonder what for so many law enforcing agencies, departments and ministries in the Indian government were? Was it also to serve the purpose of playing football amongst them with something they found inconvenient and wanted to ignore?

The letter is reproduced here for the necessary perusal of the readers. The letter reconfirms my true intentions all these years.

Shri Narendra Modi Dated: 7/7/2018

Prime Minister of India,

New Delhi.

(for his kind personal attention)

Subject: Total inaction by UOI on an on-going massive proven public fraud through the game of Cricket, now vindicated even in the Supreme Court of India.

Reference: WP(C) no. 1163/2017 in the Supreme Court of India

Dear Sir,

Your kind personal attention and that of the government including the Home Minister and the Home Ministry was drawn repeatedly since you became the Prime Minister of India to the ongoing massive fraud through the popular game of cricket. It was done through the direct letters by me to the President of India, yourself, and others, posts on some known public websites, newspaper reports now and then, and through books on the subject. **But, despite your public claim of zero tolerance against corruption, you and your cabinet/ government with full knowledge have allowed this fraud not only to continue, but prosper by each passing day.** Probably, you chose to do so to secure in your knowledge that continuation of this fraud suited the whole political class of India and the Indian media alike and, hence, no one from those quarters would utter a word against you and the government on it. You and your government didn't bother despite serious implications of this fraud including threat to the national security having been made known publicly and repeatedly. And even though this massive fraud affects the masses and millions of poor Indians adversely, you and your government have decided to continue turning a blind eye to it. Given the facts, you and your government just can't shun responsibility and complicity (through inaction) in this massive proven fraud.

Because of your and government's actions contrary to your public utterings and claims, greatly let down as a citizen of India, I was compelled to spend further considerable time and energy in filing a writ petition in the Supreme Court of India. The facts detailing the above assertions are available in this writ petition no. WP(C) no. 1163/2017. **Copies of this petition were duly served on UOI as per the Hon'ble Court's orders. Hence, your government must be well aware of the contents.** The text of the petition/mention about it is also available on the following websites/links among others:

http://www.livelaw.in/cleaning-cricket-retired-rly-officer-scribe-move-sc-seeking-stay-ipl-leagues-check-match-fixing-read-petition/

https://barandbench.com/pil-supreme-court-probe-match-fixing-cricket/

https://glaws.in/2018/02/04/pil-supreme-court-asks-sit-probe-match-fixing-betting-ipl/

Going through the facts brought out in my submissions to the Hon'ble Court would shock you and PMO to know how all the law-enforcing agencies and the police of the country have been acting blind in the face of blatant acts of cheating and fraud being committed publicly and openly, even though specific complaints have been made to them at times. For example, a twitter handle @theDcricket has not only been announcing and showing fixing of cricket matches, but also has been cheating and defrauding the gullible bettors openly for over a year now on the strength of his knowledge of the scripts of the matches, but all law-enforcing agencies and the country including the Indian media have been happy to act deaf and dumb. You may also like to have a look at the impleadment application no. 81233/18 filed by me in the C.A. no. 4235/2014 in the Hon'ble Supreme Court in deference to the Hon'ble Court's order dated 7/5/2018 in the above writ. The UOI officials can easily obtain a copy of that for your and others' perusal. A copy of that will also be served on UOI shortly/in due course.

While the Supreme Court-appointed Committee of Administrators (COA) for the BCCI also has now acknowledged the gravity of the contents in the mentioned writ petition vide their mails to me dated 9/6/2018 and 3/7/2018, UOI headed by you is still sleeping with no action whatsoever in the matter, even though the continuing fraud is greatly detrimental to the nation. **One must understand and appreciate that the COA for the BCCI and the Supreme Court have their own limitations. It was and it is for the government of the day to deal with this continuing open public fraud of monstrous proportions that undermines even the security of the country, with an iron hand.** But, contrary to your and your government's loud pretensions otherwise, you have betrayed the people of India and you have become their culprit. Your own finance minister/minister without portfolio, Arun Jaitley is clearly implicated through his past as one of the top administrators in the BCCI and for IPL for years, overseeing and administering fraudulent cricket.

You and your government pose to be champions of

Hinduism as a way of life. I am at a loss to understand which Hindu scripture/teaching supports continuance of a massive public fraud to the great detriment of the Hindus and brethren from other religions alike.

The purpose of this letter is not to put you and your government in the dock, but to make you all realise and accept your failings in this issue. **The purpose is to urge upon you and your government to wake up at least now and act and redeem yourselves since there is no escape route left for you and your government except for blatant shamelessness since everything including culpability of all concerned is docketed and beyond contention.**

The blatant fraud that cricket has over the years not only been instrumental in cheating hundreds of millions of your and my countrymen emotionally and financially, but it has also been contributing to funding the terror outfits in Pakistan led/supported by Dawood Ibrahim and others in a very big way. The sums involved are to the tune of lakhs of crores of rupees per year. This is all well established and is not an imaginary/idle talk. Compared to these sums, most of the financial data and statistics discussed so fervently by your government and the Indian intellectual class round the clock would appear very petty. This also means among other things that many of the terror strikes in Kashmir, about which the media talks day in and day out and the government and Army are much concerned, would have been funded through this fraud perpetrated by celebrity cricketers, other celebrities, top industrialists (through owning IPL teams), and the media (by hiding the truth from the public), with your and your government's apparent complicity. And the whole country makes so much noise about Kashmir and problems there, in media and in social media. **Do you realise sir what does all this mean for us as a nation with you as our Prime Minister?** While we condole slaying of police and defence personnel, and civilians in Kashmir almost on a daily basis, as a nation, we have not only been turning a blind eye to, but celebrating the massive fraud that has been financially strengthening those responsible for those continuous slayings in J&K.

The Indian Police has been dealing with betting and fixing in cricket over the years. It has either been working at the behest of the culprits or it has been totally incompetent. Otherwise, both betting and fixing in cricket couldn't have been continuously prospering. Otherwise, police couldn't have been basing its investigations on wrong pretext and in wrong directions all these years despite correct position being in the public domain. I would love to help the top police officers if they really meant to crack down on the fixing and fixers. Once fixing is cracked and controlled, betting syndicates in land and abroad will wane away by and by, freeing the millions of innocent Indians from their clutches.

With a move afoot to legalise betting on cricket in India and Law Commission finally submitting its report on the subject a couple of days ago, necessity to crack down on the continuous institutionalised fixing in cricket with the sole purpose of looting millions of gullible bettors becomes all the more important.

Through this letter, I suggest as a responsible citizen of the country that a team of suitable senior, intelligent, and upright officers/persons be formed immediately to comprehensively deal with all the aspects of the ongoing blatant massive fraud through cricket as has been brought out in the mentioned writ and my subsequent submissions to the Hon'ble Supreme Court. **Let no Arun Jaitley or M.S. Dhoni or Virat Kohli be above law and above the collective interest of the nation.** I offer myself to brief and guide such a team when formed. Or UOI may take any other action as it deems fit in the circumstances of the case, but act it must immediately, meaningfully and surely.

I look forward to a line in response. If you so desire, I can brief you or your chosen ministers/officials personally on the issue.

To sum up:

- I be allowed to brief you or your chosen ministers/officials personally on the issue so that there is clear comprehension on the subject in the minds of those who have been destined to lead/govern our nation.
- **A team of suitable senior, intelligent, and upright officers/persons be formed immediately to comprehensively deal with all the aspects of the ongoing blatant massive fraud through cricket.**
- I offer to assist such a team if need be.

Thanking you,

(Atul Kumar)

CC:

The President of India for his kind perusal and necessary intervention.

PMO

Shri Rajnath Singh, Minister for Home Affairs

CJI through the Registrar, the Supreme Court of India

Shri Vinod Rai, Head, COA for BCCI

Home Secretary, MHA, Government of India

Cabinet and other Ministers, Government of India

(Atul Kumar)

What does no action by a government for over 5 years against an on-going massive public fraud and crime mean? **Does it mean zero tolerance against corruption or does it mean zero governance; notwithstanding whatever good or great work done by the government?** A lot can be debated about governance or non-governance, but probably that all will be redundant. Here we are not concerned with any political actions or inactions, but with basic governance. **Proof of the pudding is in the eating.**

Will it open eyes of the horde of intellectuals who use up a lot of their time and energy by joining in propaganda of hailing PM Modi and his government for their great governance round the clock on the social media? There must be millions of such educated and intellectuals, men and women having achieved a lot in their lives. Will they do some objective evaluation at last? Probably not; probably the bigotry will win. Though better for us all, if the eyes opened.

□

Bureaucratic Quagmire

After the final orders by the Hon'ble Supreme Court of India while disposing of our petition, I filed an I.A. (impleadment application) number 81233/18 in the main case relating to BCCI indicated in the Supreme Court's final order, i.e., CA 4235/2014. This was done to proceed further to assist the Supreme Court in the main case concerning BCCI in deference to the Hon'ble Court's orders and to keep the door of the Supreme Court ajar for us. Side by side, I also approached the Committee of Administrators (COA) for the BCCI for a meeting since further action lied with it as per the Court's orders.

A meeting was held (on 17/7/2018) that proved to be an exercise in futility and deception, and while the COA posted its report on the website of BCCI under the link http://relaunch-live.s3.amazonaws.com/cms/documents/5bd95399b2f6c-COA%20Report%20in%20Writ%20Petition%20filed%20by%20Atul%20Kumar%20(23%2010%202018).PDF, they never posted the petition in reference to which this report was, or my rejoinder to their irrelevant report despite my specific request for doing so, thus making a mockery of the accepted norms of fair dealing and principles of natural justice. That, all telling, rejoinder is reproduced below for ready perusal of the readers.

'REJOINDER TO COA's REPORT in WP (C) 1163/2017 IN THE SUPREME COURT OF INDIA

Dated: 14/11/2018

The Committee of Administrators (COA)

Board of Control for Cricket in India

Mumbai—400,020

Subject: Continuing Colossal Fraud through Cricket

Reference: 1. Report dated 22/10/2018 by the committee of administrators in terms of the Hon'ble Supreme Court's order dated 7/5/2018 in Writ Petition (Civil) No. 1163 of 2017

2. Writ Petition (Civil) No. 1163 of 2017 and I.A.s no. 13606/2018 and 59570/2018

Dear Sir/Madam,

It is with sense of an acute pain that I have to say the following in reference to the above.

It can be well understood that it is next to impossible for COA/BCCI to publicly accept the concept of Cricket being a colossal institutional fraud, especially when one of the two members of the Committee herself is an ex-cricketer, but then Truth will have to be faced square in the face at some point of time. Then why not do it earlier than later? Can someone come along and just declare that gravitation didn't exist on earth? The COA have done something like that in their report. As some recent developments suggest, time is fast approaching when it will become more and more difficult for the cricketing world to hide from the truth. One expected a much better, more objective, and meaningful report from the man of stature that the present Head of the COA is, especially since no one else has shown much interest in curbing this nation-damaging fraud. It may be appropriate to call it a continuing national disaster. But the COA, to use Churchill's words, have acted as men of straw, at best.

The peculiarity of cricket fixing is that those who are supposed to curb it and act as authority on the subject don't know or understand much about it since they don't know much about betting, session betting, and bracket betting; whereas scripting of matches and fixing is governed by all such betting—the same being the very purpose of it. Most of cricket journalists and sports editors would also fall in that category. It is for this reason that while those in authority remain ignorant or unconcerned, many among bettors are becoming aware of cricket being an institutionalised fraud slowly but surely through my books and Facebook page of 'Bettors Beware'.

Apart from session betting, the matches are scripted with timing of wickets and partnerships to ensure movement of betting odds in matches in a way such as to trap the punters and maximise profits for the betting mafia. It is for this reason that we come across sudden flurry of wickets followed by long partnerships or vice versa, or totally one-sided matches between two equally capable teams happening quite often. The wickets tumble and partnerships blossom against run of play for this very reason. This has been illustrated and explained for many matches in my books and the Facebook page of 'Bettors Beware' earlier on. I don't do it much now because of its repetitive nature. No doubt, now and then, a few matches are scripted to make punters win and feel happy to keep them going and trapped.

It is rather strange that most of the people, especially cricket journalists, don't realise a very elementary thing, that spot-fixing—as session-fixing is popularly called—does imply match-fixing also. Whole has to be a function of its parts.

I could have appreciated if COA had expressed helplessness in tackling the fraud given how monstrous it has become, as they did during the meeting with us, rather than foolishly, haughtily, and deceitfully denying its very existence in the report now without being able to counter a single piece of evidence out of all the evidence brought out in the petition. Why did Shri Vinod Rai repeatedly tell us during the meeting that they shared our concerns if all along he had decided that the petition was bunkum? Would he please explain this? Is it not clear that COA have been under some compulsions now to give such a shabby, dreadful and deceitful report on such a grave matter?

This rejoinder to the subject report by COA will bring out how COA have gone back on their words (that is the trigger for my anger), how they have overlooked all the evidence that was before them, to suit themselves, and how they have been wilfully misleading. It will also bring out some recent international developments that further confirm the contents of the petition. This rejoinder is also being made with a hope that the COA will heed my request and will duly review their decision and report in the light of contents of this rejoinder.

I am aware that this rejoinder would sound repetitive at many places. But there is no harm in being repetitive; rather it is required to be so when those being addressed have shown themselves to be morons.

The above report by the COA is not only extremely disappointing, but also shocking.

It is shocking because I don't find anywhere in this report even mention of two specific things that the COA explicitly promised when they met with us, the petitioners, in New Delhi on 17th July, 2017. One, they promised investigation of the IPL-10 final by ACSU of BCCI, even though I wanted it to be done by outside agencies independent of BCCI. Two, on my request of getting the twitter handle @theDcricket duly questioned and investigated to ascertain what was going on behind the curtains, Shri Vinod Rai, the Head of COA, mentioned that they would do better than that. He assured that they would recommend to the Hon'ble Supreme Court to get him investigated. That gave me a ray of hope since this twitter handle is very clearly an insider who knows all about the script of matches across the world from T20 leagues to international matches, as his hundreds of tweets for over a year make abundantly clear. He must be knowing all about the scripting and fixing of matches, maybe many times more than the underground Aneel Munawar. He is available in the open. And yet while ICC is hunting for or feigning to be hunting for untraceable Aneel Munawar, they have been acting blind to the existence of @theDcricket and his tweets, in-spite of their and COA's attention having been drawn repeatedly by me to this fact. **I find this bizarre.** Turning a blind eye to the tweets of @theDcricket conspicuously shows the complicity of ICC, BCCI and now even COA/BCCI in the continuing fraud that the game of cricket has become. It is akin to the police when faced with a murder, turning a blind eye to the existence of a key witness who had seen it all and knew all about it, and whose existence is well known to the world. The fact that this open ignorance comes after the COA having explicitly suggested the opposite in our meeting (as confirmed by the brief minutes of the meeting e-mailed by me to the COA on 17/7/2018) brings to question the earnestness and integrity of the committee. That email is reproduced below verbatim:

Atul Kumar

Tue 17/07/2018, 15:32

Committee of Administrators;

Rahul Johri;

Karina Kripalani;

shantanunewshound@gmail.com

This is to convey thanks for holding the meeting today and to put the outcome of the meeting in a perspective (in confidence).

It was disappointing to learn that the purpose of this meeting was primarily only to hear us out and the meeting was not to be much interactive as COA was not to apprise us of their viewpoint. However, still the following transpired as a result of a brief discussion that took place:

1. COA indicated that it would recommend to the

Hon'ble Court to order thorough investigation into the tweets by @theDcricket for over a year now. Though it is extremely unfortunate that such an action has not yet been initiated by the concerned authorities, we applaud the indicated action by the COA. An honest and thorough interrogation/investigation of him/his affairs would definitely help spill many beans and many skeletons will come out of the cupboard. That alone will be a significant step in the right direction.

2. The COA indicated that they were as concerned about the state of affairs as us, the petitioners. Though they felt that the solutions suggested by us were rather impractical. We maintain that the solutions suggested, though may appear to be extraordinary, were necessitated considering how bad things were and given the very grave and serious implications of how things are continuing.
3. Nevertheless, we requested that the COA might please go ahead with practical solutions such that the action taken should have some telling effect given how wrong things had gone, at least to make a significant start.
4. To that effect, it was suggested to get the IPL 10 Final that was under shadow for fixing as detailed in the Writ Petition to be investigated in a transparent manner by the Police/concerned authorities, with public knowledge so that a message goes out to restore some of the public confidence. But the BCCI officials wanted the investigation to be by the ACU in a confidential manner. The COA appeared to be agreeing to that. We still feel that such an investigation may not serve

much purpose and there was a stronger possibility of things being swept under the carpet in due course with an in-house investigation by the BCCI. The COA may kindly take a final call in this regard.

5. The COA indicated their inclination to strengthen the ACU and to put a strong ACU in place to instill fear in the minds of evil-doers. This was welcome, reiterating that the implementation and putting the ACU to effective use were more necessary, mere making of regulations without implementation didn't mean much as the past results/present state of affairs showed.
6. The meeting ended on a rather positive note, giving us hope that something effective and good may eventually come out of it in the larger public and collective national interest.

It is requested that the COA while submitting their report to the Hon'ble Supreme Court in terms of their order dated 7/5/18 in WP (C) 1163/2017 may also please convey the inputs/suggestions given by me earlier in deference to the COA's desire, to the Hon'ble Supreme Court with/without the COA's comments as deemed fit.

Regards

Atul Kumar

This mail and its contents were not made public by me till date since I had felt that COA won't like it to be so, but I am compelled to do so now. This record goes a long way in calling the bluff of the subject report by the COA.

The twitter handle @theDcricket (Cricket Insider) hasn't been someone who only makes predictions about outcome of a match that may come true or may go wrong. Anyone in the street can do that. COA didn't need to tell me/us that. @theDcricket has not only been making predictions, but has been claiming a number of matches being fixed and his having confirmed information on the scripts of matches. He openly says he has to pay for getting information and it is money that makes all the merry-go-round in the world of cricket. He gives inside information not only about outcome of matches, but also on session scores. And it is not for one or two matches, but has been going on for hundreds of matches for over a year. It is a matter of record that even my specific complaints to the concerned authorities on this count have fetched nothing. There is nothing new in my mentioning this now since this all has been detailed in the writ petition 1163/ 2017 and additional documents submitted during the course of that petition. It is rather unfortunate and a waste of my time and energies that I have to repeat it all here. Repetition has become necessary to bring home the point that it was in the background of these material facts that the COA promised as they did to recommend to the Hon'ble Supreme Court to get @theDcricket thoroughly questioned and investigated. Though reasons for not mentioning of this in the above report now despite the above background will be best known to the COA, the fact does put a big question mark on the intentions and integrity of the COA themselves. The hundreds of tweets by @theDcricket for over a year have been so revealing and so clear an evidence for institutionalised fixing of cricket matches (if one had the slightest mind and could apply it) that these render anything else said/work done or anything that will be said or done to tell that cricket was institutionally fixed redundant. One will understand the import of this if one went through hundreds of his tweets, some of which were also documented in the petition and additional documents. A very few recent ones are reproduced below for ready reference:

Pinned Tweet

Cricket Insider @theDcricket Nov 7

NowmyPREMIUMLINEforcompletetwoupcoming tournaments 1. #WomensCricketTournament 2.#mzansisuperleague 15000⍰ For any single tournament PREMIUM LINE 10000⍰ FOR any single Match 4000⍰ Interested Whatsapp or TELEGRAM +91 9100544879

Cricket Insider @theDcricket 1h1 hour ago

You can't believe that I have 10K + WhatsApp contacts from around the globe. Now having 2000+ PREMIUM ✔MEMBERS#cricketinsider

Cricket Insider @theDcricket Oct 26

#PAKvsAUS Pakistan vs Australia 2nd T20I I have this match GUARANTEED REPORT with one session. PREMIUM LINE 5000□ Interested Whatsapp or TELEGRAM 9100544879.

Cricket Insider @theDcricket Oct 22

Fixing is in every sports nowadays. I'm

agree with this there is no break point for this. Even #APLFinal Match has been fixed. #spotfixing#cricketsmatchfixers#cricketinsider

Cricket Insider @theDcricket Oct 21

Congratulations! #Balkh won !! Thank you for following and keeping hope on me throughout tournament. Little mistakes and sorry for that. See you all in November for SOUTH AFRICA LEAGUE. #APLT20Final#cricketinsider

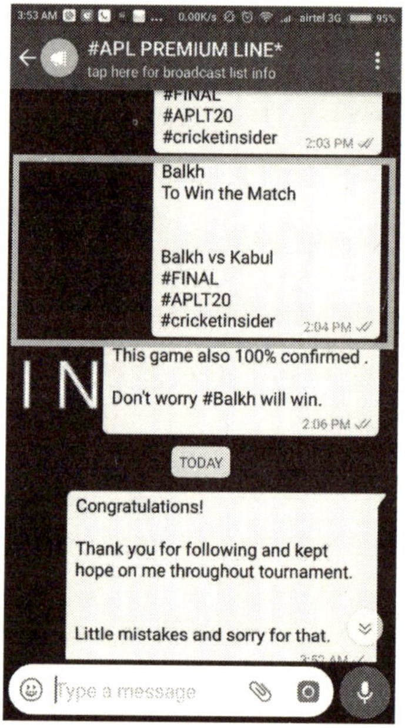

Cricket Insider @theDcricket Oct 20

Congratulations !! Kabul won !!! See you tomorrow at 3:15PM #BalkhVsKabul#Final#APLT20

Cricket Insider @theDcricket Sep 16

Trinbago WON BACK TO BACK #CPL WINNERS. THANK YOU AND BYE-BYE !

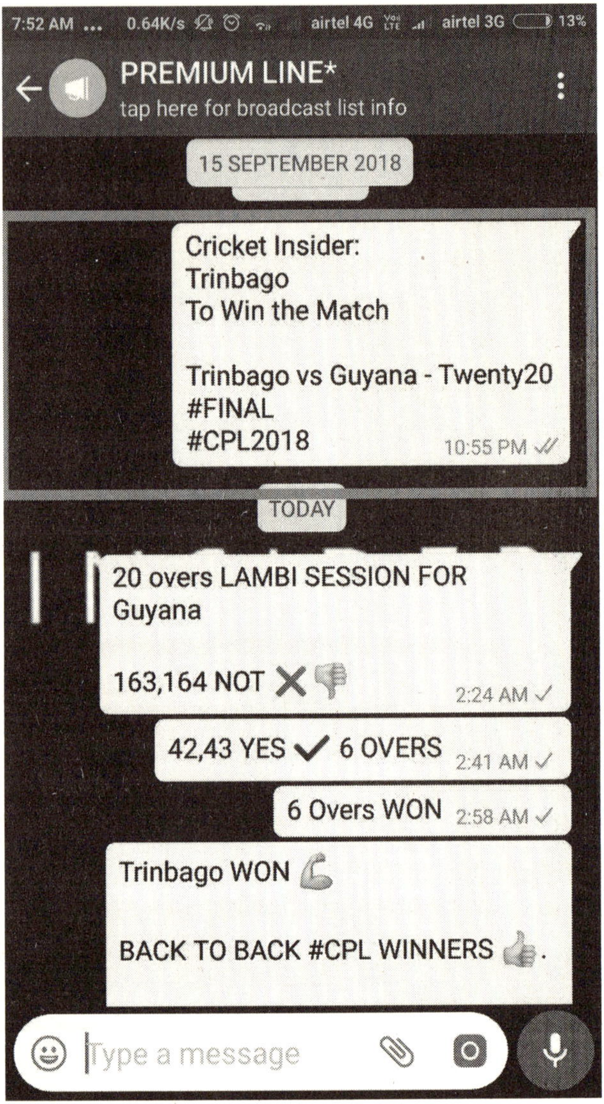

Cricket Insider @theDcricket Sep 16

#Guyana#Trinbago#GAWvsTKR#Final Final #CPL2018 PREMIUM 2000□ Will share guaranteed 3

Sessions 20 Overs lambi 15 Overs Powerplay (6 Overs) Interested WhatsApp or TELEGRAM 9100544879

These are only some sample random tweets out of hundreds of such or even more telling tweets. He has been tweeting and charging money for giving prior information about scripts of almost all T20 leagues across the world including the Indian TNPL, KPL and IPL. By his own account more than 2,000 people are paying him to get prior information about matches from him. The information given by him is often astonishingly right. After having promised in the meeting that they would recommend to the Supreme Court to get him investigated, the COA now suddenly summarily dismissed in passing that all this meant nothing and concluded that it was only a case of some predictions coming true by chance.

Acting complete blind to these explosive tweets for over a year, the world has been moving on continuing to celebrate an open and blatant fraud as a competitive sport. Didn't these tweets call for a high level thorough investigation long ago?

It is true that Shri Vinod Rai, ex-CAG of India and now the Head of the COA is a retired seasoned bureaucrat of great stature and repute, who himself had exposed a massive public scam. It is precisely for this reason that the subject report becomes more disappointing and shocking. And these are the times when even top officials of CBI have been repeatedly coming under cloud and none other than ex-CJI was publicly charged of corruption and misdeeds. Questions were publicly raised on his working by none other than a few Supreme Court Judges—the current CJI being one of them. Therefore, it would be prudent to concentrate on the facts rather than statures and reputations. And hundreds of those involved in the colossal fraud that cricket is, are celebrities and men/women of great stature and repute. The media personalities perpetrating this fraud and keeping the truth under wraps for years have no less stature. All this lies well substantiated through the petition and documents annexed therewith.

The subject report does betray lack of sense of truth, sense of responsibility, and application of mind on the part of the COA. Not only that, wilful distortion of facts and mentioning those out of context with clever manipulation to run down the petition is glaring at places (as explained in following paras). I wonder why the COA had to resort to it. Why could they not deal with the momentous issue at hand honestly? Through their report, the COA have not only insulted the petitioners, the hard work put in by them for years in order to expose and deal with a going-on massive public fraud with very grave national and international implications, and the momentous sense of the petition that goes much beyond cricket, have not only betrayed millions of honest cricket lovers, but to my mind have also insulted the intelligence and professional acumen of the bench of the Hon'ble Supreme Court that dealt with this petition.

The COA have charged now in this report for the first time that broad, sweeping, and unsubstantiated allegations to the effect that all cricket matches are scripted have been made in the petition. I do wonder if that were the case, would the Hon'ble Supreme Court of India and the bench of three judges comprising the CJI have had entertained such a frivolous petition and not fined or punished the petitioners? Not only did the Hon'ble Court entertain the petition, passed a meaningful order, but they also invited the petitioners to assist the Court in the main case concerning BCCI. Would any Court, and above all, the Supreme Court of India, do so if the petition contained unsubstantiated sweeping allegations, that too involving who's who of the country?

I am sure the Hon'ble Court would have expected the COA to apply mind in depth, and labour intensively to address the contents of the petition considering the gravity of what had been put forth, before they submitted their report. But as their report suggests and as would become abundantly clear from what follows, they chose to be superficial and casual at best. I do understand that it would not have been easy for them to comprehend the harsh reality (if they were not in the know already); if so, they could interact freely with me to understand what was what as far as our grievances and contents of the petition were concerned, but they chose to be formal and bureaucratic rather than being governed by a sense and desire to deliver in the larger public interest. They failed to appreciate that a PIL was more a matter of public interest than being something legal. To me, it is either the COA's incomprehension of reality or wilful attempt to mislead the Court and the world that manifests itself in the subject report of the COA as we have seen and would see further. The latter appears to be the more likely case since the COA have conspicuously acted dishonestly.

Is not it outright dishonest and cowardly for the COA and the BCCI to say so in their report now behind the back of the petitioners that broad, sweeping, and unsubstantiated allegations to the effect that all cricket matches are scripted have been made in the petition? If it were so, why did the COA hold a meeting with us? Why did they not mention so in their first email to me? On the contrary, in their communication with me, they categorically stated that extremely important issues had been raised by me/us. Why did they not tell us so in the meeting that the petition contained sweeping and unsubstantiated allegations? Had they given such an indication as to what they thought, we could have tried to explain or requested for another meeting to explain in detail. On the contrary, Mr. Vinod Rai repeatedly told that they shared our concerns. Our concerns had clearly been nothing, but institutionalised fixing of cricket and its implications. I got the indication of their helplessness in dealing with the problem as it was. What was the need or sense to ask for suggestions from and discuss with those who had irresponsibly made some sweeping allegations? Why did the COA not ask us how did we mean that cricket was such a colossal fraud as had been brought out in the petition, rather than asking for our suggestions? Do not the earlier actions of the COA themselves contradict what they have said now in the subject report? Could sweeping and unsubstantiated allegations on one hand, and raising of extremely important issues on the other hand go together? Is not it clear that the COA have given the subject report under some duress/compulsions rather than a sense of truth and honest responsibility?

The BCCI became a party to the petition by filing a caveat and were duly served copies of the petition and additional documents submitted subsequently. It had renowned senior advocates and a top law firm of the country at its disposal to represent it versus a common man—petitioner no. 1. If the petition contained sweeping unsubstantiated allegations as has been mentioned by the COA now, why did the BCCI not bring it out before the Court when the petition was under its consideration and before the Court passed the subject order? Surely, the BCCI couldn't know what order the Hon'ble Court would pass in the absence of any counter from them. What fear did the BCCI have? What did it have to hide from public glare? Why were petitioners not taken to task before the Court for having made unsubstantiated sweeping allegations? Won't it have been correct to resolve the issue in the open Court rather than the COA passing unilateral cowardly judgement now sitting in office? **Do the COA not understand that their saying now that the petition contained broad and sweeping unsubstantiated allegations has no sanctity whatsoever and it only shows the COA and the BCCI in poor light?** If the petition contained sweeping unsubstantiated allegations, the BCCI must have told this to the Hon'ble Supreme Court when the petition was being heard by them duly substantiating their claim and countering the averments that had been made in the petition. Countering of those averments does require and did require tearing to pieces all the evidence and arguments that had been submitted in the petition, one by one. **Even in the subject report, made after months with all the cricket experts and legal luminaries at their disposal, the COA have not been able to counter a single piece of evidence.** Leave alone countering, they didn't have courage enough even to mention and list the evidence furthered in the petition in their report.

The bottom line is that the petition didn't contain sweeping and unsubstantiated allegations. Whatever was brought out in the petition was painstakingly substantiated by facts, documents, and application of mind. Two books bringing out a lot of facts in support were submitted with the original petition and further two books were submitted with the additional documents. **In fact, the statement of the COA that the petition contained sweeping and unsubstantiated allegations itself is a highly irresponsible and sweeping statement totally unsubstantiated.** While concluding so, the COA have very conveniently picked just a few facts and mentions by me/us out of context and distorted those to state what suited them and the BCCI. They have miserably failed to apply mind and go to the depth of the matter as was expected of them.

The COA have stated that no reliable material was placed before them which would lead to the rather drastic conclusion that all cricket is a massive fraud on the public. As stated above, a lot of material including 2+2 books had been placed detailing how and why this not only drastic but unimaginable and almost incomprehensible conclusion became essential. To arrive at this conclusion didn't give any pleasure to the petitioners. Rather, they would have been delighted if they were wrong. It is regard for Truth and application of common sense that makes this conclusion essential as has been amply brought out in our submissions and as we would see again in subsequent paras.

Here I would like the COA also to understand and appreciate that whether all matches are fixed, almost all matches are fixed, most of the matches are fixed, a majority of matches are fixed, or a large number of matches are fixed, or a few matches are fixed here or there, it has implications regarding institutionalised fixing of cricket as long as no one is or has been taken to task for fixing in such matches on the initiative of the cricket administration. And that precisely is the case. **A number of matches reported to have been fixed remain unexplained with no action having been taken against players who played in those fixed matches.** On the contrary, whenever the issue has been raised by those outside cricket administration, the cricket administration has been swift to rubbish it and brush it under the carpet. The latest Al-Jazeera report as would be brought out in subsequent paras is a burning example in case. Even when M.S. Dhoni was reported to have lied under oath in Gurunath Meyappan Case, he continued to be Indian captain even thereafter. Didn't that mean mockery of the establishment?

It was for the BCCI to counter the material placed before the Court to show that the material was not reliable and all bunkum which was never done. If it were argued out in the open Court, the petitioners could bring out the reality more clearly and forcefully in full public glare. The BCCI are now trying to have the cake and eat it too. They have let the opportunity, to counter the contents of the petition and averments made, in the Court go for some pertinent reasons and now the COA are trying to crush truth passing dictatorial judgements. Even now the COA have made a sweeping statement betraying authoritarianism with no attempt to logically counter the material placed before the Court and available to them. This sweeping statement contradicts even what the COA themselves have stated elsewhere in the report. In para 2 at numbered page 2, the COA have stated that petitioners believe (the use of word 'believe' is inappropriate and mischievous) such a conclusion stands mathematically and scientifically proved in the book 'Bettors Beware'. They have conveniently forgot and overlooked to mention that the scientific proof had been got examined and found credible by a sports editor of a very prestigious English daily, and was now time tested. Without bothering to tell the world/the Court why and how that mathematical proof was not relevant and amounted only to someone's belief, they have dictatorially stated that no reliable material was placed before them. It is just one such instance.

The COA would have done well to understand that the scientific and mathematical proof mentioned by them and as mentioned by them is not something brought out anew in the petition. It has been in existence publicly duly reported in the media courtesy PTI for years and has also directly been conveyed to the BCCI and the ICC years ago. It was for the ICC, cricketers or cricket administration, or even for someone from public to counter and challenge it there and then. The continued silence of the world over this for years has already vindicated same. Even now without countering it, the COA had the temerity to say that no reliable material was there in the petition?

The COA have very shabbily, superficially, insufficiently and misleadingly summarised the contents of the petition in a small para 2 mentioned above to suit themselves. While the platform for detailed discussions and arguments on the contents of the petition was the Court and that never happened since the content was never countered in the least by the BCCI or the UOI in the Court, I would briefly list a few pertinent and important things already well documented in the petition and additional documents submitted (in addition to the continuing tweets by @theDcricket as already brought out above), off-hand from memory here which the COA have conveniently overlooked or not mentioned or not bothered to explain before making highly irresponsible sweeping unsubstantiated statements and passing unilateral judgements:

1. If all is so well and above board with cricket administration—BCCI and ICC—how is it that same Shashank Manohar, presently chairman of the ICC, who publicly demanded a CBI inquiry into all matches of IPL-2013 forgot all about it when he himself became President of BCCI thereafter and even the ICC chairman subsequently? Was he irresponsible in demanding the CBI enquiry or was he irresponsible afterwards? If he was irresponsible in demanding the inquiry, how come such a person became the President of the BCCI thereafter and has been the chairman of the ICC for two terms? How come no one else from the cricketing world or media has ever questioned such a funny behaviour of the top most official for cricket administration in the world, leaving the same to poor commoners like Atul Kumar? In the absence of any plausible explanation to such

behaviour, doesn't it show that there is something grossly wrong with the top cricket administrators?

2. The Cricket Insider @theDcricket tweeted a number of very peculiar predictions (detailed in the petition) before IPL-10 final in 2017 as to who would score how many runs, or hit how many sixes, or how teams will score and win/lose which proved true to the hilt except for one regarding some run-rate. Could there be any other explanation for that under the sun other than that the IPL-10 final was fixed and scripted beforehand? The only other explanation could be that the tweets were made after the match and doctored/engineered to look as if those had been made beforehand, but nothing of the sort ever came out or was explained by the authorities. No one was ever taken up for making such doctored tweets and misguide and mislead the public. All have only maintained a deafening silence on it till date. Was it not imperative for the BCCI/IPL Governing Council to respond when these prophetic tweets were reported in and by responsible media? Doesn't the silence of all concerned—the Shastris, the Gavaskars, the Pontings, the Laras, the Sehwags—the cricket world—alone amply show that cricket is an institutionalised fraud with complicity of all concerned? And now even the COA have apparently backtracked on their promise/ inclination to get this match investigated even in-house.
3. It was none other than an ex-Pakistani captain Amir Sohail who during Champions Trophy last year (that was eventually won by Pakistan defeating India in

the final) publicly asked Sarfraz Nawaz, the Pakistani captain, in a sudden spontaneous outburst, that he should not let his team winning go to his head since the match results were governed by outside forces—something to that effect. None of that was doing of a commoner like Atul Kumar. Why has the cricket world remained silent on that? Why has no one been able to explain what that outburst meant?

4. An ex-international Australian cricketer, and one who had participated in Bangladesh Premier League (BPL), Dirk Nannes, came on record recently to tell the world that fixing and fishy things happened in BPL matches, team managements also being involved. Why has ICC and cricketing world been silent about it if cricket was not an institutionalised fraud?

5. It was not someone from the street but another ex-Pakistani cricketer and captain, Rashid Latif, who years ago explained through an article titled 'How Cricket Matches are Scripted' how session scoring showed scripting of the matches and how matches were scripted to manipulate session scoring. What is the explanation of the COA to the contents of that article (copy of which lies annexed with the petition)? Why has the cricketing world been silent on it all these years?

6. Have the COA fully understood the mechanics of session betting and bracket betting before concluding that session scoring meant and indicated nothing? What is the explanation of the COA to tens of specific instances from all sorts of matches over the years illustrated in the documents submitted with

or referred in the petition to show how correlation between session betting and plays in the field showed institutionalised fixing of matches? These have not been vague or theoretical narrations, but specific instances from real-time matches.

7. Why have the COA overlooked the fact of confirmation by an internationally acclaimed betting expert, Edward Hawkins, that the patterns of session scoring as occurred were not possible without scripting and fixing of matches? He understood when things were explained to him briefly.
8. Earth revolves round the Sun and the Sun rises in the East are scientific facts. These facts stand out not because some Court decided these to be so. These are facts that no human being in senses can deny. Similarly, theory of probability also doesn't have any subjectivity and is a science. It doesn't depend on whims or judgements of any individuals. Petitioners would have welcomed if the COA had been able to find loopholes in the claim of scientific proof in the book 'Bettors Beware' which they have mentioned. Even while acknowledging the existence of a scientific proof, they have concluded that no reliable material was available. How bizarre and what a contradiction! That too when the proof of this scientific evidence having been got examined and found credible by a veteran sports editor was readily submitted in the petition. The same got corroborated again and again by a lot other evidences also, some of which has been listed above and some will follow.
9. The COA have miserably failed to apply and address

themselves to the contents of the chapter 'Large Scale Fixing Gets Established but All Look the Other Way' in the book 'Bettors Beware'. This relates with the fixing episode during IPL-6 in 2013 involving Sreesanth and others. It was clear as explained in this chapter that a good number of batsmen, and some very big international names like Adam Gilchrist as a batsman, and Rahul Dravid as a captain of the bowling team had to be involved in those incidences of fixing termed as spot-fixing and widely reported in the media. Why has the cricketing world been silent on this fact? Why has the media been silent? Why have many of those cricketers continued to play or act as coaches, and were never questioned? Does the fact of everyone continuing to look the other way even today not announce the existence and continuation of an institutionalised fraud? How come without even any attempt to counter that irrefutable logic, the COA arrived at a conclusion that no material evidence was available? Have the COA not been conspicuously despotic?

10. It has been reported that Mudgal report brought out the fact of one Javed Chutani, a Dawood aide, routinely opening rates for betting in cricket matches to key bookies in some south-east Asian countries. Nothing else but Mudgal report contains that '***Chutani was sure what would happen in a match and rates were opened accordingly***'. What is the explanation of the COA to this if it didn't establish institutionalised fixing of cricket?
11. The book '**Fixed! Cash and Corruption in Cricket**'

is a book of non-fiction written by an eminent awarded journalist, Shantanu Guha Ray and published by a reputed publisher, Harper Collins in early 2016. It brings out a lot which still awaits explanation from the cricketing world, and the authorities. But all have been silent as if this book and its contents didn't exist. There is more than enough in this book that tells one of continuing large-scale fixing and corruption in cricket. What is the explanation of the COA to the contents of this book when they claimed not to have found any reliable material placed before them? If cricket was not an institutionalised fraud, why had all been keeping quiet on this book? Why were investigations not taking place based on the contents of this book?

I can go on and on if I started mentioning how specific matches over the years were nothing but fixed and scripted cricket, as has already been brought out in my books and posts on the Facebook page of 'Bettors Beware'. All that forms content of the petition. Here I have listed only a few points off-hand (that are already detailed in the petition with the necessary documentary evidence) without having gone through the petition that should make sense to any intelligent mind that the COA had at best acted irresponsibly in making and submitting the subject report. To my mind, each and every one of the above points is independently sufficient to establish that cricket today is an institutionalised fraud or at least to raise a genuine question to that effect. The COA have not bothered to address or explain any of these and considered it prudent to say that petition was all bunkum and nonsense. I do hope that the COA will realise their foolishness and foolhardiness at least now. The complete petition and additional documents submitted contain a lot more material not only to substantiate the averments made, but also to make one understand what is what. It is really strange and most unfortunate that the COA preferred to go with the common pre-conceived notion and decided that they couldn't accept that all cricket was part of a massive ongoing fraud without applying mind to the contents of the petition.

The COA have not only been foolish and foolhardy, but they have also been mischievous and misleading in their report by wilfully concealing a lot and distorting some other content of the petition. In para 9 b) at numbered page 9 of their report, the COA have attempted to totally trivialise a laboriously detailed petition—totally substantiated as above glimpses would have conveyed to any intelligent mind—by conveying to the world as if the petition was mainly based on nothing but a foolish logic that if someone made some off-hand correct prediction, then that meant the match was fixed. I do wonder what made the COA try to mislead the world through such blatant falsehood and misrepresentation of the contents of the petition. Similarly, in para 9 a), they have tried to convey as if stray underperformance by world-class players or unexpected scoring in some sessions were the main reasons furthered by the petitioners to jump at the conclusion of cricket matches being fixed. There could be nothing farther from the truth and the COA must be knowing how misleading they have been. The COA have summarised the content of the petition their own way out of context and distorting its sense and essence, excluding everything which conveyed the essence of what was said. The above were never mentioned as proof, but were stated differently and in more detail with scores of supporting examples in the documents submitted or referred, only to bring home how an alert viewer could also see fixing taking place straightaway without having to go into details of mathematical evidence.

I do repeat that wilful underperformance by cricketers in all departments of the game, i.e., bowling, batting or fielding, especially highly trained and experienced bowlers (since batting outcome and underperformance may be explained away to have been a function of the ball received, but a bowler can bowl how he likes independent of anything else) is too conspicuous at times in all matches day and night—once one understood it. Fielding lapses also may be explained as momentary lapse of concentration, and that may definitely happen so naturally at times, but very often, such lapses are too blatant to get explained. Many times, performances are termed as 'inexplicable' by commentators also. And yet we know that everything man-made does have an explanation. The plays in the field are very often so inexplicable, unnatural, and absurd that even housewives can and do see through the scripted cricket. For example, wilful crawl by set batsmen in slog overs of limited overs' matches has no explanation other than that it was done for non-cricketing reasons. This is what was meant to be explained in the petition and to the COA while conveying my suggestions to them in this regard.

It is repeated that these narrations have never been

meant to be the evidence and were necessary to make one understand and appreciate the overall scenario. It could not be that cricket was institutionally fixed and yet there was no manifestation of the same in the field. The bad and wrong intentions of the COA become too obvious by the fact that while they have quoted out of context and distorted such narrations, painting such distortions to be the essence of petition, they have conveniently skipped to even mention many irrefutable pieces of evidence in the petition before declaring to the world that the petition was nothing but bunkum non-sense. **And the million-dollar question remains, why did every one remain silent in the Court if petition was all bunkum?**

While the COA have discovered that there was no reliable material before them to conclude that all cricket was part of a massive ongoing fraud on the public, I reproduce the below excerpts from a very recent article in The Statesman dated 11/11/2018 titled **'When you have a lot of money, you needn't be a stickler for probity'** by Mr. Pulakesh Mukhopadhyay. The article was in the aftermath of the recent tweet by Gautam Gambhir against inviting Mohammad Azharuddin to ring the bell to get the India-West Indies T20 international at the Eden Gardens on 4/11/2018 going and response to that by a CAB heavyweight saying that Gambhir had better shut up given that he had long been in the Indian Premier League with its make-believe cricket.

"*...Well might Gambhir too have his own riposte to the IPL jibe, but when you come to think of it, global sport, rich and powerful, had got, long before this Indian barb-trading, to a point where it could be seen and felt* *to have out-grown both probity and even the illusion of it.* ***A conveyor-belt supply of evidence will fill up encyclopaedias galore, if attempted****...*". Mr. Pulakesh Mukhopadhyay is a veteran sports editor of 'The Statesman'. He is no relative of mine.

Since the BCCI have posted this unilateral dictatorial report of the COA on their website without posting the contents of the referred petition, it becomes crystal clear that the COA have acted so mischievously to mislead not only the Hon'ble Supreme Court, but also the public and the world, and, thus, to sub-serve the interests of the fraudsters and the mafia.

Fate acts beyond the wildest imaginations of man and Truth has its own way of seizing up with Falsehood. As luck would have it, the biggest ever exposé yet by some journalists on fixing in cricket (https://www.aljazeera.com/news/2018/10/exclusive-spot-fixes-15-international-cricket-matches-181020142431726.html) was probably just waiting for the COA to finalise the subject report that was to summarily dismiss much wrong-doing in cricket and show the petitioners in poor light despite overwhelming evidence to the contrary before them, so that they would subsequently stand ashamed for having pursued the path of falsehood.

First, I reproduce below the latest report dated 29/10/2018 on this exposé from the link: http://www.espncricinfo.com/story/_/id/25115953/al-jazeera-criticises-icc-ca-ecb-responses-spot-fixing-allegations

"Television news channel *Al Jazeera* has hit out at the manner in which the ECB and CA dismissed allegations of spot-fixing involving their teams in its documentary, *The Munawar Files*, adding that the ICC had failed to answer questions about the alleged "match-fixer at the centre of our investigation" Aneel Munawar.

The documentary, the second on corruption in cricket by Al Jazeera, claimed that up to 15 international matches—several of them Tests—in the 2011-12 period had been subject to spot-fixing. Munawar was also at the centre of their first documentary, which alleged that the Chennai Test in December 2016 and the Ranchi Test in March 2017 had been subject to spot-fixing by England and Australia players.

The ICC, CA and ECB said Al Jazeera had refused to share information regarding various corruption allegations despite repeated requests, and the two national boards said there was no credible evidence to support claims of spot-fixing.

In a statement, a spokesperson for Al Jazeera's Investigative Unit said it had been five weeks since the channel put certain questions to the ICC, and now urged them to answer the following:

- "When did the ICC first become aware of Munawar and his activities and what action was taken?
- "What action has it taken to track down Munawar since our first documentary was broadcast on May 27, 2018?
- "Is Munawar on the ICC's list of known match-fixers?
- "Is it the ICC's view that some formats of international cricket, including Test matches, are not vulnerable to spot-fixing?

- "Is the ICC confident that match-fixers cannot get close to international players?
- "How many players, international and others, has the ICC found guilty of match-fixing or spot-fixing in the past five years?
- "Who are those players and what were the punishments handed out in each case?
- "Given the ICC's limited investigatory powers, what should be done to tackle the organised criminals behind match-fixing?"

In the documentary, Al Jazeera claimed that the ICC's ACU had been aware of Munawar being linked to corruption in cricket as early as 2010, when the Oval ODI between England and Pakistan was under scrutiny and subsequently cleared of suspicion. The documentary also showed photographs—supposedly taken in Colombo around the 2012 World T20—in which Munawar appeared in the same frame as several top international cricketers.

Al Jazeera, in its statement, said the denial of the allegations from the boards "simply failed to engage with the specific and compelling evidence".

"We are particularly struck by what appears to be a refusal in some quarters even to accept the possibility that players from Anglo-Saxon countries could have engaged in the activities exposed by our programme and that the evidence we have uncovered even merits appropriate investigation," Al Jazeera said. "Rather than merely dismissing our findings, we would urge our critics to engage with their detail and, if they remain determined to argue that the spot-fixes suggested by the evidence never took place, to explain how it was that Munawar was able to predict what would happen in 25 out of 26 cases before the sessions in question had even begun, notwithstanding that the odds of this happening were many millions to one."

Al Jazeera claimed that Munawar was associatcd with South Asian mafia organisation D-Company, and that they had recovered a cache of recorded phone conversations between him and clients, in which Munawar detailed the specifics of pre-arranged spot-fixes during matches.

Al Jazeera has claimed and continues to do so that it does not have confidence in the ICC to be able to police the game.

"The ICC has repeatedly 'demanded' that we hand over our evidence to them," Al Jazeera said in its statement. "We have always said that we will hand over our material to the relevant authorities. However, no reputable broadcaster does this before broadcast and, furthermore, as our inquiries have progressed, we have become increasingly concerned at the ICC's ability and resolve to police the game; its failure to respond to our simple, factual questions shows a disturbing lack of transparency and only aggravates those concerns.

"It is for this reason that we are in discussions with Interpol about handing over the evidence to them. We are not ruling out handing over material to the ICC—but feel that it must first accept some accountability and answer the legitimate questions raised by our investigation."

The ICC is not expected to issue a response for the moment. Further, it is believed that Munawar does not feature as a top corrupting threat in the 20-plus live investigations the ICC's anti-corruption unit is currently undertaking, other than through the Al Jazeera investigations."

Now let us try to examine and analyse above report of espncricinfo.com. If one applied a little mind to it, it confirms everything brought out in the petition. This is something that has happened thousands of miles away from us and independent of our petition. I am sure Al Jazeera would even not be knowing about the existence of such a petition. And yet it corroborates not only the fact of cricket being nothing, but an institutionalised fraud, but also grave implications of this fraud as brought out in the petition. Very briefly we shall understand that.

We shall consider here that the exposé by Al Jazeera is very unlikely to be bogus and they won't have claimed what they have without having supporting evidence. A channel just won't come out with some explosive claims out of thin air and telling white lies. And, of course, they won't have been contemplating going to Interpol if they were not having the necessary evidence.

So, what did Al Jazeera people tell us? They told us this vide their report dated 21/10/2018:

"Al Jazeera Investigative Unit's latest documentary, *Cricket's Match-Fixers: The Munawar Files,* contains recordings of an Indian match-fixer phoning in details of spot-fixes in 15 international matches to a notorious bookmaker.

The match-fixer gave a total of 26 predictions, of which all but one turned out to be accurate.

The spot-fixes were all session fixes, predicting what would happen in a specific session of six, eight or ١٠ overs.

Many of the matches involved multiple spot-fixes. In some cases, fixes were delivered by both teams.

Due to the gravity of the accusations and the prospect of criminal investigations, we are not, at present, naming the fixed sessions nor the teams perpetrating the fix because that would identify the batsmen suspected of fixing.

The 15 matches in question are:

1. Australia vs. England, ODI, 21.01.2011
2. Australia vs. Zimbabwe, ODI World Cup, 21.02.2011
3. England vs. Netherlands, ODI World Cup, 22.02.2011
4. Australia vs. Kenya, ODI World Cup, 13.03.2011
5. England vs. South Africa, ODI World Cup, 06.03.2011
6. England vs. Bangladesh, ODI World Cup, 11.03.2011
7. England vs. India, Test, 21-25.07.2011
8. South Africa vs. Australia, Test, 09-11.11.2011
9. Australia vs. New Zealand, Test, 09-12.12.2011
10. England vs. Pakistan, Test, 17-19.01.2012
11. England vs. Pakistan, Test, 25-28.01.2012
12. England vs. Pakistan, Test, 03-06.02.2012

13. Sri Lanka vs. Zimbabwe, T20I World Cup, 18.09.2012
14. England vs. Afghanistan, T20I World Cup, 21.09.2012
15. South Africa vs. Pakistan, T20I World Cup, 28.09.2012"

Sessions of 6, 8, or 10 overs are, thus, known to have been fixed in 15 international matches in 2011 and 2012 that included matches of the ODI World Cup, T20 World Cup, and Test matches involving teams that are considered most prestigious in international cricket. The matches mentioned are also considered most prestigious in the game. Undoubtedly, top international cricketers from many countries mentioned must have been playing in the matches mentioned.

Let us now see very briefly what fixing of sessions means. Session fixing means it is fixed how many runs will be scored in the session spanning a number of continuous overs. No one or two players can ensure that. A lot many players on both sides including fielders have to be involved. All the batsmen on the crease and bowlers who bowled during those overs have to be necessarily involved. (It all lies explained in the book 'Bettors Beware' mentioned by the COA). And it is not only the final session score that is fixed or can be fixed. How the scoring continues in that session ball by ball is also to be fixed since session betting continues ball by ball throughout the session. It can also be understood this way that the desired final score can't be attained suddenly until the scoring is controlled throughout the session.

For example, suppose it has been fixed to score 47 runs in a session of 10 overs. That can't be achieved if 48 or more runs are already scored in first, say, 8 overs of that session.

Then, will this fixed session not necessarily have a bearing on the final result of the match? It certainly will have. Whatever happens during a part of a match is bound to affect the match as a whole. So, we can clearly see that the term spot-fixing implies fixing of the match as a whole also. It should be rather simple to understand it.

It is only today, after 6-7 years, that we are being told that these prestigious international matches were fixed. But commentators must have commented on these matches that time as if competitive matches were being played. Many expert comments must have been made all along and columns written analysing these matches as competitive ones for the world. Won't coaches and captains of the team have known when fixed cricket was being played in the open continuously for many overs? This is how colossal and mind-boggling a fraud-fixed cricket is.

Is it difficult to understand that we know today about above matches having been fixed in all probability only because someone or some people in Al Jazeera toiled hard and did some extraordinary work? That it doesn't mean that only these matches were fixed and others were not? It is like a thief or murderer is caught for one crime, but could have committed many crimes in the past. In this case, the crimes continue to be committed, since the fixers and actors in crime happily continue to be at large, courtesy those in authority like the current COA of the

BCCI who when called upon by Providence to deliver, chose to protect the crime and, therefore, the criminals through reports, such as the subject report.

What this Al Jazeera report brings out is confirmation of what the petition contains and conveys, and what stands mathematically and scientifically proven years ago from the application of principles of probability to the score sheets of cricket matches. The difference is that this Al Jazeera report is comparatively given better cognizance by media and, therefore, people are more likely to become aware as a result of this report. This report also tells us that the match-fixer was connected with D-company. That confirms the serious implications of the fraud that Cricket is as brought out in the petition.

The beauty of that scientific proof given years ago is that it not only applied to matches in the past that time, but also to the matches of the future. **It is compulsion arising out of session betting and bracket betting that session scoring and, hence, the cricket matches have to be scripted.** Since session betting has been continuing, the match-fixing has also been continuing.

I feel really glad that apart from exposing fixing in international cricket, Al Jazeera have also exposed inaction all these years and cover given to fixing by cricket boards and ICC through their questionnaire as reported in the above espncricinfo report. That is another confirmation of the contents of the petition. **And I stick my neck out to say that like many exposés in the past this all-telling exposé will also lie buried or brushed under the carpet, howsoever easy or difficult it may be, and unsuspecting masses will continue to cheer**

when their opponents get bundled out for 104 (like in the 5th ODI India vs. WI at Thiruvananthapuram on 1/11/2018) in an ODI for betting syndicates to make a killing on the bets of that innings score as well as bets on outcome of the match. The COAs of the world would not feel ashamed of continuing to act as total morons.

I do hope that at least after going through the above, the COA would realise they have been incorrect, if not outright foolish, in dismissing the petition as bunkum through the subject report. I marvel at their audacity to do so even when the Hon'ble Supreme Court had given due respect to the petition. And now they stand slapped in the face by the Al Jazeera exposé. Rightly so.

The COA have been mischievous also in reporting on suggestions made by me in para 6 at numbered pages 6–7 of the report. They have quoted only a part of the suggestions made out of context. The suggestions were made on being asked and with a view of same to be a matter of inter-active discussion with the COA. The COA never adopted much interactive approach in discussion as accepted by them in the report. The alternative suggestions to the ones brought out in the report have not been mentioned and discussed. Why? Many other suggestions have not been touched upon, why? The COA have used words like 'insisted upon', 'would have us do' for the suggestions made by me. The suggestions are and were suggestions and the use of phrases as above for the same is inappropriate. That is wilful misrepresentation in their attempt to show me in poor light, as someone obstinate and impractical. It was during limited discussion on suggestions in the meeting that two specific, not practically difficult, actions were promised by Shri Vinod Rai, and now there is no mention of the same in the report. I could never imagine that someone like Mr. Vinod Rai could stoop so low. In reference of this, I have already reproduced above the minutes of the meeting with the COA that I had e-mailed to protect me against such potential misdemeanour by the COA.

I am not saying much about various measures suggested by the COA because that is nothing but a futile bureaucratic exercise and an eye-wash. The suggested measures aim at dealing with stray cases of fixing by some stray players. The reality is much different. Institutionalised fixing and fraud are things at a totally different pedestal. **The measures suggested/ recommended by the COA are like a doctor suggesting a patient to take *Disprin* for curing terminal cancer since without proper check-up or without applying mind, he had diagnosed cancer as headache.**

This report by the COA in totality could also be termed as an exercise in taking bath while wearing a raincoat. If there was nothing drastically wrong in cricket as concluded by the COA, and nothing serious involving reputed players has ever been detected by the BCCI and the ICC either, then what for high-powered Mudgal and Lodha Commissions formed and why did they make recommendations for some stringent rules? And now the COA makes some recommendations to send a strong message against fixing; Why? Clear that not only the COA, but the authorities at large are victims of self-contradictions and self-deception. Icing on the cake is that while Commissions are being formed and they are submitting their reports, the fixed fraudulent cricket is not only continuing unabated, but prospering with mushrooming leagues like KPL and TNPL. Even as I draft this rejoinder, fixed matches in the interest of betting syndicates and mafia are being played all around.

Another recent eye-opener coming to light as I draft this rejoinder is the case of a lead investigator in 2013 IPL probe, Mr. B.B. Misra, now retired IPS officer. About only a couple of months earlier, he is reported to have told The Indian Express that he couldn't investigate a certain link between an Indian player from the 2011 World Cup winning squad and a bookie to a logical conclusion because of paucity of time and because it was not in his brief. Suddenly, he has taken a U-turn as he was reported by PTI on 2/11/18 having said that time was never an issue and he couldn't complete his investigation because he didn't have enough evidence. This is the level of integrity/credibility of our chosen lead investigators in the past! Or is it not a matter of integrity of individuals, but strength of the fraudulent forces that they can succeed in pressurising or tempting almost any mortal to say or do anything? Whatever it is, it is another confirmation of the contents of the petition. And it puts one at loss as to what to make out of the investigations done by such investigators.

And an investigator, who was really succeeding with investigations against Gurunath Meyappan, had got evidence against M.S. Dhoni, the IPS officer, Mr. G. Sampath Kumar was implicated, suspended, and shunted out of the probe. Today, he stands vindicated, but the damage was done as the probe got tempered with and scuttled. M.S. Dhoni continued to captain India.

Apart from suggesting cosmetic changes to the organisation and functioning of ACU/ACSU that has been good for nothing all these years as above clearly reveals, the COA have also made some farcical recommendations of some iconic players having indisputable integrity educating the players. Are there any such players in existence? Gilchrists and Dravids clearly stand implicated. Tendulkar was coach/mentor of Mumbai Indians when they played and won fixed final of IPL-10. At least, they all are under cloud. All legendary players get connected one way or the other with the institutionalised fraud that cricket is.

I have had first-hand experience of how good-for-nothing ACSU/ICC and ACU/BCCI have been. Years ago, before publication of the book 'Bettors Beware', when I met Shri Y.P. Singh, the then Head of ACSU/ICC at New Delhi in order to explain to him how session betting meant institutionalised fixing in cricket, he washed off his hands saying there was no proof for session betting. My experience of that interaction has been chronicled in the book 'Bettors Beware' mentioned by the COA. Today, session betting is openly taking place on-line. Why is ACSU silent now? Now, ACSU don't even respond to my mails. When fixing is so rampant, they have found it convenient to become deaf. They become blind to existence of Cricket Insider (@theDcricket) and hunt for untraceable Aneel Munawar. ACU/BCCI are no better as my recent interaction with them has told me. Only a couple of days back, someone contacted me over phone for the first time and went on to tell me that he had contacted ACSU of ICC and when he told them that he would like to demonstrate and explain to them that cricket was institutionally fixed, he was disconnected. Probably, these anti-corruption units are well aware that they are redundant in the face of institutionalised fixing of cricket. Their only role appears to be to keep a watch on players so that they don't go astray and do something other than the roles prescribed for them from match to match as per pre-written scripts or don't divulge scripts to bookies or others unauthorised.

Almost every IPL season matches are reported to be fixed and under investigation. But then no one hears further or of any logical conclusion. ED had told that 5 matches of IPL were under scanner for fixing in 2015. No one knows what happened thereafter. A lot many IPL matches were widely reported to have been fixed in 2013. At least a couple of matches including final were publicly known to have been fixed last year in 2017. No one was ever found guilty for these numerous reportedly fixed matches. Cricket continued to be reported upon as a competitive sport in the same breath by the media.

I have mentioned a lot in the petition and now that I could know from my limited sources of information. There may be a lot more reports on fixing I am not aware of. It is only a couple of days ago that I came across a report that Shoaib Akhtar, the Pakistani internationally famous fast bowler, had told in 2011 that match-fixing was taking place all the time. That reminds me that around the time he retired, Adam Gilchrist was reported to have said that it would be naïve to think that matches were not fixed or that no fixing was taking place. Then has all fixing been taking place in some vacuum or at some another planet, since no match in the last decade or more has been accepted or mentioned to have been fixed by cricket administration anywhere in the world?

The COA need to ask themselves some simple questions. Is it possible that when fixed cricket was taking place in an open ground, the players in the ground, the team managers and coaches, the cricket experts would fail to notice it and won't know anything about it? If fixing were taking place only sometimes involving only some players at the behest of some bookies—as is popularly believed—how come that other players and coaches have always remained silent spectators to that? How is it that when so many matches are reported to have been fixed, no player has ever been hauled over the coals apart from some fringe action once a while (to misleadingly show that anti-corruption bodies were at work) and the same players who had played in those matches reported to have been fixed continue to play for years thereafter?

As things stand, isn't a very high-powered SIT including sufficiently intelligent individuals of impeccable and unimpeachable integrity the minimum necessity to go to the bottom of the matter and bare all regarding cricket? It is a many-faceted, multi-dimensional fraud, with mind-boggling implications. Today, it becomes imperative in the larger public interest that people should know the truth from the authorities. Almost everyone is aware of existence of fixing and corruption in cricket, but they are aware only in a vague way. Not many are aware of its extent and depth. At least, people deserve to know what is what.

SIT is also necessary to unearth detailed modus-operandi of this mind-boggling fraud. While we know that cricket is fixed and fraudulent, we don't know the details of modus-operandi.

Presently, it is under consideration of the authorities in India whether cricket/sports betting should be legalised or not. Necessary call in this regard must be taken considering all pros and cons with full awareness that cricket was a massive fraud taking place with the main purpose of looting bettors and punters. To my mind, the poor bettors may have better opportunities for redress of their grievances if betting were legal. This may be just one point, the authorities will have to consider other pros and cons, but they must be fully aware as to what is what before taking decisions.

I have used up 10 precious years of my life (since I started writing my first book 'Inside the Boundary Line' on the subject) and a significant part of hard-earned money in pursuing efforts to bring an end to this colossal fraud that is continuing to great detriment of the nation and its people. It has not been for fun and it has not been fun. To successfully file such a detailed PIL has been very laborious and not a child's play. It took months, almost a year or more since I first decided to go ahead with PIL. In fact, I have been quite miserable for most of the last few years. I have been trying to tell a serious truth to the world, but all have been happy in their collective degradation, mainly because media in self-interest has been happy in continuing to be the preacher of falsehood selling a massive fraud as a competitive sport. It is not a joke for one man to take on combined might of all the institutions that join hands in self-interest for continuation of a public fraud. **I doubt if there is any such precedent in human history.** The real possibility of being harmed by the betting mafia was also always there. Still, I took this up since I could see that there was no one else to take this up, and since I have felt concerned about far-reaching and very serious national, political and international implications of this colossal fraud all along. In the process, I have not only become a target for the establishment, but have also become a pariah not only in the society, but also among family and friends. Still, I have continued in the hope that Truth will prevail one day and a blow to this massive fraud that goes on with the active and passive complicity of mighty institutions and hundreds of mighty celebrities and political leaders whenever that happens shall give rise to a sort of revolution that will bring an end to the culture of crony capitalism that is today ruining all institutions slowly but surely. But, probably, that was not to be.

I have no one else but myself to blame for my miseries since I went ahead, though aware of the warning by the bard: '*Sachchi baat kahi thi maine, logon ne sooli pe chadhaya…*'

Those who are today supervising and looking over the continuation of colossal fraud through cricket are probably unaware or unconcerned that they are sounding the death knell of the very institutions they are part of today.

Nothing exposes the present Modi government in India on its claims of zero tolerance against corruption more than its wilful protection to this continuing massive public fraud through institutionalised fixing in cricket despite matter having been brought to the notice of the PM and the government repeatedly. It goes without saying that the present finance minister of India, Arun Jaitley, has been one of the kingpins of this fraud through his long association with cricket administration and IPL. Unfortunately, through this report, even the COA have acted as stooge of the fraudulent and rogue establishment.

I am already 61 and my time may be up anytime, or my faculties may cease to be what they were or are. Also life has its own uncertainties. Even otherwise, I don't know how longer I can go on like this or what else I can do. The question also arises why I should go on when whole world is happy with this manifestation of human degradation. But, then, is the world of intellectuals the whole world? Masses are not even aware since they are not told the truth. As Providence would have it, the COA failed to understand and appreciate the contents and spirit of the petition knowingly or unknowingly and failed to rise to the occasion. They rather chose to be ordinary mortals looking after only self-interest and self-preservation.

It is incidental that I am alive today and drafting this rejoinder. Life has no guarantee. It was not for me but for the world to act after publication of the book 'Bettors Beware', rather after publication of my first book on the subject 'Inside the Boundary Line' and my first Press Conference thereafter in January 2013, to take on this massive fraud. Alas! The world has miserably failed itself.

I appeal to the good sense of the COA to kindly excuse me for my anger that has been natural and well placed. In the final analysis, individuals and their egos don't matter. What matters is what we could get out of life and what we could do for the humanity, especially from position of authority or knowledge that we got blessed with. We all have same destination. Burial ground/ crematorium remains the last destination for us.

Today, the COA may feel intoxicated with power, but tomorrow history may rightly judge them as villains.

And if I had been making false noise publicly knowingly or unknowingly about cricket being institutionally fixed for the last 7 years through my books, published interviews, and press conferences, I deserved to be publicly hanged for harming the great game of cricket by bringing it into disrepute and for falsely poisoning people's minds all these years.

Those who die—almost on a daily basis in J&K—as a result of terror activities, substantially funded by dirty money (lakhs of crores of rupees per year) earned by betting syndicates and mafia like D-company, may not be our nears and dears; but they are and had been men and women of flesh and blood, nears and dears of some. Only very recently, on 1/11/2018, even a BJP leader and his brother were killed in Kishtwar.

And like drug-addicts, there are millions of betting-addicts who get trapped jointly by betting the mafia and cricketing world to lose their wealth almost on a daily basis throughout and out scripted and fixed cricket. Most of them remain unaware of how they are trapped and looted, and those aware don't know what to do. While the society is concerned

for the drug-addicts, it remains unconcerned for the millions of victims of cricket betting. To continue to suffer becomes their fate. Those millions are also our brethren, men of flesh and blood.

Any scope for me to doubt that cricket was a colossal fraud totally vanished when I was told by a responsible friend on 17th July, 2018, later in the day after the meeting with the COA, that in a chance meeting, a ward of a Cricket Test player who played for India in the 90s had told him (the friend) that contents of my books and petition were all correct since that player had told that ward that the players just played as per some orders and no competitive cricket on their own. I was also surprised a bit to know how old the continuing fraud was. It could well be older than the 90s also. Unbelievable, but true! Hope that the COA or anyone won't quote me saying that I considered it as evidence. I am fully aware that it is no evidence till people deposed officially, but it did further confirm and corroborate for me what was already so clear otherwise.

God alonc knows how much longer this institutionalised fraud—a very sizeable manifestation of human degradation—will continue. Though the same is not necessary, my challenge as mentioned in the petition stands, from recordings of any match (whether a league match or an international match) over the last decade or so, I can show any panel of cricket experts or jury how scripted cricket and not competitive cricket was taking place all along.

To bring home the import of how big a scam the continuous institutionalised fixing of cricket for

decades is, it would suffice to say that it is a scam hundred times bigger than the currently much-publicised alleged Rafale scam in India both in magnitude and reach, and many times bigger than all the scams known to man till date put together including 2G scam which Mr. Vinod Rai himself was instrumental in exposing.

Cricket being said to be the second religion to Indians, the fact of cricket being a fraud also has a tremendous emotional bearing for the masses across all religions.

Through this rejoinder, I urge the COA to come out of slumber, go through the petition once again and this rejoinder word by word with an open intelligent truthful mind and review their decision and revise the report in the larger public interest. In case they still have any genuine doubts about what has been stated or in understanding and appreciating what is what, I offer to come and explain across the table.

That Cricket is a colossal institutionalised fraud is as sure as Sun rises in the East or 2+2 = 4. No autocratic statements can keep the truth under wraps for eternity, even though it may not be easy for one to comprehend the harsh truth since it shatters what one has been made to believe all his life and believing what one has grown up, more so without knowing at least a bit about betting, especially session betting, which is the cause behind this fraud.

Al Jazeeras may go to sleep over their own reports (media and the cricketing world are already sleeping), the crusaders may take U-turns like B.B. Misra did or may go into oblivion; there may not be any further reports about matches being fixed; viewers may continue to bite nails while regarding absurd wilful performances by teams to lose as competitive cricket; the media and cricket experts may continue to sell a colossal fraud as a great sport filling columns and air-time with reports, analyses, and statistics and creating fake heroes; there may not be any more outbursts like Amir Sohail's or Dirk Nannes'; twitter handles like @theDcricket may stop tweeting, delete their tweets, their twitter handles may be suspended, abandoned or manipulated; Cricket administrators of the world may continue to act blind or go back on their words; the whole world may join to echo the COA's decision that cricket was not an institutionalised fraud and contents of writ petition (Civil) 1163/2017 were nothing but unsubstantiated sweeping allegations; everyone including me may go dead quiet; **but score books of cricket matches will continue to speak to those who wish to listen and objective application of the basic principles of probability to these (as detailed in the book 'Bettors Beware') shall continue to illuminate the world with the truth of cricket being a massive institutionalised fraud as long as it continues to be so.**

Since the subject report of the COA has been uploaded on the BCCI's website, the fair play would require this rejoinder also to be uploaded alongside. In fact, they must have uploaded the petition in reference to which this report has been made, before uploading the report. Had they done so, many intelligent minds could straightaway see the COA's bluff. There has not been any response from the COA even to my specific request to them to do so after they had uploaded the subject report on the BCCI's website.

Let people judge for themselves after this rejoinder is uploaded.

Thank you.

(Atul Kumar)

CC: Registrar, The Supreme Court of India in reference to references above and CA no. 4235/2014. He may please connect it and put it up to the appropriate bench that is considering the report of the COA under reference.'

The committee of administrators never responded to this painstaking detailed rejoinder, and my subsequent communications to them, displaying a skin much thicker than of a rhinoceros. It had issued a meaningless bureaucratic report under the leadership of famous Mr. Vinod Rai, ex-CAG (Comptroller and Auditor General) of India, and its job was done. **It had carried the orders of the Supreme Court on paper, howsoever facetiously and stupidly. The continuing fake cricket was none of its concerns; the committee belonged to a world that patronised bogus and phony cricket and took pride in drowning itself in bureaucratic quagmire.**

□

The Deaf Statesmen

"We can easily forgive a child who is afraid of the dark; the real tragedy of life is when men are afraid of the light."

—PLATO

The COA's report and my rejoinder were later on duly filed by me in the Supreme Court also in continuation of the IA (Impleadment Application) in the main case of the BCCI. Since then, nothing further fruitful has happened despite me virtually charge-sheeting the Hon'ble Supreme Court of India repeatedly; the issue remains dead and well buried even though my subsequent various letters to the Hon'ble Court are duly registered under their grievance management for many months; the fraud not only prospering but becoming more and more open through advent of further open instruments/ games cheating the masses like Dream 11, 11 Wickets, My 11 Circle, etc. It has been brought out/explained in my various communications to the Hon'ble Court sent as notes for assistance to it. The same can be accessed through the link given in this book for the same.

A lot happened before that. After the final order of the Supreme Court in our PIL, I was acting on two fronts. One, I tried to pursue with the committee of administrators so that it could act meaningfully in the matter. Side by side, I filed an IA in the main case of the BCCI, case no. CA 4235/2014. The acceptance and registration of the IA by the Supreme Court wasn't without drama and delay. My letter in early August 2018 to the bench that passed the order in the PIL brings that out:

Hon'ble the Chief Justice dated 7/8/2018

Hon'ble Mr. Justice A.M. Khanwilkar

Hon'ble Dr. Justice D.Y. Chandrachud

The Supreme Court of India,

New Delhi.

(through: The Registrar, the Supreme Court of India)

Subject: A puzzling order by the Supreme Court of India and implementation thereof by it.

Reference: 1. WP (C) no. 1163/2017 in SCI

2. The Supreme Court Order dated 7/5/18 in this case

Sir/s,

You are requested to kindly peruse the following brief facts and concerns and do the needful.

1. I had filed the above writ successfully along with a co-petitioner as party-in-person.
2. The writ brought to fore a massive on-going national and international fraud through the game of cricket.
3. The serious and grave implications of this fraud were also brought out, same including fleecing and looting of tens of millions of Indians to fill the coffers of betting syndicates connected with underworld and terror funding, mostly operating from enemy lands, **to the tune of estimated lakhs of crores of rupees**

or more per year, through fixed and scripted cricket matches.

4. The fraud is going on brazenly because of the clear complicity of the three pillars of democracy—media, executive, and legislature (actively or passively). A plethora of powerful Indian politicians across political parties, top industrialists, media barons, celebrities from and outside cricket are and have been involved. **Therefore, judiciary and, hence, the Supreme Court of India remained the last hope.**

5. It is a matter of record that even though the Court itself had ordered the above writ to be listed after 2 weeks vide their order dated 16/2/18, I had to fight it out with the Supreme Court of India for getting the case listed next before it ultimately got listed on 7/5/18.

   As if an on-going massive national fraud was just my personal concern and no concern of the Supreme Court or the rest of the country.

6. Not a single word was uttered/submitted by the respondents (BCCI and UOI) or anyone else against the contents of our submission in the Court or elsewhere, nor our averments ever contested by anyone, before the Hon'ble Court passed the order vide reference 2 above in this case. **That does mean vindication of the contents of our submissions in the subject writ petition.** Not only that, subsequently in their communication dated 3/7/18 to me, the Committee of Administrators (COA) for

the BCCI themselves acknowledged that extremely important issues had been raised by me in the Writ Petition/my letter to them.

7. The Court also very kindly took due cognizance of the petition and didn't find anything amiss with it.
8. The Court passed the summary orders and not speaking orders.
9. The text of the order passed by the Hon'ble Supreme Court is reproduced below for your kind ready reference:

   "Heard Mr. Atul Kumar, the petitioner No. 1 appearing in-person, and Mr. Parag P. Tripathi, learned senior counsel appearing for the Committee of Administrators. In our considered opinion, the Committee of Administrators may take a decision with regard to the grievance made in this writ petition and submit a report, which shall be considered in the main proceedings that relates to the BCCI. The petitioners are at liberty to assist in the main case. With the aforesaid liberty and direction, the writ petition stands disposed of. There shall be no order as to costs. The interlocutory applications, if any, stand disposed off."
10. Despite what got established through the petition, the above order cut no ice to arrest ongoing massive fraud (IPL 11 was allowed to go on and now TNPL matches are going on). **Still, there was a big silver lining that opportunity was given to the petitioners to further assist the Court in the matter concerning BCCI and that the issue**

remained alive before the Court.

11. Knowing very well the gravity of the issue for my country and its people, in deference to the Hon'ble Court's order, in further follow-up, I wrote to the COA. I got a reply through email after about a month, after sending a reminder.
12. In the meantime, I also filed an impleadment application in the main case relating to the BCCI, i.e., CA no. 4235/2014, in deference to the Hon'ble Court's orders to enable me to assist the Court.
13. The impleadment application was filed by me as party-in-person on 4/6/18, a month before the next scheduled hearing on 5/7/18 in that main case CA 4235/2014. My impleadment application was duly received by the concerned counter and numbered 81233/18. I live in Kolkata and I had to toil a lot again and spend in order to be able to file the impleadment application in the Supreme Court at New Delhi. Anyhow, I was happy that I had done the needful in deference to the Hon'ble Court's orders and that my intention to assist the Court as desired by it was very much in place and on record.
14. It was only on 4/7/18 at Kolkata (a month after filing) that I received a letter from the Supreme Court informing me that there were defects in my impleadment application that needed to be cured. There was no way that it could be done before 5th July, when the case was scheduled to be heard in which the Supreme Court itself had invited the petitioners to assist it.

15. When I subsequently came to Delhi and took action to cure the defects, submitted the necessary documents for curing vide no. 97646 and interacted with the concerned section III of the Supreme Court over phone from party-in-person counter in this regard on 18/7/2018 (when the website of the Supreme Court was showing the case CA 4235/2014 listed for 20/7/18 next), the section behaved strangely. First, I was told that there was no order dated 7/5/18 in CA 4235/2014 by which the Supreme Court had invited me to assist in that case. When I insisted on their seeing the necessary order in the WP (C) 1163/2017 as had been clearly mentioned in my impleadment application also containing a copy of that order as an annexure, they were not prepared to listen and subsequently told me that since hearing in the main case CA 4235/2014 was already over on 5/7/2018, no impleadment by me was now possible. I was left helpless, bewildered, and wondering in and by the Supreme Court of India.
16. My subsequent emails dated 26/7/18 and 30/7/18 to the Supreme Court to advise me how I could assist the Court in terms of its order have also elicited no response. As on date, the case CA 4235/2014 is listed for 21/8/18 next as per the Supreme Court website.
17. It was only yesterday on 6/8/18 that I received a letter no. D. No. 24114/2013/Sec. III dated 25/7/2018 from Assistant Registrar, the Supreme Court of India. The contents of this letter confirm what has been stated above in para 15 regarding the concerned Section III of the Supreme Court refusing to see and connect

the relevant order under reference for reasons best known to the concerned officials. Either they are grossly erring or there is some technical lacuna in the order itself. Whatever it is, I, the poor petitioner, find myself at the receiving end having toiled hard and spent personal money in national and public interest.

18. In the meanwhile, to the credit of the COA, they held a meeting with me and my co-petitioner at Delhi on 17/7/2018 in response to my request earlier to them in order to search for the remedies to the ongoing menace of institutionalised fixing in cricket. Shri Rahul Johri, CEO/BCCI and Shri Ajit Singh, Head/ACU were also present in the meeting along with some other officials and legal advisors of the BCCI. **The essence of the meeting was that the COA were at the same page with us regarding our concerns, but appeared to be at a loss as to how to deal effectively with the problem given its magnitude. It also transpired that solutions lied with agencies other than the BCCI also.** (A copy of this communication is also being marked to Sh. Vinod Rai, Head, COA/BCCI.)

19. **As things stand today, with the clearance of my impleadment application having been delayed (no communication is being made with me over phone or through email by the concerned office of the Supreme Court) and the same not being cleared for undue reasons, whatever happens further in the Supreme Court in the matter brought out in WP (C) 1163/2017 will be behind**

the back of the petitioners against the basic principles of natural justice. We may not even come to know what report the COA submits to the Hon'ble Court and whether the suggestions given by me to them prior to the meeting as desired by them would be conveyed to the Hon'ble Court. My mails to the COA in this regard remain unanswered. In the background, the massive fraud in the name of cricket, **as clearly visible as the shining sun to anyone who cares/bothers to open eyes**, is continuing as unbridled as ever. And that is the biggest concern.

20. **To sum up, sounding fair, the Court had ordered for the report of the COA to be considered in the main case relating to the BCCI, inviting and allowing petitioners also to assist/implead in that case. But, in effect, the hearing in that main case concluded with only some isolated impleadment applications pending (as told to me by the concerned section) even before the COA submitted its report, and the Supreme Court itself has ensured so far through its acts of commission and omission that the petitioners couldn't implead in that case. In the face of what followed, doesn't the order (under reference) by the Court No. 1 of the Supreme Court become a bit farcical and a slap on the face of the judicial process in India (even though if the order itself in essence was a very sound one)? All the while the powerful of the country involved in a massive public fraud, resulting in looting**

the tens of millions of people and financially strengthening the underworld and terror outfits that in all probability are also involved in killing Indians (defence personnel and civilians alike) and challenging the security and integrity of the country, are continuing to be free and unquestioned. To name a few top celebrities, they include Reliance Industries/Mukesh Ambani (by virtue of being owner of Mumbai Indians), Shah Rukh Khan (an owner of KKR), Arun Jaitley (a top cricket administrator for years), Rajiv Shukla (IPL Chairman), Sachin Tendulkar (ex-Indian and IPL player and mentor of IPL team Mumbai Indians), Virat Kohli, M.S. Dhoni (top cricketers), Ravi Shastri, and Sunil Gavaskar (top cricket experts and commentators). The complete list will run into pages.

21. Once again, I wrote to the Government of India through PMO, MHA and PM requesting them to act after the continuing fraud through cricket got established at a platform not less than the Supreme Court of India through the subject writ petition, endorsing a copy of that letter to the Hon'ble CJI also. But the Government of India has continued to turn a deaf ear to the matter of a massive anti-national fraud that is prospering with each passing day.

In the light of the above facts and concerns, you may please like to do the needful in larger public and national interest and also ensure that I am allowed to assist the Hon'ble Court in the main case concerning the

BCCI, CA 4235/2014, without further unnecessary delay in deference to the Court's order under reference.

With kind regards,

(Atul Kumar)

CC: President of India

Chairman, Bar Council of India

Shri Vinod Rai, Head, COA/BCCI

As nothing moved, I decided to write an open letter to (or meant for) all the sitting judges of the Hon'ble Supreme Court of India, since the issue appeared to have become dead at the end of the Hon'ble Court. This letter attempted to comprehensively apprise all the esteemed sitting judges of the august Court as to what was happening, urging them to consider the whole thing in the larger perspective. I did hope that there would be at least some statesmen amongst the sitting judges of the august Supreme Court of India to take forward this very grave issue, but that was not to be! This letter got registered twice with their Grievance Management as Diary Nos. 18182/SCI/PIL(E)2019 and 18183/SCI/PIL(E)2019. That has been the fate of this letter till date. Needless to say, the monumental fraud and crime have been continuing unfettered. However, going through this letter should give one gist of everything.

AN OPEN LETTER TO THE HON'BLE CJI AND ALL OTHER HON'BLE JUDGES OF THE SUPREME COURT OF INDIA

Hon'ble Mr. Justice Ranjan Gogoi

The Chief Justice Of India, 27th March, 2019

Hon'ble Mr. Justice Arjan Kumar Sikri,

Hon'ble Mr. Justice Sharad Arvind Bobde,

Hon'ble Mr. Justice N.V. Ramana,

Hon'ble Mr. Justice Arun Mishra,

Hon'ble Mr. Justice R.F. Nariman,

Hon'ble Mr. Justice Abhay Manohar Sapre,

Hon'ble Mrs. Justice R. Banumathi,

Hon'ble Mr. Justice Uday Umesh Lalit,

Hon'ble Mr. Justice A.M. Khanwilkar,

Hon'ble Dr. Justice D.Y. Chandrachud,

Hon'ble Mr. Justice Ashok Bhushan,

Hon'ble Mr. Justice L. Nageswara Rao,

Hon'ble Mr. Justice Sanjay Kishan Kaul,

Hon'ble Mr. Justice Mohan M. Shantanagoudar,

Hon'ble Mr. Justice S. Abdul Nazeer,

Hon'ble Mr. Justice Navin Sinha,

Hon'ble Mr. Justice Deepak Gupta,

Hon'ble Ms. Justice Indu Malhotra,

Hon'ble Ms. Justice Indira Banerjee,

Hon'ble Mr. Justice Vineet Saran,

Hon'ble Mr. Justice K.M. Joseph,

Hon'ble Mr. Justice Hemant Gupta,

Hon'ble Mr. Justice R.Subhash Reddy,

Hon'ble Mr. Justice Mukeshkumar Rasikbhai Shah,

Hon'ble Mr. Justice Ajay Rastogi,

Hon'ble Mr. Justice Dinesh Maheshwari,

Hon'ble Mr. Justice Sanjiv Khanna'

The Supreme Court of India,

New Delhi.

Subject: Fate of Writ Petition (C) no. 1163/2017 in the Hon'ble Supreme Court of India on continuing Fraudulent Cricket—a source of terror funding.

Dear Sir/Madam,

I write this with a sense of awe, considering your stature and power, but as the Nobel Prize Laureate, Gunter Grass had said in his famous poem 'I'll say what must be said'. I shall divide my submission in three parts: A. The Bare Facts, B. The Meaning Thereof, C. Summing Up.

(A) The Bare Facts

It was recently reported that on 13th December, 2018, a bench of Justices Madan B. Lokur and Deepak Gupta told a petitioner seeking directions for the immediate execution of the four death row convicts in the 2012 Nirbhaya gangrape and murder case, "....You are making the court a joke."

A few days earlier to that, the Hon'ble CJI, Justice Ranjan Gogoi was reported as having quoted in late November 2018, "It is in our best interest to heed to the advice of the Constitution. If we do not, our hubris will result in a sharp descent into chaos."

About a week later, the retired Supreme Court judge, Justice Kurian Joseph was reported having said in reference to their much publicised and controversial press conference (by him and three other Supreme Court judges including the present CJI) in January 2018, that they felt the then CJI was being remote-controlled.

Against the above background, kindly peruse the

following bare facts that are a matter of record in relation to a PIL filed in the Supreme Court of India through the subject petition WP (C) 1163/2017.

I, along with a co-petitioner, the eminent journalist and writer, Mr. Shantanu Guha Ray, filed the above-mentioned writ petition. The following link gives the full text of it: https://www.livelaw.in/cleaning-cricket-retired-rly-officer-scribe-move-sc-seeking-stay-ipl-leagues-check-match-fixing-read-petition/ I reproduce below the synopsis as filed to give you a sense of the PIL and the issues involved:

"On the very outset, the petitioners aver that in filing this petition they are acting with utmost sense of responsibility. This is a petition in the public interest by two petitioners, Atul Kumar and Shantanu Guha Ray, seeking action/intervention by the Hon'ble Supreme Court to put a break to the ongoing open massive fraud through cricket that is mostly scripted and fixed. The fixing and fraud are so deep-rooted and institutionalised that one would find it very difficult to imagine and believe. The petitioners have been compelled to petition the Hon'ble Court since all the agencies who should have acted to stem this rot have failed to do so despite repeated pleadings to them by the petitioners for years and despite fraud having become brazen. The agencies include the ICC, the BCCI, and the Government/Union of India.

Sufficient material has been brought on record through this petition to bring above home to a logical mind. A lot more lies in the public domain through books, press coverage and public posts on the subject. No one in authority has been looking at it or applying mind to it. Mathematical and, hence, scientific proof for continuous institutionalised fixing of cricket matches is in the public domain unchallenged and uncontested for more than three years and has withstood the test of time.

This massive fraud continuing through cricket is immensely harmful to the masses and the nation in more ways than one. Masses who don't bet on cricket matches get cheated emotionally, the most telling recent example being inexplicable and conspicuous underperformance by World number one Indian team against Pakistan in the ICC champions Trophy final in June 2017. This match was widely believed to be fixed and millions of Indians suffered emotionally. Masses still don't know and don't realise that fixing of that match was no exception. They are unaware what and how serious the implications of fixed cricket are.

Those who bet on cricket matches get cheated financially as well. There are millions of them in India alone. Matches in all the formats of the game are so scripted as to make bettors addicted and make them lose heavily to the betting syndicates match after match, session after session. Law Commission of India has termed illegal betting market in India as parallel economy. SIT on black money appointed by the Hon'ble Supreme Court itself has estimated the Indian cricket betting market to be more than ₹ 3 lakh crores per year. With other estimates, it is likely to be much more than that. The Hon'ble Supreme Court itself has found even IPL team owners guilty of betting on IPL/cricket matches in the past. Dawood

Ibrahim has been known to have been controlling cricket betting syndicates, and an unknown chunk of big money earned by betting syndicates through fixed cricket goes to terror funding. The cricketing legends, cricket experts, cricket broadcasters, cricket commentators and cricket journalists are acting akin to drug peddlers selling fake cricket for the benefit of the betting syndicates to the gullible masses hooked on to it.

Turning of almost a blind eye by the media at large to institutionalised total fixing of cricket even though it throws up sporadic news on fixing now and then, and inaction by the highest authorities of the country, both executive and judicial, so far on all that is in public domain and on the repeated pleadings by Petitioner no. 1, who has been acting as a responsible member of the society exposing for years this massive fraud with very grave national and international implications at great personal cost and risk (acting against the interests of a big mafia) with no protection and without much support from any quarter in the society, has brought the things to such a pass that people without any fear are today openly telling and showing using social media that matches were fixed and charging money for giving inside information, purposefully wrong at times, to rob the addicted and trapped bettors for the benefit of betting syndicates linked to terror funding. Matches are so scripted that addiction continues reinforced. The fraud and the crime are being flaunted openly as if there is no governance left in cricket and in the country. All the authorities, multitude of them in India alone, seem to be taking pride in acting blind.

With overwhelming material on record to establish all above, the petition primarily requests for a thorough, meaningful and honest investigation by a Court-appointed SIT to unearth the total modus operandi of this massive fraud through continuous fixing in cricket matches to bring all the culprits to book. It also requests for a stay on IPL or any other such leagues. like KPL, TNPL, etc., from taking place in the country till culprits are brought to book or the SIT formed decides and recommends lifting the stay. Strictly speaking, other international cricket matches should also be stayed from taking place in the country if so possible. That will go a long way in controlling this monstrous fraud and stem the rot.

Immediate effective action is a must since big crime continues to take place openly in the country through almost every match being played and broadcast. A body blow to this monster will send a strong message to all those in authority as well as the masses in the country that '*der hai andher nahin*' and will desist them from corrupt practices and activities that appear to be becoming the order of the day. Vice versa of it will also hold. If this brazen massive fraud, with more and more people becoming aware of it, continues unbridled, demoralisation and degradation of the society as a whole will continue to increase."

The case was first listed on 2/2/2018 in Court no. 1, the bench comprising HON'BLE THE CHIEF JUSTICE, HON'BLE MR. JUSTICE A.M. KHANWILKAR and

HON'BLE DR. JUSTICE D.Y. CHANDRACHUD. The Court passed the following order:

"Let a copy of this petition be served on the Central Agency so that it can make arrangements for the counsel for the Union of India to assist the Court. List on 16th February, 2018."

The case was then listed on 16th February, 2018, but, unfortunately, I had to seek adjournment due to the sad demise of my mother in the early hours of 13th February, 2018. Accordingly, the Hon'ble Court passed the following order on 16th:

"List the matter after two weeks."

Before the next listing, the BCCI also themselves became a party to the case through filing a caveat. The copies of the petition and the As (interlocutory applications) were duly served on them by us.

Thereafter, the listing of case continued to be postponed repeatedly. I continued to pursue through letter after letter, through email and post, to the Registrar, the Supreme Court of India and the Hon'ble Chief Justice. The correspondence between me and the Hon'ble Court in the intervening period should be available in the case file. At last, the case was suddenly listed on 7th May, 2018, the listing date having been shown to be in October 2018 on the Supreme Court's website prior to that.

Not a word was uttered or submitted in writing either by the UOI or the BCCI against the contents of the petition, nor did the Hon'ble Court make any comment at all, before passing the following order on 7th May, 2018:

"Heard Mr. Atul Kumar, the petitioner No. 1

appearing in-person and Mr. Parag P. Tripathi, learned senior counsel appearing for the Committee of Administrators. In our considered opinion, the Committee of Administrators may take a decision with regard to the grievance made in this writ petition and submit a report, which shall be considered in the main proceedings that relates to the BCCI. The petitioners are at liberty to assist in the main case. With the aforesaid liberty and direction, the writ petition stands disposed of. There shall be no order as to costs. The interlocutory applications, if any, stand disposed of."

Mr. Parag P. Tripathi briefly argued against this, but the Hon'ble Court went ahead with the above order.

As a follow-up to this order, I wrote to Shri Vinod Rai, the Head of the Committee of Administrators (COA) for the BCCI, requesting him to give me a hearing to be able to explain things to him across the table through a letter dated 14/5/2018, bringing out the salient points of the petition also for his ready reference. Not hearing from him, I sent a reminder dated 31/5/2018. Finally, I got the following e-mail dated 9/6/2018 from the Committee of Administrators:

"*Dear Mr. Atul Kumar,*

1. The Committee of Administrators has received a letter from you on 18th May, *2018 enclosing a copy of the order dated 7th* May, *2018 ("****Order****") passed by the Hon'ble Supreme Court in Writ Petition (Civil) No. 1163 of 2017 ("****Writ Petition****"). The Committee of Administrators has also received your second letter dated 31st* May, *2018 on 4th* June, *2018.*

2. The Committee of Administrators is aware of the gravity of the issues raised in the Writ Petition and is currently in the process of reviewing the existing rules regulations/mechanisms/measures that have been put in place by the BCCI to prevent and/or otherwise deal with fixing and other similar corrupt activities in cricket matches.

3. The Committee of Administrators believes that it will be more fruitful and constructive to have a discussion/hearing on the issues raised in the Writ Petition once the above exercise has been completed. Please be assured that no decision/report in terms of the Order will be taken/submitted before such discussion/hearing with you.

Thanking you.

Yours faithfully,

The Supreme Court-Appointed Committee of Administrators"

Further interaction took place between the COA and me, the COA asking for my suggestions as below before the meeting:

'*(a) Your suggestions/inputs on what mechanisms/measures the BCCI can put in place to prevent and/or otherwise deal with fixing and other similar corrupt activities in cricket matches; and*

(b) Your suggestions/inputs on what assistance/support other agencies (including agencies of the Government of India and/or States) can be requested to provide to the BCCI for the purpose of preventing and/or

otherwise dealing with fixing and other similar corrupt activities in cricket matches.'

I sent them the necessary suggestions which were relevant to the issue as brought out in the petition. Finally, the meeting took place between us—the petitioners—and the COA along with paraphernalia of their officials and legal advisors on 17th July, 2018 in New Delhi.

I briefly summed up and recorded what transpired in the meeting through an email to the COA and copy to others on the same afternoon. The same is reproduced below:

"Atul Kumar

Tue 17/07/2018 15:32

Committee of Administrators;

Rahul Johri;

Karina Kripalani;

shantanunewshound@gmail.com.

This is to convey thanks for holding the meeting today and to put the outcome of the meeting in a perspective (in confidence).

It was disappointing to learn that the purpose of this meeting was primarily only to hear us out and the meeting was not to be much interactive as the COA was not to apprise us of their viewpoint. However, still the following transpired as a result of the brief discussion that took place:

1. The COA indicated that it would recommend to the Hon'ble Court to order thorough investigation into the

tweets by @theDcricket for over a year now. Though it is extremely unfortunate that such an action has not yet been initiated by the concerned authorities, we applaud the indicated action by the COA. An honest and thorough interrogation/investigation of him/his affairs would definitely help spill many beans and many skeletons will come out of the cupboard. That alone will be a significant step in the right direction.

2. The COA indicated that they were as concerned about the state of affairs as us, the petitioners. Though they felt that the solutions suggested by us were rather impractical. We maintain that the solutions suggested, though may appear to be extraordinary, were necessitated considering how bad things were and given the very grave and serious implications of how things are continuing.
3. Nevertheless we requested that the COA might please go ahead with practical solutions such that the action taken should have some telling effect given how wrong things had gone, at least to make a significant start.
4. To that effect, it was suggested to get the IPL-10 Final that was under shadow for fixing as detailed in the Writ Petition to be investigated in a transparent manner by the Police/concerned authorities, with public knowledge so that a message goes out to restore some of the public confidence. But the BCCI officials wanted the investigation to be by the ACU in a confidential manner. The COA appeared to be agreeing to that. We still feel that such an investigation may not serve much purpose and there was a stronger possibility of

things being swept under the carpet in due course with an in-house investigation by the BCCI. The COA may kindly take final call in this regard.

5. The COA indicated their inclination to strengthen the ACU and to put a strong ACU in place to instill fear in the minds of evil-doers. This was welcome, reiterating that implementation and putting the ACU to effective use were more necessary, mere making of regulations without implementation didn't mean much as the past results/present state of affairs showed.
6. The meeting ended on a rather positive note, giving us hope that something effective and good may eventually come out of it in the larger public and collective national interest.

It is requested that the COA while submitting their report to the Hon›ble Supreme Court in terms of their order dated 7/5/18 in WP (C) 1163/2017 may also please convey the inputs/suggestions given by me earlier in deference to the COA›s desire, to the Hon›ble Supreme Court with/without the COA's comments as deemed fit.

Regards

Atul Kumar"

There was never any rejoinder to this by the COA or anybody else. The Committee of Administrators finally made and submitted their report dated 22/10/2018 on the subject petition and also posted its text on the website of the BCCI, the link for the same being: http://relaunch-live.s3.amazonaws.com/cms/documents/5bd95399b2f6c-COA%20Report%20in%20Writ%20Petition%20 filed%20by%20Atul%20Kumar%20(23%2010%20 2018).PDF.

I sent rejoinder dated 14/11/2018 to this report bringing out how it had been nothing but a sham, a conspicuous act of cheating, and a mockery of sense of justice, requesting the COA to post this rejoinder also on the website of the BCCI. Neither that has been done nor any response to the rejoinder has been received by me till date. The text of rejoinder is also available on my blog http://atulonly.blogspot.com/ through a post dated 28/1/2019. This rejoinder was also duly sent to the Registrar, the Supreme Court of India through post as well as email.

In the meantime, to be able to assist the Hon'ble Supreme Court in the main case concerning the BCCI in deference to the Hon'ble Court's order dated 7/5/2018 in WP (C) 1163/2017, on 18th July, 2018, I filed Impleadment Application, i.e., IA (no. 91439/18) in that case (no. CA 4235/2014) pending before the Court. But that IA is not yet listed, the Registrar's office continuing to insist that there was no order passed by the Court giving me liberty to assist in that case. The relevant portion of letter no. D. No. 24114/2013/Sec. III dated 25th July, 2018 from Assistant Registrar, the Supreme Court of India is reproduced below verbatim:

" ...you have stated in the letter that regarding permission to implead in the matter, the Hon'ble Court vide order dated 7/5/2018 has already permitted you to assist in the above-said case, but there is no order passed by the Hon'ble Court for the above-said date..." (The Registrar's office, thus, refused to take any cognizance of the Hon'ble Court's order passed in WP (C) 1163/2017 giving petitioners the liberty to assist the Hon'ble Court in the main case concerning the BCCI, despite the copy of that order having been documented in the IA (impleadment application), and my repeatedly having drawn attention to that in answering the objections thereafter.)

My last few letters and emails to the Registrar further on this remain unanswered for more than two months now. There has not been any response from the Supreme Court to my rejoinder to the COA's report either till date. While following status of case CA 4235/2014 on the Supreme Court website on 22/02/2019, it was only by chance that my name among the list of counsels caught my attention and then I came to know that sometime back, my IA had been tagged with this case with no information to me.

(B) The Meaning Thereof

The above are the bare facts. Now we must examine what these facts mean and what questions arise. We must do so objectively, with an open mind, without prejudices and mental blocks, and in the larger perspective. **We must keep in mind that the Supreme Court of India is (or supposed to be) a man-made institution created to sub-serve nothing and no one but Justice and Truth** (यतोधर्मस्ततोजयः)

I have tried to be as brief as possible while bringing out the above facts. But some detailing would be necessary now so that everything is correctly understood in the larger perspective, especially since what comes out is beyond one's wildest imagination and normal human comprehension.

As the intelligent minds of the addressees would have already discerned, is it not a clear case of even the Hon'ble Supreme Court of India at times failing to take the cognizance of its own orders? **Can there be anything more bizarre**? Why did it happen so? What does one do in such a situation? Another thing that is very loud and clear is cheating by the Supreme Court-appointed Committee of Administrators for the BCCI with the petitioners. Why did such a high-powered committee have to stoop so low? **They acted with utmost irresponsibility, if not like third-rate goons, in giving the report as they did. In essence, the report by the Committee of Administrators (COA) and as things stand amount to a total joke of judicial process in India.** How and why so?

It was after repeated requests by me that the COA agreed to have a meeting with me, subsequent to the Court's order dated 7/5/2019. I meant the meeting to serve the purpose of a meaningful interaction and exchange of ideas. I had hoped that the COA would take the right call keeping in mind the gravity of what the subject writ petition had brought out. The COA were well aware that the contents of the petition remained totally unchallenged in the Court, the BCCI themselves having been one of the respondents. Above anything else, the order of the Hon'ble Supreme Court dated 7/5/2018 clearly implied that the contents had withstood the scrutiny of the Hon'ble Court. If it were not so, the Hon'ble Court couldn't and wouldn't have given the petitioners the liberty to assist (for all purposes it amounted to an invitation to assist) the Court in the main case concerning the BCCI.

As per the Hon'ble Court's order, was not the COA to take the decision for the action to be taken in the face of what had been brought out in the petition rather than passing their dictatorial farcical judgement on it? It is a matter of record that in their interaction with me leading to the meeting and during the meeting with us, they repeatedly indicated such an intention (to take the necessary action) all along. They are on record having repeatedly stated that very important issues had been brought out/raised in the petition. But, in the report they submitted, they went back on their words and took a U-turn, **the report being a futile bureaucratic exercise and totally irrelevant to the contents of the petition**. If the contents of the petition were unsubstantiated as unilaterally concluded by the COA in their report, what for did they hold meeting with us? Do you give value to someone who makes unfounded bogus allegations? Do you ask for suggestions from such wasters? Why so much contradiction between their statements and actions leading to the meeting and their report afterwards? **The million-dollar questions remain: having Mr. Vinod Rai, Head of the COA assured us that they would request the Supreme Court to get 'Cricket Insider' investigated, what made them forget all about it afterwards? What happened to investigation of IPL-10 final as they had assured and promised us in the meeting?**

Then could the COA be at liberty to term the contents of the petition as unsubstantiated behind the back of the petitioners, that too having kept quiet in the Court when facing the petitioners, making a mockery of the Hon'ble Supreme Court itself who had invited the petitioners to assist in the main case concerning the BCCI? And, above all, not having been able to counter a single piece of evidence in the least when an encyclopaedia of it including scientific evidence existed before them? Did it not amount to an act of utmost cowardice and making mockery of natural justice, fair play, and normal human-behaviour? In doing what they did, the COA have not only proved themselves that fraud was institutional as brought out in the petition, but have also indicated their own complicity as well. Futilely, they have tried to deny a fact as sure as that Earth revolved around the Sun or 2+2 equalled 4. That people remain largely unaware is another matter.

Has not the COA's report amounted to the thief himself passing a dictatorial judgement that no theft had taken place rather than constructively advising the Supreme Court as to what could be done in the face of what the stark reality was, as the Hon'ble Court must have implied through its order dated 7/5/2018?

While seeing the obvious acts of commission and omission by the Supreme Court-appointed Committee of Administrators, let us not overlook what has happened in the Supreme Court itself with regard to the subject petition. While entertaining/implicitly admitting the writ petition 1163/2017 vide its order dated 2/2/2018, the Hon'ble Court had desired counsel for the UOI to assist in the case. What happened to that thereafter? There was no assistance whatsoever from counsel for the UOI before the case was disposed of on 7/5/2018. The petitioners remained in the dark in that regard. So much so that the UOI didn't even say a word about its own acts of commission and omission as had been brought out in the petition, and was nowhere in picture when the Hon'ble Court passed the final order in the case on 7th May, 2018. And while the Hon'ble Court passed a seemingly meaningful and fair order clubbing the matter of WP (C) 1163/2017 with CA 4235/2014 for further consideration after the COA's report for all practical purposes giving liberty to the petitioners to assist the Hon'ble Court in that case, no such order existed for the Assistant Registrar of the Supreme Court himself! The Supreme Court itself failed to take cognizance of its own orders for months; closing the door on the petitioners after having invited them to assist in the main case concerning the BCCI—making the petitioners lose all the enthusiasm and momentum in a massive public cause. Has anyone been held responsible and hauled over the coals for this serous lapse/act of commission and/or omission? And I was never informed when the door was surreptitiously opened months after the invitation. Then, matter was to be listed after two weeks as per the Hon'ble Court's order dated 16/2/2018, but it is a matter of record that I had to fight tooth and nail to get it listed thereafter. Those defying Hon'ble Court's orders are liable for Contempt proceedings, rightly so, but what when the officials in the Hon'ble Supreme Court of India defy the Court's own orders?

All above could only be routine bureaucratic muddle (though considering the issues involved, it looked very unlikely that it had not been motivated and on purpose). Whatever be the reasons behind, as a result, the momentous issues brought out through WP (C) 1163/2017 lie totally forgotten, if not dead and buried. The colossal public fraud through cricket, robbing the tens of millions of people not only in India alone but in the world, of thousands of billions of rupees per year (money—a substantial part of which goes to terror funding), through cricket betting, as a result of continuous institutionalised fixed and scripted cricket globally, continues not only unfettered and unbridled, but prospering by each passing day. **The biggest manifestation of this fraud—another version of IPL—IPL 2019—has recently started on 23rd March, 2019 with great fan-fare even after none other than much-reputed former Indian captain, Bishen Singh Bedi publicly termed IPL as the biggest scam India had ever seen as per a news report dated 19/11/2018 (https://m.dailyhunt.in/news/india/english/catch+news+new-epaper-catchne/ipl+is+the+biggest+scam+india+has+ever+seen+says+this+former+indian+captain-newsid-101848173?ss=pd&s=a).**

This is when the whole country of India, the authorities and public alike, is extremely concerned with terror and terror funding in the aftermath of the Pulwama attack. Now through this IPL same country is daily celebrating big-time contribution to the same terror-funding. Would there be a bigger joke on earth? Such is the sheer power of the continuing colossal fraud through Cricket. Terror activities haven't ceased after Pulwama nor are those going to cease. **It is money that makes the mare go**. The Indian authorities remain happy to keep eyes closed to a big source of Terror funding—

the backbone of all terrorist activities—while making so much noise all over the world against terrorism.

It could genuinely be argued that there is a benevolent face also of this colossal fraud. It is a fraud that has unprecedented binding and uniting power in times of all-around fighting and in-fighting. It unites top political leaders across parties like Sharad Pawar, Arun Jaitely, Jyotiraditya Scindia, Rajiv Shukla, etc., as administrators of cricket over the years. It unites top industrialists like Mukesh/Nita Ambani, Bollywood superstars, like Shah Rukh Khan, media-houses like Sun Network, etc., as co-team-owners in IPL. It unites and bonds cricket players across teams and nations as one in a crime. So, it does for cricket experts, commentators, administrators, and coaches. Fiercely competing media channels and their highly vocal editors and anchors; the eminent newspaper editors—they all mysteriously unite in keeping their mouths tightly shut and pens down when it comes to this all-pervading colossal fraud. Not only does media keep mouth shut unitedly, it also continues to fill its coffers through marketing of this criminal fraud. It binds all above and more across professions and stature. And it unites them all combined with the world's underworld. It unites cricketers and cricket boards across the third-world and the first-world countries in continually perpetuating the international fraud. **And if so much unity were not sufficient, it unites even the enemy and warring nations like India and Pakistan in continuously playing fixed cricket matches between them.**

Apart from this, the scripted and fixed matches also keep the masses entertained and enthralled through periodic last-over and last-ball finishes. The dramatised cricket keeps masses in countries like India under its opium-like effect and helps them keep forgetting their travails and day-to-day exploitation by the haves of the world, and non-governance or misgovernance by government after government. They remain mesmerised under the aura of purposefully created fictitious Indian demi-gods, like Tendulkar, Dhoni and Kohli.

But this benevolent face that a common educated Indian sees or can see to feel happy about continuance of this colossal public fraud is only the by-product. The main product, that still remains hidden from public at large, is frighteningly malevolent.

That main real product, the purpose of it all, is to addict the masses in cricket-betting and then loot them through ball-by-ball scripted and fixed cricket. That is akin to infamous Saradha Scam of West Bengal in effect—this one being pan India and beyond, at much larger scale and thousand times magnified—the scam still continuing and kicking. And a substantial part of these mind-boggling sums of lakhs of crores of rupees per year finds its way to terror-funding. Hundreds and thousands of lives continue getting ruined through people getting bankrupt from betting on matches designed to render them so. Other telling implications of this malevolent product that readily come to mind are:

1. A continuing open public fraud, especially one as mammoth as the scripted cricket, is bound to degrade the society, especially the conscience of the young generation hooked on to it, in a very big way, with or without society realising so.

2. National anthems are routinely abused, when teams swear by the national anthem to play competitively for the honour and prestige of the country, but in reality play only scripted cricket, match after match.
3. All law-enforcing agencies in India are totally defunct, one can depend only on self-guard or God's mercy for help against public frauds and crimes.
4. Everything being and having been said about cricket—performance of players, cricket statistics, player or team standings, team selections, speculation on winning or losing of teams etc.—has been nothing but bunkum, nonsense, and gibberish.
5. Through its reporting on fixed cricket matches as a competitive sport, media has been acting criminally while subjecting the masses to a mammoth fraud round the clock.
6. Thousands of those indulging in and facilitating this fraud are, thus, **criminals with no fear of any authority or law**, hundreds out of those being our top celebrities and superheroes from various walks of life, many of those being the recipients of our top public awards. **That makes us an absurd entity.**

To my mind, and I hope no one will disagree, for humanity the implications of this fraud continuing with gay abandon, even years after it was brought to knowledge of the authorities, the members of parliament and the government in India, after it was exposed repeatedly in public for years and brought to knowledge of press and media, and even a year after all above was well apprised to the Hon'ble Supreme Court of India with irrefutable evidence and necessary documents through a laborious writ petition (WP(C) 1163/2017), are far more serious than this massive, mammoth, and colossal public fraud itself. That means:

1. **There is no institution in India that can guard its Constitution or its billion-plus people from being exploited by a few (hundreds/thousands) mighty fraudsters/criminals.**
2. There is no credibility whatsoever even of highly renowned journalists, and eminent editors across the nation since they all have chosen to keep quiet on and keep ignoring this colossal public fraud.
3. **Only money and power matter, nothing else matters.**
4. Mahatma Gandhis, Vivekanandas, and Baba Bhimrao Ambedkars have no relevance whatsoever in today's world except for being a topic of hollow and time-passing discussions.
5. There is no credibility whatsoever of institution of the Parliament of India as well as the present Union Government under PM Modi.
6. **PM Modi has been cheating India and the Indian public by repeatedly proclaiming outside and inside the Parliament that he and his government had zero tolerance against corruption. If not a cheat, he certainly doesn't know meaning of zero, or of tolerance, or of corruption.**
7. The Holy Scriptures like Rama, Ramayana, Mahabharata and Vedas are all totally irrelevant since they all propagated Truth, we collectively having chosen to shun it.

8. All literature, art, and human evolution become meaningless since we have decided that Falsehood should reign supreme. Literature or Art or even human existence itself has any meaning only if mankind strives to pursue Truth.

And so on.

Here it should be clear that the fact of cricket being an institutionalised fraud lies well established, **beyond any doubts and questions now**, with the arguments and evidence given in the petition, in my rejoinder to the COA's report, and otherwise available in public domain. Above everything else, one has only to open one's eyes, literally and figuratively, when watching telecast of cricket matches—to see that it was no competitive cricket, but drama being unfolded match after match. Only the last match before my penning these lines, the first T20 match between South Africa and Sri Lanka on 19/3/2019 that ended in a tie was another such match. That it was scripted to result in a tie out of blue became too conspicuous; and then Sri Lanka choosing not to compete in the super-over was an anti-climax to the thrilling drama a few minutes ago—the betting syndicates filling up their coffers in the bargain at the cost of the fooled bettors.

Going through the tweets of @theDcricket for last more than a year-and-a-half and applying mind to that alone should suffice for anyone to understand that there could be no explanation for these tweets other than that cricket was nothing but an institutionalised fraud. **I don't hesitate in saying that these tweets have rendered all my painstaking efforts over the**

years in exposing the colossal continuous fraud through scripted cricket all around the world redundant. His many tweets have repeatedly made it abundantly clear that cricket matches were scripted with scripts known to him beforehand. Pre-scripting of any match necessarily means active involvement in the fraud of all the players and coaches in both the teams, and many others related with conducting of the match. **While on the very face of it, it looks preposterous and impossible, there is no way or no possibility that it could be any other way**. Yes, @theDcricket does make wrong predictions once a while. He has to; otherwise shops of betting syndicates would get shut. He has to be one belonging to the gang to have knowledge beforehand of the scripts of the matches to unfold. The whole aspect of his tweets has been detailed and explained in our writ petition. Here it should suffice to say that we must understand that one can give wrong answers on purpose while very well knowing the right answers; but one cannot give right answers repeatedly if one didn't know the right answers. Many of his prophetic tweets have been such that those could not be dismissed as flukes.

While the tweets by @theDcricket are an open, sufficient, easier to comprehend, and readily available proof of institutionalised fixing of cricket globally (**it is another matter that the COA of the BCCI, the ICC, the cricket world, Indian Police, Union of India, and all other authorities in India are happy to feign blind to these**), the scientific proof worked out by me has its own value simply because it is scientific and, therefore, eternal. And though the world has chosen to ignore it so far, it is no mean achievement. I do understand that it was something new, unprecedented, beyond what we have been trained or taught to consider as evidence or proof. But can and should humanity refuse to evolve, refusing to heed to and apply mind to any novel ideas that appeal to common sense? Gravitational Force and Archimedes' principles were also once unknown to man.

Through simple application of the basic principles of probability to score books, we can know for sure that our superhero cricketers have only been stage performers, and that cricket has not been a competitive sport at least for the last few decades, but has only been a staged drama performed with very serious and grave ulterior motives. No one needed to be grilled and agencies didn't have to investigate for years with or without success for knowing this truth. **All scope for vested interests to create all possible bureaucratic and legal muddle vanished**. And, today, the scientific proof also lies repeatedly corroborated by ex-cricketers, bookies in custody, stings, and other exposés coming to light now and then. **Closing eyes in the sun didn't mean that it was dark.** As mentioned in my rejoinder to the COA, while all other people may take U-turns or proofs may vanish, this scientific proof will always be there to enlighten one.

I do feel happy that the mathematical/scientific proof that occurred to me has withstood the biggest Test—the Test of Time, no one from the cricket world or cricket establishment, ICC included, ever challenging it even though its existence was sufficiently reported in the media and brought to the cricket authorities' notice directly by me repeatedly. It was not countered even in the Supreme Court of India, or in the report of the COA—with the whole world including top mathematicians and advocates available at the disposal of the powerful respondents. They had no legal luminary to beat, but only a commoner—the petitioner-in-person—armed with nothing but common sense and Truth.

Whatever might have been the game-plan of the respondents in dealing with the subject petition; time to counter the contents of the petition for the concerned parties or the Hon'ble Court itself was there and then in the presence of the petitioners, before the Hon'ble Court passed order in the petition. No one has any right thereafter to counter or challenge the contents of the petition (WP (C) 1163/2017), not even the Supreme Court of India. It can't be an unending process. I may not be conversant with the legal nuances, but this is what I am entitled to believe as a man of common prudence and as a petitioner. **Though we often tend to forget, everything is a function of Time.** It is only incidental that I am still alive and writing this letter. The blot on the world for its failure to wake up to the massive public fraud through cricket and act to arrest it years ago when it was first exposed is not washable. And anyone even now having doubts about veracity of the contents of the petition has to be an incurable blockhead.

The cricket legend M.S. Dhoni was very recently reported having said, "*The biggest crime that I can commit is not murder, it is actually match-fixing.*" In light of this, one should try to visualise and understand how big a crime the institutionalised fixing of matches involving hundreds of Dhonis day and night is from the perspective of the public. For Dhoni and players like him, the fixing must be meaning fixing outside institutionalised fixing, i.e., acting to play outside the script given/dictated by the team management/coaches to them.

Now let us briefly see the larger overall picture on the canvas of India today.

24 × 7, day after day, month after month, and year after year, through the media or social media all our surplus energies are spent in discussing as to who is bigger rogue or rascal? A, or B, or C? Or which political party is greater rogue? X, or Y, or Z? We fail to discuss our collective systemic problems, ills, and evils, and discuss for solutions for our collective good. All the time we are indulging only in blame game. Led by our media, the public discourse has been reaching lower levels each passing day. We continue to be divided by religion, caste, and states. Reservation—leading to divisive politics—remains our main issue rather than personal development and advancement. The gap between the Haves and Have-nots has been widening all the time. Even though the Constitution desired us to be a Socialist State, wealth is more and more accumulating in the hands of a few. Corruption, and big time corruption at that, is the order of the

day—a rule, rather than an exception. As a routine, bigwigs charged of corruption and misdoings continue to enjoy five-star life style for years, hardly ever coming to any harm except for a few exceptions here or there. Crony-Capitalism rules. Slavery is deep-rooted in our DNA as evident from the fact of single family continuing to rule us or remaining to be the top contender to rule us since independence. Judicial systems are overdue for overhaul and revamp. Public is constantly at the receiving end for medical support or for civic amenities. There is hardly any ray of hope for the unemployed youth, the poor, and masses at large for improvement of their lot.

We just keep changing ruling dispensations through our votes to govern/mis-govern us and feel happy about it. The backbone of governance, bureaucracy and bureaucratic systems remain same, continuing to rot at large, as exemplified by the Supreme Court's Registrar's office, as illustrated in this letter (not to go far). Despite my successful crusade years ago against systemic corruption in procurement in the Indian Railways causing leakage of taxpayer's money worth ₹ 5,000 crores and more per year, the leakage continues even today increased a few times. **No one is bothered either in bureaucracy or outside it.** That too when this leakage was later on confirmed by the Metro Man E. Sreedharan and a detailed report suggesting solutions was submitted to the Railway Board before I took voluntary retirement 7 years ago. **Our daily narrative set by self-serving employees of native**

or foreign corporates owning the media is often sponsored, bogus, petty, divisive, self-abusive, and self-defeating. Self-seeking and self-service are the virtues most sought after by man today.

Public scams and frauds worth hundreds or thousands of crores of rupees are reported with regular periodicity, many more remaining unreported. The agencies meant to control those are either themselves mired in corruption or otherwise inadequate. The present state of the CBI and those having been at the helm of its affairs for the past few years themselves having been charged/under suspicion is a burning example.

Therefore, in the present scenario, nothing but renaissance has become a necessity. (All this doesn't mean that nothing good is left in the world). In the absence of that, the rut is bound to continue and multiply.

It was for this reason that I have pursued the cricket fraud for years, with single track mind, at great personal risk and cost, often ridiculed by family and friends, my efforts culminating with the filing of the subject writ petition in the Hon'ble Supreme Court of India. **Against all odds, I continued to be driven by my sense of proportion.** If people came to know of this fraud and understood its implications and involvement of big political leaders across parties, top industrialists and celebrities, etc., that, in all probability, would have been the starting point for the renaissance. People would have known for sure that all or almost all those with might were one in fooling the masses and that **media and those flaunting moral authority were most immoral**. As we have seen above, the fraud and its continuance have relevance and implications on a very wide horizon, much beyond the game of cricket. But alas! Those who control the world have been successful in ensuring that people remained ignorant and the word 'renaissance' never occurred to them.

This leads to a very relevant and big question: When the fact of cricket being thoroughly scripted and being an institutionalised fraud lies so exposed and unchallenged, how and why is it that masses still remain largely ignorant of the truth? For most of the cricket lovers, fixing takes place as an aberration only at times, involving only a few players at the behest of some bookies from outside. It is so because masses come to know of things only through the media and this is what the media has kept telling the world to keep it fooled. Like thick-skinned rogues, the cricket journalists and cricket experts keep analysing and discussing cricket for the masses as if competitive cricket was taking place all the time. Pages of newspapers and hours of air time on various sports and news channels are devoted daily to such analysis and discussions. The cases of much lesser importance in the Supreme Court are reported widely in the media. But there was hardly any coverage in media even after such a momentous petition as WP (C) 1163/2017 on cricket being an institutionalised fraud was entertained by the Hon'ble Supreme Court of India except for one or two news items here or there. And after that those controlling media ensured that there was total black out on any coverage related to this petition in the media. So much so that even the meaningful final order by the Hon'ble Court in the petition found no mention anywhere in media (to the best of my knowledge). That was so when media otherwise talks so much about cricket—fall of a wicket in an ongoing match becoming news headline on TV channels. The vocal news channel editors including Nevika Kumar, Rajdeep Sardesai, Arnab Goswami, Ravish Kumar, Rahul Kanwal, Bhupendra Coubey, etc., can be frequently seen making mountains out of mole-hills and then forgetting everything at their convenience. **When confronted with a real mountain, they all chose to become total blind.** The media ensured that the public largely remained ignorant of the petition, of any talk on fact of cricket being an institutionalised fraud for years, some coverage here or there in some obscure columns notwithstanding, **thus, by itself proving its complicity in the continuance of cricket as a colossal public fraud.** Even the explosive recent public assertion by Mr. Bishen Singh Bedi that IPL was the biggest ever scam India had seen didn't find much mention in our press and media at large that contrarily continues to market IPL to the hilt. The explosive exposé by Al Jazeera also had more or less similar fate. The inherent absurdity of media as an institution is best exemplified by the Statesman, only independent major newspaper in India with the best credibility today. Its sports editor, Mr. Pulakesh Mukhopadhyay has been exposing thorough corruption in cricket including it being scripted and being a farce, and the complicity of media at large in that, silently with perseverance for years, probably since earlier than my books, through his weekly column '**Short Point**'. And yet the Statesman also like other press continues to report daily with prominent headlines on cricket matches across the world as if competitive matches were being played all along.

And this established complicity of the Indian media beyond any doubt in one of the biggest ongoing public frauds on earth raises a very big question and concern for the mankind. **How to protect the masses from the media-controlled misinformation and frauds?** What is media today? All or almost all media is controlled by self-serving big or small corporates or the government. There is nothing like independent press or media. As a result, a person like me who needed only half an hour or so to interact with the public to make it understand how cricket was institutionally fixed to arm the people against the fraud—has no platform to do so. It may not be wrong to say that in today's world, the media is the multi-headed monster. Solutions will have to be found to control this monster, if mankind has to survive the onslaught of total falsehood.

What could be the possible solutions? A solution that comes to mind is that let there be a multilingual TV channel under control of office of Lokpal or so where any responsible citizen from society can tell and convey to the world what he wants to on first-come-first-serve basis on payment of predecided fees as per some chart depending on the duration asked for. Simple rules could be framed to ensure that such a facility was not misused, nor any genuine request was turned down. The people will, thus, have prior knowledge where to look for insights from the public. Such a channel could also show commercials to earn the necessary revenue. By and by such a provision would be widely used by the millions of well-meaning

Indians, especially the educated youth, to tell and to know. Simply, the existence of such a provision would go a long way to keep the monster media under check. It is just an idea that occurred to me. Better minds may find better solutions. What was necessary was awareness and acceptance of the problem and a will to find workable practical solutions.

(C) Summing Up

To sum up, the bottom-line is that a colossal public fraud—**a very potent source of terror funding globally**—lies publicly exposed and established beyond any doubt for the past few years, and yet it continues to prosper unfettered and unbridled even after the Hon'ble Supreme Court of India having been fully apprised about it through the subject writ petition, and, thus, being fully aware of it for over a year.

Turning of a total blind eye to this fraud and crime by the present government under PM Modi tells one how bogus and laughable are propaganda of nationalism and '*main bhi chowkidaar*' by PM Modi and his government.

The possible solutions to arrest this fraud have been suggested in my IA 81233/18 in case CA 4235/2014. The easily implementable and the best one to my mind is to make it mandatory for the authorities to issue a simple statutory warning during any telecast of or reporting on cricket matches: '**the cricket matches could be totally fixed and scripted**'. I had suggested this in one of my Press Releases also during one of the Press Conferences years ago. Though a very practical and effective solution, to implement it will require a very strong will and decision-making.

Still there will be bettors like there are smokers and drinkers, but they would remain sufficiently warned and cricket will cease to be a fraud even if it was fixed. The volumes of cricket-betting across the world are likely to reduce drastically. The continuing terror funding by betting syndicates, etc., if any, will have to be dealt with separately by the law-enforcing agencies of the world. This is not an ideal solution, but probably the only possible one considering how deep-rooted and vast the fraud is and considering who all are involved in it. Again, better minds can think of better solutions.

In light of all that has been brought out in this letter, the Hon'ble judges will have to put their minds together and think hard as to what has gone wrong with the Constitution of India that it is possible for a mammoth, massive, colossal public fraud and crime to continue totally unfettered even after lying publicly exposed for years, with no one in authority bothering the least. That too when the fraud is so big and all-pervading that it threatens the very security of the country and its people, and when attention of the authorities, the Supreme Court-appointed high-power Commissions, the Supreme Court itself, and the media had been drawn to it repeatedly during all those years.

Through this letter, **probably as a last resort**, I appeal to the collective wisdom of the sitting judges of the august institution of the Supreme Court of India to come to the rescue of the ignorant people of this country when all the offices including that of the President of India, and the Prime Minister of India have miserably failed.

I do hope that the world will act on this open letter and won't leave it for aliens, whenever they descend on earth, to find it and know how degraded and foolish the mankind was in the early 21st century.

Thank you.

(Atul Kumar)

The Supreme Court of India and its statesmen judges found their fulfilment in assigning diary numbers to this letter and forgetting. That necessitated me to write further as follow-up.

□

Hopelessness at its Extreme

Sensing that my well-meaning open letter addressed to more than a score of the esteemed judges of the Supreme Court of India also had disappeared in the bureaucratic quagmire, and nothing appeared to move, I wrote another letter to the then Chief Justice of India (CJI), Ranjan Gogoi. The letter was written as from a man to another man, and should be worth a read: Expectation of a better response from the new CJI could also have been at the back of my mind.

Shri Ranjan Gogoi Date: 16/5/2019

The Hon'ble Chief Justice of India

The Supreme Court of India

New Delhi

Sir,

Subject: Monumental fraud in the name of Cricket–Continued inaction from the Supreme Court reg.

Reference: 1. The Supreme Court order dated 7/5/2018 in WP (C) 1163/2017

2. My open letter dated 27/3/2019 addressed to sitting judges of the Supreme Court of India and registered

under the Grievance Management with diary nos. 18182/SCI/PIL(E)2019 and 18183/SCI/PIL(E)2019

I write this to you as one man to another man in the interest of the society and humanity we both belong to and indeed should feel indebted to. I write to you secure in my knowledge of what lies established, beyond any doubt, about what is going on in the name of cricket, but under the circumstances, the authority to act lies with you alone.

With reference to 1 above, I had filed an IA (Impleadment Application) 81233/18 in the BCCI main case number CA 4235/2014 in June 2018 and on my initiative held a meeting with Committee of Administrators/BCCI in July 2017. Developments, thereafter, further compelled me to write an open letter under reference 2 to all the sitting judges of the Supreme Court including your good self. I was informed through messages by the Supreme Court in Mid-April that this letter had been registered as Diary Nos. 18182/SCI/PIL(E)2019 & 18183/SCI/PIL(E)2019 under Grievance Management. And there it lies, apparently forgotten, without any further action for about a month now. And this appears to be a dead end.

I hope your honour have had time to go through the open letter under reference. If not, please do find time to go through it along with various references brought out therein. I am sure it will be a big eye-opener even for a man of your stature and experience.

And your honour will know what needs to be done.

There is no greater test than test of time and the exposure of the monumental public fraud through cricket years ago based on even scientific evidence has passed that test with flying colours. What remains to be initiated is only action to stall the public fraud and crime, but that hasn't been forthcoming from any quarters. This letter is aimed at impressing upon your honour once again the absolute necessity for the Supreme Court to act purposefully in the matter.

Fortunately enough for me, I wrote and sent the open letter under reference well before the eruption of headlines-making controversy with someone levelling an allegation of harassment against your honour; else the culprits and the cynics would have found it very convenient to dismiss my open letter as a mere attempt to fish in troubled waters. Interestingly, the Supreme Court and many of its sitting judges swiftly acted, or rather reacted (and rightly so), on this complaint of harassment since it was directed at 'one of them' and mouthed by some in media who matter; but the same Supreme Court and all its judges have chosen to be silent on my letter, even after more than a month has gone by, in spite of it bringing to the fore much graver issues of critical national and international importance—**an ongoing mind-boggling public crime that is clearly a joint venture of the betting mafia, ICC/BCCI, Corporates, Media and the Establishment.** Also, the same media that so eloquently highlighted the complaint of harassment against you has chosen to keep totally mum about this letter, further confirming its complicity in the ongoing massive fraud and crime.

Does silence of the Supreme Court even on my open letter not imply that it doesn't have much regard for Truth and Justice per se and is controlled, after all, by political and money power only and considers itself answerable only when there is some hue and cry in the media? Is it not contrary to some recent public statements by some of the apex court judges that **'SC can't be run by money or political power'** while reacting to a recent affidavit by a lawyer Mr. Utsav Bains in the aftermath of the above allegation of harassment? It is worthwhile remembering here that the affidavit, as I learn, claimed that the allegation was part of a conspiracy to frame the CJI and that there had been rampant fixing of the Supreme Court benches and even judgements for cash, Dawood Ibrahim and some Corporates being behind that.

It is even more amazing that while the Supreme Court of India has been very swift in ordering an all-encompassing inquiry into the contents of this affidavit by an advocate, rightly so, it never considered it necessary to act similarly when a much larger fixing issue, aiding terrorism and having much greater national and international implications, was brought to its knowledge through a detailed writ petition (Civil) 1163/2017 a year and half ago, reiterated through the above mentioned IA in June 2018, and again highlighted through the above-mentioned open letter more than a month ago! Is not the Supreme Court of India, by its very actions, confirming the contents of the affidavit by Adv. Bains, the same being much more grave and serious than the allegation of harassment by an individual? After all, that affidavit exposes the whole institution of the Supreme Court of India as never before.

The facts brought out in my open letter would have clearly indicated to any receptive mind how none other than Court No. 1—the bench of 3 prominent judges headed by the then CJI himself—changed course for no apparent rhyme or reason after their first order dated 2/2/2018 in WP (Civil) 1163/2017. Was that also a result of forces as brought out in the affidavit of Adv. Bains at work? And are the same forces still at work in causing all the sitting judges of the Supreme Court of India to act unconcerned even after registration of my open letter addressed to them despite its explosive contents?

Why and how is it that the Supreme Court acted almost instantly on the affidavit of an advocate, but has failed till date to deal comprehensively with much graver issues brought first to its notice one and a half year ago, by me along with a co-petitioner, through the above-mentioned writ petition? Do only Advocates, rogue politicians, and biased media hold worth and value for the Supreme Court of India with other responsible citizens (even those with credentials of having done exemplary work in public interest) considered worthless? In writing the open letter to the sitting judges of the Supreme Court, I expected at least some—and especially your honourable self – to act and react suitably considering stature and calibre of you all; but the deafening silence of you all has conveyed to me that your honourable selves are after all also like other ordinary mortals next door with the prime objective of self-preservation and self-service.

I have already spent more than 10 precious years of my life—not to mention a lot of money and energy—and risked the lives of myself and family in exposing a massive public crime, a blatant joint venture of the betting mafia, ICC/BCCI, corporates, media and the establishment as mentioned above; a crime immensely harmful not just to followers of the game or to those involved in cricket betting, but also to the hundreds of millions of unsuspecting and ignorant people in India and abroad. Knocking at the door of the Supreme Court has been especially arduous for me, and pursuing further in the Supreme Court even more arduous. To my mind, the Supreme Court of India should have taken over the issue after it was apprised through our detailed petition of what was happening in the name of cricket and its grave implications. But that was not to be and I had to continue running from pillar to post, and am being made to do that even today. **I cannot go on indefinitely and forever; I am not immortal either.**

While on the subject of risks, another question arises; have my and my co-petitioner's lives no value? I learnt from the media reports that police protection for Adv. Bains was ordered by the Hon'ble Supreme Court after his filing of the above-mentioned affidavit; why is there no protection for us when we exposed a much bigger crime involving hundreds of much more powerful criminals including dreaded mafia dons, top political leaders and the central cabinet ministers, corporate giants, superheroes, celebrities, and the media big-wigs, etc., through our writ petition? We had to fear retaliation not just from the Mafia alone, but also from the establishment, both being partners in the crime. A recent Hindi movie '*Tashkent Files*' becomes very relevant here. Thankfully, none of the culprits has bothered so far – probably secure in the knowledge that no one including the mighty Supreme Court or its eminent judges was going to lift a finger while the fake, scripted cricket show rolled on unhindered, continuing to be celebrated across the length and breadth of India by the ignorant and unsuspecting masses. The IPL Final even day before yesterday was nothing, but shameless and blatant display of a scripted drama—as some could clearly see, and many more must be wondering. The Cricket Insider has again claimed through his tweet that he knew it in advance and had told his clients so. His tweet is reproduced below:

Cricket Insider @theDcricket 40m40 minutes ago

#MUMBAI WON✓ is it fixed? I knew something better than you ! #MI #IPL2019Final#cricketinsider

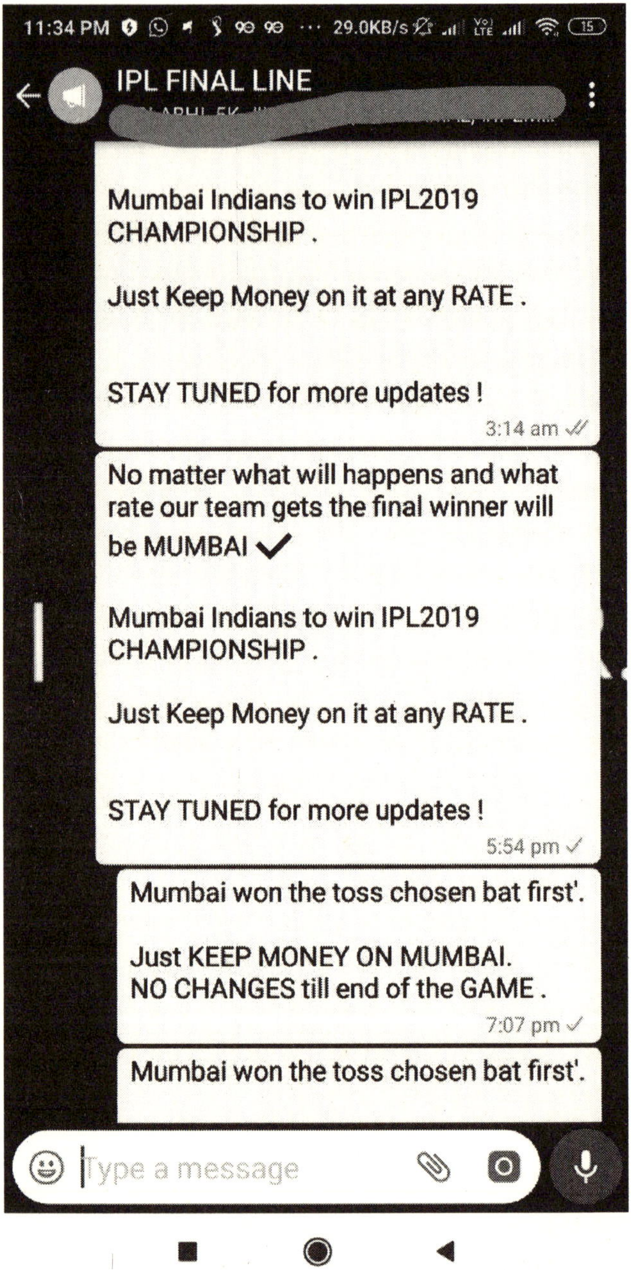
11:34 PM
29.0KB/s
IPL FINAL LINE
Mumbai Indians to win IPL2019 CHAMPIONSHIP .
Just Keep Money on it at any RATE .
STAY TUNED for more updates !
3:14 am
No matter what will happens and what rate our team gets the final winner will be MUMBAI
Mumbai Indians to win IPL2019 CHAMPIONSHIP .
Just Keep Money on it at any RATE .
STAY TUNED for more updates !
5:54 pm
Mumbai won the toss chosen bat first'.
Just KEEP MONEY ON MUMBAI.
NO CHANGES till end of the GAME .
7:07 pm
Mumbai won the toss chosen bat first'.
Type a message

Such a big paraphernalia of BCCI including ACSU, CEO, COA, Ethics Officer, Ombudsman, etc., and the ICC boasting of an international ACU, and multitude of law-enforcing agencies in the country—all continue to look on shamelessly.

Your Honour might be wondering what has prompted me to write this letter so close on the heels of my open letter, and in such a tone. I am perfectly aware how the Supreme Court and its judges have their hands full with the recent controversies and many highly important cases; but what has prompted me to write again are a series of unbelievable actions of commission and omission by the Supreme Court of India even after receipt and registration of my open letter and despite the recent public claims by its top judges.

As per the Supreme Court's order dated 7/5/2018 in our writ petition mentioned above, the Committee of Administrators (COA) for the BCCI was to take a decision on our 'grievance' and was to submit a report to the Court which was to be considered by them in the main case concerning the BCCI. We were also given liberty to assist the Court in that case. That case happens to be CA 4235/2014, and COA did submit a report in October 2018. No one knows what the Court has done with that report and my rejoinder to that of November 2018 which was also duly sent to the Court.

I have also tried to contact Senior advocate P.S. Narasimha, the Amicus Curiae appointed by the Supreme Court in the BCCI main case, but he too chose not to respond at all to me.

While my IA 81233/18 is listed now in the case CA 4235/14, the Court's order dated 14/3/2019 in that case clearly suggests that the amicus curiae and, hence, the Court were not even aware of the existence of any such IA in the case. Till date, the Court doesn't appear to have taken any cognizance of that IA. Having been invited to assist the Court as per its own orders, I wrote to the Registrar on 6/4/2019 requesting to be apprised of the case as a whole, while expressing my desire to assist. The copy of that letter is enclosed for your ready perusal and is self-explanatory. I have received no response to it whatsoever till date. As a common man, **I fail to understand how the Apex Court of this country can pass an order and then refuse point blank through its actions to honour its own order. Doesn't the sanctity of the Supreme Court of India and, hence, the Constitution of India lie openly abused here?**

I am not blaming any individual, but only bringing to your honour's kind personal notice through irrefutable facts and documentary evidence what the Supreme Court of India as an institution has been reduced to today, to a great disappointment of citizens like me. And I hope that it becomes a matter of great concern for Your Honour and the fellow judges, that Your Honour understands what it means for a country of 120+ crores.

The cricket matches are so blatantly fixed today that anybody asking for proof would amount to one asking for proof of existence of the Sun even while it was shining brightly in the sky. None other than the legendary cricketer of yesteryears, Shri Bishan Singh Bedi also independently said so in November 2018, as brought out in my open letter. **And yet everyone in the media, BCCI and ICC has been deadly quiet.** Not only that, the media reports reveal that the BCCI has even entered into partnership with gambling businesses (in effect, if not strictly legally) like Dream-11. I don't know whether to laugh or to weep. I am sure your honour will also have similar emotions. And for the proof for the blind (as Shri Bishan Singh Bedi put it), there is no dearth of that either; as a veteran sports editor put it not long ago, an encyclopaedia of proof exists now.

India has shown itself to be a country of the gullible made to believe in the enmity between India and Pakistan all these years. Can two countries playing fixed cricket matches between them, year after year—that too in a period when the matches were considered to be a big prestige issue by their populace—ever be enemies? Developments and politics in the aftermath of Balakote strikes both in India and Pakistan have, therefore, been nothing but a false narrative created with the complicity of pliable media to fool and emotionally exploit people, especially in India during the election times, **at the cost of scores of innocents killed on both sides**. Again the movie '*Tashkent Files*' becomes very relevant.

While round-the-clock scripted and fixed cricket matches by themselves are a massive and monumental fraud and crime nationally and internationally, with many very grave implications, I specifically mention above so that the seemingly incomprehensible enormity of the writ petition we filed in the Hon'ble Supreme Court in November 2017 may dawn upon your honour, though it appears not to have impressed the bench dealing with the petition then. As the things have unfolded, it could be that the bench did come under some outside influence after first ordering the UOI to assist it in the case. That order clearly indicated that the bench could see it was quite a significant case. It is also probable that the bench could indeed sense the significance, but not the enormity of the issues involved, otherwise it wouldn't have dealt with the petition as casually as it eventually did. I know, and records of the case would reveal to anyone how hard I had to fight for even listing of the case after ٢٠١٨/٢/١٦. Being an insider, Your Honour would be the best judge in this regard.

We all are born once and death is inevitable. Yet we all spend life time in pursuit of Falsehood, governed by hypocrisy and our inflated and misplaced egos the most! How amazing!

Under the circumstances, in light of the response of the Supreme Court of India so far, as narrated above, I shall have no option left but to call it a day on the subject if you still choose not to act as you must. One can't go on indefinitely and I can't wait till eternity for people to wake up and the Supreme Court of India to stir. Let people continue to rejoice at their own degradation and continue to celebrate their folly. All I will have to say is, 'Congratulations to the Hon'ble Supreme Court of India for having succeeded in wearing me out as probably it set out to do!' On my part, it is highly gratifying to have succeeded against all odds in irrefutably establishing the existence and continuance of a monumentally blatant public fraud and crime, involving the combined might of the rest of the world at large—**with the BCCI and**

the Supreme Court of India both revealing their own complicity in the crime and unconcern through their own acts of commission and omission—as I probably set out to do as the next best option to try and bring a halt to the massive fraud and crime! It is another matter that the sustained efforts have cost me dearly.

Sir, I am just a medium and can only hope this letter is treated as a portent of stern disapproval of the actions and attitude of the Apex Court from the Gods of Truth and Justice, whom the Court has failed miserably to protect so far. It is true that it was for the ICC, BCCI, law-enforcing agencies, and the Government of India to act in the matter rather than the Supreme Court of India. But with their complicity in the crime established through their deliberate inaction over the years, and the media also shamelessly parading its complicity, it was imperative for the Supreme Court of India to act when the matter was brought to its knowledge—to act at least to stall the ongoing massive fraud and crime if not to bring culprits to book immediately; after all, the Supreme Court is supposed to be the last resort for a hapless citizen.

The refrain we keep hearing from various quarters, including the Apex court, is that "**the show must go on!**" Why and what for? To continue cheating hundreds of millions of unsuspecting and hero-worshiping fans? To continue to lead ignorant people to commit suicide and murder driven by desperation resulting from huge losses and bankruptcy as a result of betting on fake matches being designed for that very purpose? To get our fellow citizens killed and endanger national security by continuing to facilitate flow of funds to the underworld and the neighbouring country for fostering terror in our country and the world?

If the show is indeed to be allowed to go on, it is imperative that this game is first made clean again and that certainly cannot be achieved by keeping envelopes sealed and continuing to ignore painstakingly compiled books and petitions which establish how the whole system is rotting. Bogus reports by the culprits aimed at self-preservation won't help either. The monumental task of cleansing needs to start now, without any more delay!

I appeal to Your Honour one final time to go through all that is available in the records of the Supreme Court of India in respect of the subject matter, apply your highly judicious and experienced mind, and act as you must. Your Honour alone, with the fellow judges, can act in the matter since none other than the present Finance Minister Arun Jaitley, India's top industrialist Mukesh Ambani/Neeta Ambani (to name a few) in addition to almost all cricket legends and superheroes, have been/are involved in this monumental crime that has been going on unbridled for over at least a decade now.

It is all the more imperative for you to act since the media itself is the biggest facilitator and marketer of this continuing monumental fraud and crime, even though, in doing so, it exposes itself and becomes guilty of everything it has accused anyone else in the world ever of. The media leaders own/have stake in IPL teams, and some teams even wear media logos. One can say 'SHAME to MEDIA', but that doesn't help.

The greater question worrying us all should be "how can a civilisation blatantly continuing to feast on

Falsehood deal truthfully with any issues confronting it, especially challenges from Nature?"

I am quite aware that I am nobody to question the Hon'ble Supreme Court's orders. It is the Hon'ble Court's prerogative as to what orders it passes. But reason and Truth must prevail, and serious questions are bound to arise when the Hon'ble Court fails to honour its own orders. Why should such an extraordinary thing happen? I don't know if there is any such precedent in the past.

One never knows if this letter will find a place in some book some time and, if so, how posterity and the present-day intellectuals including thousands of advocates will react to it. Hope being what leads us all forward, I do hope that someone else will take up the baton and reach the finishing post.

Thank you.

Regards

(Atul Kumar)

Encl.: As above

CC: The Registrar, the Supreme Court of India

(Atul Kumar)

The following letter was enclosed with the above letter to CJI Justice Ranjan Gogoi:

SPEED POST

The Registrar Dated: 06/04/2019

The Supreme Court of India

New Delhi

Subject: Order of the Hon'ble Court dated 7/5/2018 in WP (C) 1163/2017; and the main case concerning BCCI, i.e., CA 4235/2014

Dear Sir,

The following order dated 7/5/2018 was passed by the Hon'ble Supreme Court in WP (Civil) no. 1163 of 2017:

"*WP(C) 1163/2017*

ITEM NO.6 COURT NO.1 SECTION PIL-W SUPREME COURT OF INDIA RECORD OF PROCEEDINGS

Writ Petition (Civil) No. 1163/2017 ATUL KUMAR & ANR. Petitioner(s) VERSUS UNION OF INDIA & ORS. Respondent(s) (With appln.(s) for permission to file additional documents)

Date : 07-05-2018

These matters were called on for hearing today.

CORAM : THE CHIEF JUSTICE HON'BLE MR. JUSTICE A.M. KHANWILKAR HON'BLE DR. JUSTICE D.Y. CHANDRACHUD

For Petitioner(s) Petitioner-in-person

For Respondent(s)

Mr. Parag P. Tripathi, Sr. Adv.

Mr. Adarsh Saxena, Adv.

Mr. Vikas Kumar Jha, Adv.

Mr. Prabhjyot Kaur Chhabra, Adv.

Mr. Nikitha Shenoy, Adv.

Mr. Kunal Bahri, Adv.

M/s. Cyril Amarchand Mangaldas

UPON hearing the counsel the Court made the following ORDER

Heard Mr. Atul Kumar, the petitioner No. 1 appearing in-person and Mr. Parag P. Tripathi, learned senior counsel appearing for the Committee of Administrators. In our

considered opinion, the Committee of Administrators may take a decision with regard to the grievance made in this writ petition and submit a report, which shall be considered

in the main proceedings that relates to BCCI. The petitioners are at liberty to assist in the main case. With the aforesaid liberty and direction, the writ petition stands disposed of. There shall be no order as to costs. The interlocutory applications, if any, stand disposed of.

(Chetan Kumar) (H.S. Parasher) Court Master Assistant Registrar"

This order is also available on your own website and in your own records.

This order gives liberty to me to assist the Court in the main proceedings/case related to BCCI, i.e., case no. Civil Appeal (CA) 4235 of 2014. I do intend to assist the Hon'ble Court and to that effect, I also filed IA no. 81233/18 in CA 4235/2014. It took months for your office to register/list this IA, and I remained in dark when it was listed. After I incidentally came to know about the listing of this IA, I have also filed interlocutory application no. 53616/19 dated 30/3/2019 seeking permission to file additional documents and bring additional facts on record—consisting of the COA's report on the writ petition and my rejoinder to that.

Our writ petition earlier and now the IA 81233/18 by me have brought a massive mind-boggling ongoing public fraud through cricket involving the present government, top political leaders, top industrialists, media barons and media, larger-than-life cricketers and other top celebrities of the country, to the door/knowledge of the Hon'ble Supreme Court of India.

Anyhow, since the IA is now listed, I would like to assist the Court with respect to the case CA 4235/2014 as a whole in terms of order dated 7/5/2018 mentioned above. For that purpose and towards that end, kindly make all the papers relevant to the case bringing out all the developments in this case available to me at the earliest and give me sufficient reasonable time to apprise myself fully of the case so that I could assist the Hon'ble Court meaningfully.

My emails to you, with copies to the *Amicus Curiae*, the learned advocate Shri P.S. Narasimha, dated 30/3/2019, 1/4/2019, and 3/4/2019, making the above request have not been responded to.

It is requested that no further proceedings may kindly be made in the case Civil Appeal (CA) no. 4235/2014 till such time that copy of the complete case file and all the papers relevant to the case bringing out all the developments in it are made available to me and sufficient reasonable time is given to me to apprise myself fully of the case so that I could meaningfully assist the Hon'ble Court to the best of my capabilities in further proceedings in terms of the Court's own

orders.

Thank you.

(Atul Kumar)

CC: Learned Advocate Shri P.S. Narasimha, *Amicus Curiae* in CA 4235/2014. I also tried to contact and meet him during my visit to Delhi last week, but didn't get any response from him.

(Atul Kumar)

The above letter to the CJI also elicited no response, though I continued pursuing whichever way I could. One fine day, out of blue, I got the following email from the Supreme Court. It gave me renewed hope.

SCI <supremecourt@nic.in>
Fri 12/07/2019 16:29

To:

• You

All communications should be addressed to the Registrar, the Supreme Court by designation, NOT by name. Telegraphic Address "SUPREMECO"

By E-Mail

THE SUPREME COURT

OF INDIA

NEW DELHI

80/Copying/2019

Dated: 12/07/2019

From: Assistant Registrar

Copying Branch

To: Mr. Atul Kumar,

Email : atulrailways@hotmail.com

Sir,

With reference to your email dated 30.03.2019 requesting therein to apprise the case history and make all papers related to the case available in CA No. 4235/2014 entitled BOARD OF CONTROL FOR CRICKET AND ORS. Vs. CRICKET ASSOCIATION OF BIHAR AND ORS., I am to inform you that in the above-mentioned case, file is voluminous in many parts. You are, therefore, requested to specify the documents so that your request can be processed further.

Yours faithfully

--sd/--

Assistant Registrar

The hope was to be very shortlived. I responded promptly, but once again didn't get any answers to my repeated mails. I then took the plunge and the trouble of going to the Supreme Court of India, New Delhi, all the way from Kolkata to be able to inspect the necessary documents so that I could assist the Hon'ble Court to the best of my abilities. I was treated as persona non grata, and was told verbally that the above mail from the Court had been issued by mistake. Can you believe it!

Meeting PRO also didn't help.

Here was a citizen of India who had successfully alerted the much extolled Supreme Court of India about an ongoing monumental international crime and fraud—spending his time, energy and money for the benefit of the humanity at large—and now he was being conveyed how unwanted and unwelcome he was! Consequently, the following email was issued by me to the Hon'ble Court.

The Registrar Dated: 29/7/2019

The Supreme Court of India,

New Delhi.

Subject: To assist the Supreme Court of India in CA 4235/2014

Reference: 1. Email dated 12/7/19 no. 80/ Copying/2019 to me from Assistant Registrar, Copying Branch

2. My email dated 23/7/2019 to you.

Sir,

In reference to reference 1 above and pursuant to my mail under reference 2 above, I visited the Supreme Court of India today. I came all the way from Kolkata to Delhi in order to inspect the subject case file so that I could apprise myself better of the case and assist the Hon'ble Court more fruitfully in terms of its own orders in WP (C) 1163/2017. But even on contacting PRO in person, and Shri Ram Ratan, Asst. Registrar copying through your intercom from pass section counter no. 41, I was not allowed. He made it appear to me that his mail under reference 1 above was just like that meaning nothing, and, thus, probably a big joke.

Finally, I was advised by PRO to lodge a formal application for inspecting the case file. Hence this mail. This may please be treated as a formal application and I be advised well in advance the time and dates for me to inspect the subject case file. Thank you.

Regards
Atul Kumar

A hard copy of the same, dated 30/7/2019, was refused by the receipt window of the Court the same day (PRO's advice meant nothing!) and was subsequently sent through post by me. It was registered under the Court's grievance management with diary number 41148/SCI/PIL(E)/2019. Nothing was to happen, nothing happened. Feeling highly aggrieved, I wrote a stinging letter to the CJI (Chief Justice of India) through the Registrar. I demanded a compensation of ₹ one crore from the Supreme Court of India for willfully harassing me. The letter remains unanswered till date though duly registered with the Court. Going through this letter, one can well appreciate the state of mind under which this was written. How could one ever imagine for the Supreme Court of India to act as it had done? The letter is self-explanatory and here it is:

The Hon'ble Chief Justice of India 7/8/2019
The Supreme Court of India
New Delhi
(Through the Registrar, the Supreme Court of India)

Subject: Unimaginable high-handedness and shamelessness by the Supreme Court of India in harassing a well-meaning senior citizen of India—compensation thereof

References: 1. My email dated 29/7/2019 to the Registrar, and earlier mails mentioned therein.

2. Assistant Registrar (Copying)'s email to me dated 12/7/2019.

3. Order dated 7/5/2018 by Court No. 1 in WP (C) 1163/2017.

4. My open letter dated 27/3/2019 to the Supreme Court judges and registered with diary nos. 18182/SCI/PIL(E)2019 and 18183/SCI/PIL(E)2019 under Grievance Management

5. My letter dated 16/5/2019 addressed to the Hon'ble Chief Justice of India

Sir,

I do hope that this email/letter will be put up to you, the Hon'ble Chief Justice of India, early and will not have a fate similar to the letter by the mother of Unnao Rape Victim as was very recently in news. I write this not because I have been/am being harassed, but because it could be anyone in my place and because it shows how the Supreme Court of India, and, hence, the country of India has gone to the dogs (I doubt if any other phrase would be more appropriate, given the unfortunate facts). Please do read on.

Only last week there was a news item that told us that you had said there were some fundamental problems in your registry and you found yourself helpless to do much/anything about it. Did your responsibility end with that, giving your registry even more freedom to continue acting like buffoons? Like high-handed monsters? That too, even months after my letters under references 4 and 5 above. Not very long ago, we learnt that CBI had been deputed to see/investigate what wrong had been going on in the Registrar's office of the Supreme Court of India. But, certainly, it has had no deterrent effect. Are CBI officials there to crack jokes with the registry officials?

It is evident now from the Unnao Rape Victim case that the Supreme Court of India acts only when there is noise in the media. Does that mean it will never act on a matter in which the media itself was the culprit? What have you and your Court done on letters under references 4 and 5 even after precious months elapsing, even after registering one of these? Only you would know whether, for some reason, you couldn't go through those or you didn't consider it worthwhile to do anything about it. But since there is no noise in the media about those, and won't be any—media itself being a major culprit—will the Supreme Court of India never act? Is this the nation our freedom fighters had fought for, had dreamt of?

On the contrary, your registry is now acting with even greater criminality and shamelessness. Rather than acting to curb a monstrous proven public fraud and crime, the Court is finding novel ways of harassing me, the messenger. It is true that powerful politicians like Arun Jaitely, Sharad Pawar, and many others cutting across political parties are/have been at the helm of this monstrous fraud and loot, and top industrialists and celebrities including Mukesh Ambani and Shah Rukh Khan are a part and parcel of it, not to mention the powerful cricketing world. But, is the institution of the Supreme Court of India to act as their keep? Is that the oath you people take when assuming office? Don't you people have any conscience of your own and/or shame left?

This is not about some high-handedness by some police officials somewhere, some jungle raj somewhere in the country, crimes of rapes and murders taking place somewhere. Nor is it about disputes, some minor or massive public frauds, or scams worth thousands or lakhs of crores of rupees coming to light now and then, or about some injustice taking place somewhere. Those are unlawful acts indulged in by people to be brought to justice. Here we are talking of extreme high-handedness and jungle raj in your own courtyard, in the Supreme Court of India—the ultimate destination to seek justice in the country—in a desperate attempt to shield trillions of dollars' worth continuing loot from the poor addicted bettors, a substantial part of which goes to terror funding.

I have come across many people jumping and saying, "So what? Why should people bet? They are responsible if they lose money." They say so out of ignorance. First of all, they are ignorant, with Ajit Dovals and PM Modis choosing to be blind for reasons best known to them, that a substantial amount out of these mind-boggling sums finds way to terror funding. It is not my imagination; it is a matter of record by police and mentioned so by judges in their judgements. So, even if bettors solely were to be blamed, to allow it to continue was highly damaging to us as a people. Secondly, are bettors alone to be blamed? Don't we hold drug peddlers also accountable for drug addiction of our brethren and sisters? And here matches are so scripted and fixed round the clock that the bettors are not only looted, but are also made addicts. Enough has been brought out by me in the public domain over the years to show it irrefutably and all that, including the scientific proof of out-and-out scripted and institutionally fixed cricket across formats and across countries arrived at by me and brought out in the media as well years ago, remains uncontested and undisputed till date; even after detailing of the same in my petition to the Hon'ble Court a couple of years ago.

There are many journalistic accounts of young people losing large sums and people losing lives because of fixed matches and cricket betting. I have personally come across promising youngsters who have been the victims of institutionally fixed cricket. They are men of flesh and blood. And there are not hundreds, not thousands, but millions and millions like them in our own country alone. Not much comes out because of stigma attached with betting/gambling in India. Many bettors are quite aware what goes about in the name of competitive cricket matches. But they are not a united lot and most of them don't have means and knowhow to fight this massive fraud being perpetrated by a powerful nexus and facilitated by the media. The Supreme Court of India remains the only hope for them at present.

I am sure people are still largely unaware that there is nothing illegal about betting on cricket per se; they are unaware of ruling dated 25th July, 2015 by the Patiala House Court, New Delhi in SC No. 115/13 (it is the order by which Sreesanth and others were acquitted). Betting on Cricket was found to be excluded u/s 12 of Public Gambling Act, Cricket being a game of skill. I myself was unaware till recently. So, those betting on cricket all these years, thinking it to be a competitive sport as being marketed by the cricket world and the media, have been continuously cheated through institutionally fixed cricket. Those betting have not been the culprits, but all those responsible for continuous dishing out of fixed and scripted cricket in the garb of a fair and competitive sport to fool the bettors have been the culprits. Their crime has been phenomenal such that many would find it difficult even to comprehend it. This crime even extends much beyond national boundaries.

Court number 1, the CJI's Court, passes order in May 2018 in WP (C) 1163/2017 inviting me as a petitioner in that case to assist the Court in a particular case. But your section III dealing with that particular case doesn't recognise this order for months. Finally, it does and allows my IA (Impleadment application) in that case CA 4235/2014. Then I request for case details in order to assist further in deference to the Court's orders. I get a mail from Assistant Registrar after months, that too only after my letters under reference, asking me what documents I required. I pleasantly thought someone responsible in the Supreme Court was finally awake, but how wrong I was! There is no response again to my several mails in reply. I come all the way to the Supreme Court from Kolkata (after having duly informed the Registrar) to inspect the case file so that I could know what documents were to be required by me, carrying a load of related papers myself, but am told by the same Assistant Registrar, Mr. Ram

Ratan that now suddenly, after his email, I had no locus standi in that particular case for which the Court had given me the liberty to assist in, since some official in section III was telling him so. Even if it was the case (though anyone would fail to see how it could be so), then why the hell did he/the Supreme Court of India send me email dated 12/7/19, to someone who didn't have any locus standi? Is it the Supreme Court of India or a circus manned by a bunch of jokers?

Or am I a joker? I don't know. For the world I may be. I have been spending my own money, substantial amounts of it (though I don't mind it, still getting enough to make our both ends meet), running from pillar to post at this age, allowing myself to be harassed by all and the Court under your charge, the Supreme Court of India, fighting almost single-handed against the combined might of the world in exposing the largely unknown blackest face of corporatisation and capitalism so that the necessary corrections in the interest of humanity could set in. Probably, not even a joker would dare do what I have been doing for some years now. I had gone to the Supreme Court only after exhausting all other possibilities over the years, the world including President and Prime Minister of India and the Supreme Court-appointed Commissions on the subject (or their offices) acting totally dumb.

For whatever it is worth, I am a retired joint secretary-level officer from the Indian Railways, who successfully exposed a massive systemic scam in Railway procurement while in service (the same was later confirmed by the Metro Man E. Sreedharan in a report on the Indian Railways), a responsible senior citizen, a recipient of the national-level award for crusade against corruption, a poet and writer, and one who has exposed and proved trillions of dollars (yes, you have read correctly—a conservative estimate based on real data helps us arrive at this figure) loot of bettors' money and cheating of hundreds of millions of cricket fans through institutionally scripted and fixed cricket round the clock. And here I find myself being harassed by your officials (seemingly having very low IQ or having been bought out by the powerful mafia). And while that happens, apparently you, your fellow judges and registrars, all sit tightly in air-conditioned surroundings, well pampered using public money, conveniently acting deaf, dumb and blind.

Don't those shielding the monstrous fraud and crime, in and outside the Supreme Court of India, understand that they are fighting a losing battle? Whatever anyone does, can one keep hidden for long something as sure as the shining sun? Even the whole cricketing world and the world together hasn't been able to counter my exposé on cricket for the past 6 years, nor can it ever do so. It is only continuing with the monster crime nonchalantly, with people like Shashank Manohar and Vinod Rai at the helm, duly supported by the media and the establishment. The childish action by the Supreme Court of India in blowing hot and blowing cold repeatedly, in not honouring its own order, only exposes it more and indicates its own complicity in the phenomenal crime, fraud and loot.

On second thought, it helps the cause (our cause).

Now without going into petition and without applying mind to all that is in record and in public domain, people should readily know that I had been right. If not, why would the Supreme Court of India have been behaving as it has to expose itself? Why would the apex Court of the country openly act as an antagonist to a well-meaning and bonafide petitioner who had brought a colossal and monstrous public fraud and crime to its knowledge? Why would people of the stature of Vinod Rai expose themselves losing all their credibility?

Does anyone realise what the Supreme Court of India not honouring its own order means? It implies total collapse of the legal system in India. And this collapse becomes more pronounced since this dishonouring of its own order by the Supreme Court of India continues unashamedly even months after my letters under reference. It amazes me and should amaze anyone how the learned judges of the Supreme Court of India and the rest of the legal fraternity of the country have been happily digesting such a state of affairs.

Your PRO didn't have much time to listen to me either on 29th July, 2019. He advised me to buy a Supreme Court rule book and lodge a formal application for inspecting the documents in the subject case CA 4235/2014, without bothering to know and understand the background. And, then, the other officials refused even to accept such a request/ letter as had been advised by the Court's own PRO. Even when an advocate friend tried just to submit such a request letter from me on 1st August, 2019, he was denied (though the contents of that letter were already emailed by me to the Registrar on 29th July itself, as per reference 1 above). Does it make you stir in your chair?

Probably, I should have expected all this—for the Supreme Court of India to act for the powerful lobby that appoints/has a major say in the appointment of the Supreme Court judges themselves. Let me share with you, I did feel fulfilled and pleasantly surprised on successful filing and listing of our WP (C) 1163/2017. Since that itself created a permanent and irrefutable record of a massive public scam by the most powerful from various spheres in the country combined. After that, the Court had only two choices: either to act honestly and purposefully in the matter or expose itself. Sadly, after taking the first few steps in the right direction, now under some duress or temptation, the Court feels compelled to expose itself, unfortunately forgetting its own motto '*Satyamev Jayate*'.

First Vinod Rai, as the head of the COA/BCCI danced naked in serving the interests of the cricket mafia and now the Supreme Court of India as a whole is following in his foot-steps. There is a necessary documentary evidence to show this. Probably, the word 'shame' belonged to different times and cultures. Those feeling power-drunk (the mafia masters and their stooges alike) are forgetting that **'The evil that men do lives after them'**.

But what do I do now? Do I say 'BALLS' to all and everything and go to sleep, forgetting the plight of hapless cricket fans, especially the tens of millions of bettors being robbed day and night through a puppet show controlled by a powerful nexus of mafia-politicians-industrialists-cricket world-media? **Forgetting how the world including millions of highly learned and intellectuals, including the learned judges, learned advocates, and all the officials of your Court also, has been allowing it to be fooled day and night by the cricketing world and media combined?** Or do I fight on, first and foremost demanding a reasonable token compensation, say ₹ one crore (I don't want to be greedy—haha!), from the Supreme Court of India for unduly harassing me? As of now, I go for the later course and request you to order the compensation as above to me.

Under the media pressure, you have acted in the Unnao Rape Victim case now, so belatedly, announcing compensation and giving a very severe target to CBI to complete the investigation. I still hope against hope that in this case, you will act like-wise on the merit of the case even though there is no media pressure, and there won't be any media pressure. The deafening silence of the media on the subject since filing of our PIL loudly announces its own culpability.

Do you find this letter unpalatable? I shall be happy if it is so. That would mean some shame is still left somewhere. Did the Supreme Court of India expect me to take its inexplicable behaviour lying down? You will find that for the past two years and more, I have been persevering in the most appropriate and submissive way, under the provisions of the law of the land, despite apathy of the world and continuous harassment by your registry, but the latest unimaginable act of high-handedness by them causing me utmost discomfort and harassment—both physical and mental—has compelled me to write the way I have done. And I am confident this will not be the last the Supreme Court of India will be hearing on the issue and the subject, even if I am dead. Because at the core is a monster very much alive, engulfing millions of victims every day. It will have to meet its end one day. God/Nature will act through someone else. There will be a public outcry sooner than later.

I urge your kind Honour to go through the whole case file personally, and put yourself in my shoes. It will consume your precious time, but I assure you that it will be worth it. I had expected commendation from the Supreme Court of India for all the trouble taken by me for years in exposing and proving a monstrous continuing international public fraud and crime, and taking further trouble in knocking the doors of this august Court. And here I find myself being treated like an antagonist and dirt by its registry. But all the more painful is the fact that all this while, the colossal fraud and crime merrily go on.

Thank you.

Regards

Atul Kumar

This letter was also registered under the Supreme Court of India's Grievance Management with 3 diary numbers 41789/SCI/PIL(E)2019, 41150/SCI/PIL(E)2019, and 41151/SCI/PIL(E)2019. That's its fate till now.

Taking that the Hon'ble Supreme Court's order dated 7/5/2018 giving me the liberty to assist the Court still held, I sent three communications in succession to it towards my notes on assisting it in the main case concerning the BCCI. The case was lying dead at the time of finalising the draft of this book and cricket was continuing as such, the media and the world excited at the announcement of dates and venue for IPL 2020—at the staging of the biggest event governed by the underworld mafia—the reported explosive revelations by Sanjeev Chawla also having not made even an iota of difference. The notes sent by me can be accessed through the link https://drive.google.com/drive/folders/1UH6MJWeqDi91yqaM5SPbZukR_0NquXcf?usp=sharing.

This is the working of the top Court of India, registrar's office and judiciary all included. This is how a continuing trillion-dollar fraud and a big-time crime involving hundreds of celebrities and others concerns the 'Hon'ble Supreme Court of India'! It is the Supreme Court of India that is Supreme! No one can question if it gives immediate priority to cases concerning big names; and consigns cases/issues involving terror funding, country's security, criminality of hundreds of luminaries, loot of hundreds of billions of dollars from unsuspecting populace, something concerning millions, concerning the masses—to side bins or dust bins. It's entirely its prerogative. I did wonder—did the public fraud, deceit, scam, crime—all and more in one—not affect the officials and judges of the Supreme Court of India? Was it a crime only for me? Was it my personal problem? **How absurd the society and its existence were? Was indulging in long hollow intellectual discourses, pursuing non-issues, making cartoons, joking, and mouthing or writing satires the ultimate in accomplishment, while the humanity went on degrading more and more?**

The international cricket continues to be as fake and as bogus as it was, no authority feeling bothered in the least. **Yet the documents reproduced or referred above will forever be a testimony to failure and inadequacy of the evolved human systems and to existence of a highly degenerated world in the second decade of the 21st century.** Does people, media and authorities making noises about thousands of other things, while showing scant sensitivity to an all-encompassing monumental crime and fraud, really matter or mean much?

Is there no world beyond the Supreme Court of India? What is the Supreme Court of India? Is it not merely an institution developed or created to achieve some purpose in the larger interest of the society? Can it be bigger than the spirit of Truth and Righteousness? What does the Supreme Court of India acting as it did mean? Is it failure of an institution or is it failure of those who value it so much? We need to ask ourselves these questions, a few more, and we do need to think hard.

□

We the Oodles

"One of the saddest lessons of history is this: If we've been bamboozled long enough, we tend to reject any evidence of the bamboozle. We're no longer interested in finding out the truth. The bamboozle has captured us. It's simply too painful to acknowledge, even to ourselves, that we've been taken. Once you give a charlatan power over you, you almost never get it back."

—Carl Sagan

Often we forget, but Time remains the essence of all or most of our activities. Here an international fraud at a massive scale has been taking place. It was publicly exposed in 2013, but nothing changed then, and nothing has changed even after 7 years or more than 2,500 days, though the fraud continued to be repeatedly highlighted in all public forums and officially during this long time. That meant daily loot of millions of dollars from ordinary mortals continued unhindered despite all my efforts as documented in previous chapters. It was not that only I continued to harp, but the fraud continued to be exposed and highlighted time and again from many different quarters—well known and/or having the necessary credibility. **Inaction and total lack of reaction by the world even for a few days after**

a massive public fraud is exposed is not only inexplicable and unpardonable; but makes a mockery of all systems, all intelligence, all professionalism, even all spirituality—in short, of the complete human world. This is because the world we are talking of consists of advocates, judges, activists, doctors, engineers, entrepreneurs, professionals, journalists and editors, shrewd businessmen, self-proclaiming righteous people, preachers, celebrities, parliamentarians, politicians, leaders, intellectuals, scholars, bureaucrats, serving and retired—many of them with distinction attached to them, executives and CEOs, sales and marketing experts etc., and the masses. All these great minds who had excelled in their respective fields and served the society—tens of thousands of them—continued talking about everything on earth all these years, continued discussing right or wrong about any number of issues with heated arguments, in media as well in social media, or in private talks, but remained saintly unperturbed by being fooled day and night through cooked-up or pre-scripted cricket matches being sold to them as competitive matches—as if being played for prestige—and all bogus talk in print and on air about team selections, strategies, individual performances, team performances, pitch conditions etc.; remained unperturbed by the massive crime rocking the society and the human world 24x7.

So, there are two aspects. One, the intelligentsia of the world that virtually controls and runs the world being not concerned of something they must be. Two, they are widely fooled. This means that those whom we consider as cream of the society—very intelligent and learned people—are basically nitwits—lacking the basic common sense. That is none of their doing, they are made that way. But they and we must know it. Yes, that's right, we are being run and governed by silly people, silly because they feel happy to be blind, and like to be stupid.

We are talking here of real human world—what it has been, not of a fairy tale. This colossal continuous fraud never bothered all the cream of our society, though so many petty crimes and almost any other issue did continue bothering them. India is a peculiar country where advocates abound and amongst them brilliant advocates abound. Various advocates go on taking up almost every issue of public interest. Yet no advocate, none of the renowned advocates, ever cared in the least about a continuing open fraud and crime of extraordinary proportions!

As this book gets ready to go into print, many advocates are coming to limelight and getting accolades in the now famous Prashant Bhushan contempt case. That's good. There have been hundreds of advocates who have been signatories for and against Mr Bhushan. Comparisons are being made to Mahatma Gandhi. But day in and day out, questionable, yes, quiet questionable orders are passed and blatant misuse of power is visible in Indian courts, yet we don't hear anything from these advocates or in the media. The delays by decades in Indian courts are a matter of folklore. This in no way means to convey that nothing good happens in the Indian courts. But question naturally arises; **why have these great and thousands of now vigilant advocates been unaware or unconcerned about the supreme shame in their own backyard as has sufficiently been brought out in this book? Where were they all who are now coming out with eye-catching impressive statements when I was knocking at the doors of the Bar Council of India even?** While some of them may feel offended by my saying so, as the media and many of the intellectuals of the world also may by the contents of this book; that will neither help them nor the world we all live in. Only an objective honest contemplation will!

I am sure there won't be any dearth of blockheads who would even today readily dismiss the fact of cricket being institutionally fixed as some hallucinations of a mad man without bothering to know what all existed in record to show and prove otherwise or bothering to apply mind even a wee bit. They would even have no regard to the fact that this had already been vindicated at a platform no less than the Supreme Court of India through a detailed petition bringing out the necessary evidence. Sure that could not be a joke and could not be for a joke. I say so because I have personally been having such friends—men of exceptional intelligence, knowledge, and genius—failing to see something very obvious or refusing to apply their minds out of conceit or because of the inability to overcome the conditioning of their minds, steeled over the years. The more we close our eyes, allowing something to rot, the more damage it causes and the more difficult it becomes to tend it. By ignoring such a massive open crime not for days but for years, we, the people, have been committing nothing but hara-kiri, whether we realise so or not, whether we accept it or not.

The world is full of people far more intelligent and knowledgeable than me—by millions. They vividly analyse everything and understand almost everything. They know what wrongs were happening and why. I do wonder of what use that is except for gratifying their ego. They feel happy and satisfied with their knowledge. But, they accept things as these are, either unconcerned or with a resigned attitude. Many of them are not interested in doing anything to bring about the required changes, others just find themselves helpless. Their egos don't allow them to join forces with others for common good. At times, their self-interest comes in the way. At times, it's both. The good people don't combine; the bad do. We have seen it clearly how hundreds or thousands combine to make cricket a successful international fraud for more than a decade. **But where are even one hundred out of hundreds of millions of the good people who inhabit the earth, to jointly raise a voice against it?**

A few renowned philosophers/thinkers have also said that more than evil doers, the silence of the good men is responsible for the evils. Why do good men keep quiet when they should not? Is it self-preservation or conceit? Conceit or ego, a predominant trait in humans, works in more ways than one. It is ego in us that mostly stops us from freely acknowledging the good work done by those around us. It doesn't let us appreciate that someone was more endowed than us in certain aspects and respect him/her. I was ridiculed by almost everyone around me a decade ago when I started telling them that cricket was fixed ball by ball. Even today, years after I stood vindicated, hardly anyone of them has conveyed regrets to me accepting or realizing how wrong they had been. Egotism, false ego, a major driving force, comes in the way. Most of them are good men of the world. We forget that we all are equal before death, and we must combine for the right, for the right cause, for the common good; irrespective of our status.

The narcissism in man drives him to any extent to argue. I have met many who never had a word of appreciation for my efforts, but would say, 'yes, cricket is a big scam, so what? There are many bigger scams.' Some would cite 'football', some would say 'stock market', and some would say defence deals! They could be right, and, in good probability, are right in their citations. But, how could they or anybody say 'so what?' One, if one can say 'so what?' to this, then he or she must say 'so what?' to any crime/any fraud/any deceit, even if he/she is personally affected. Secondly, **they forget the difference between something suspected, may be widely believed, but not proven, and something having been proven mathematically and also vindicated in a top Court**. They don't realise the difference because the narcissism in them doesn't allow them to appreciate what it takes to expose and prove a fraud of this magnitude, being committed by such mighty people? It is beyond me how anyone can say 'so what', even when the Supreme Court of India acts as blatantly as has been amply shown? How can the world accept it so nonchalantly and move on?

It is not some odd person who utters, 'so what?' Rather it would be very few who don't say, 'so what's in it for me?' That has been my experience over last many years. Think of it, what do these people, most of the intelligentsia and good common men and women around me and you included, do? They are not only accepting one evil - the open crime and fraud through cricket - but also many other evils. They are justifying and accepting another evil coming to their knowledge, because so many more evils exist, already accepted by them. And we don't tire of flaunting our knowledge of scriptures and of great teachings there in endlessly, while accepting stinking evils around us so very casually! It is here that we fail ourselves as common men, and find our fulfilment in giving sermons and blaming others throughout our lives. It can be easily understood that what is happening in cricket would be happening in many other sports also, with varying degrees. But does that mean we should deceive and defeat ourselves saying, 'so what's the big deal?' and doing nothing? **No wonder, collectively as humans we continue to degenerate more and more.**

It must be a combination of various human traits and compulsions that we tend to ignore the fundamentals and basics, and prefer to pose, to show off, and to be ostentatious. I give a very germane real-life example to illustrate. As mentioned elsewhere and in some of the documents, while working in the Indian Railways, I could bring out and highlight more than a decade ago that there was an estimated loss of ₹ 50,000 million per annum to public exchequer due to systemic wrongs in procurement policies—from organisation-induced cartels. Neither the authorities nor hundreds of my peers ever bothered to correct these, though these wrongs were commonly known and accepted. These also got confirmed later in due course, just like institutionalised fixing in cricket. But those wrongs are still continuing, no one ever bothered; even though, in this case, the corrections were suggested in detail by a committee formed for the purpose. During the last decade, ostensibly, many improvements and advancements must have been done in public procurement and Railway procurement. Many officers and officials must have received accolades for such upgrades. Yet the basic fallacies resulting in much higher leakages by now remain as such. All this is doing or undoing not of the masses, but of the intelligentsia, of the cream of the society. We most often neglect and overlook the primary concerns and issues, and keep worrying about tertiary matters.

We forget and overlook the basics also since often we crowd our minds with things of no consequence; or rather we are made to do so by the vested interests. As a result, we lose out on the essentials and pay the price throughout our life. The propaganda machinery works thus through social media and media. All the camouflage is created following this principle on purpose. Most of the political leaders world over thrive on this failing of human mind. Democracies, even the large ones, have been evolving on this fallacy. Power is captured by the undeserving through exploiting this human frailty. For example, the bogey of Ram Mandir in Ayodhya so assiduously created in modern India didn't address any of the basic problems confronting its billion plus populace, but kept captivated the masses and the elite alike. The delusion of enmity with Pakistan is another gleaming example. Cricket per se also falls in this category. The public is kept busy in worrying about Kohlis and Dhonis so that it can forget its own hardships.

Bhoomipujan for Ram Mandir at Ayodhya could be a great way forward for a country of 1.3 billion plus, but that hardly appeared to be the case; because side by side, same people were keenly looking forward to the magnum opus of a fraud, scam, and crime in the form of IPL-2020. Nothing could abuse the *maryada* of Purushottam Ram more!

Don't we come across people, the common men and women, lamenting about many wrongs around them through letters to editors, in print, in TV talks and debates, and above all, in social media? The forwards and discussions in social media abound, criticising judiciary and judicial systems, police and its high-handedness. The false talk, deceit, and loot by leaders constitute majority of such chats. Financial irregularities by institutions, black money, scammers and fraudsters escaping the legal net are cribbed a lot about. Nothing wrong happening in any corner of the earth and coming to light escapes the wrath of the people. The same people don't tire of eulogising and clapping for those at the helm of wrong-doings. Taking on the ongoing open monumental scam and fraud in the name of cricket could and would have helped all such people in striking at the roots of everything wrong from black money to ransom by the so-called professionals in various fields to police atrocities to judicial inadequacy and high-handedness to deceitful leaders. But, inherent duplicity of human nature makes us say one thing and do the opposite!

People not only talk a lot about wrong-doings around them, but also suffer a lot in their day-to-day lives by rampant high-handedness, cheating, and deceit. The rampant corruption at times destroys lives, destroys families. Books can be written on how people get adversely affected by the devolution and corruption around them. When those very people exhibit total detachment to a very big fraud and crime, an epitome of many an evil they suffer from, it is astounding. Even more mystifying is the fact that many of such people don't think twice in rooting for the felicitated criminals and the imposing crime.

In today's world, someone's worth and success is judged by a number of followers on social media or in life. It doesn't matter what is the worth of those followers. What is their intellect or what is their depth? How many of them can't see beyond their nose and how many have a broader perspective? Whether they are law-abiding or not? Those worthy because of their popularity become role models for the youth, for the future of the society. Almost all the celebrities from various fields qualify so. They themselves may be worthless, cheats, fraudsters, scammers, liars or criminals. Almost all cricketers, a number of politicians, journalists or editors, activists, and many more will qualify so. This is the vicious circle that has evolved, probably without our realising so, almost imperceptibly.

When a crime is committed and known, it is to be tackled immediately in a civilised society. We all have grown up learning so and believing so. For example, if a murder is committed, the law-enforcers will have to come into action immediately. They can't allow the murderer to be at large to cover up his/her tracks, to destroy clues, and continue committing more and more murders. In cricket, the known fraudsters are allowed to be at large not for a few days, but for years, month after month, year after year, free to commit more and more crime. They are very happy in increasing the scope and reach of their fraud each day. There is no one to question them. Today they must be more than happy as they have seen that even the mighty Supreme Court of India hasn't bothered to touch them. They have absolutely nothing to fear now. Any revelation, like the recent one by Sanjeev Chawla as reported, or by the ex-Pakistani captain Aamer Sohail on Pakistan's performance in the last ICC World Cup, or by Vindu Dara Singh in 2013, or by the Sri Lankan sports minister in June 2020 that Sri Lanka had lost the 2011 World Cup final on purpose to India, or by Bishen Singh Bedi in 2018, many more by cricketers and others, **has absolutely had no impact on the hardened collective shamelessness and degradation of the world**.

Sports and competitive sports are the best or one of the best expressions of a civilised society. And cricket is no ordinary sport. As we all know and the governments know, in India and in the sub-continent, cricket is a religion by itself for the teeming masses—the cricketers being gods and demi-gods. And it is this sport that lies thoroughly abused. Thorough corruption in the same turning it to a massive fraud makes it the worst manifestation of decadence of the same society. The most worrisome is the folly/self-deception of the intellectuals of the world, especially those belonging to the world of media, in not grasping that all the institutions that have not only failed so miserably in putting a stop to this fraud but have sided with it actively or passively can never be relied upon to do any real good for the humanity. For example, how self-deceptive it is for us to allow the same media to set our daily agenda and govern our consciousness whose credibility has been torn to shreds through unashamed facilitation by it of the 'biggest known' and continuing public fraud on earth. But it is so; knowingly or unknowingly, the consciousness of the educated remains under the control of the rogue media. This aspect has been dealt with in some detail by me in my open letter to the sitting Supreme Court Judges in 2019 (documented in the chapter 'The Deaf Statesmen'), suggesting a solution also as it came to my mind.

Today's world doesn't end with the media. Social media—the hundreds of millions on WhatsApp, Facebook, and Twitter—the man next door—is a force to reckon with. **It is the whole—media, authorities, government, judiciary are just parts; subsets of this whole.** Rather interestingly, the whole has always been blaming the part for any adversity; never resorting to introspection or realising that it was the whole that had been giving shape to the parts which it later on blamed for all the ills. Has it not been a fashion for decades for the people to blame politicians and leaders for everything? Forgetting that no one could become a leader on his own until the people/the masses accepted someone as the leader? We enjoy the satires and the jokes on the politicians and clap; in the bargain, reinforcing our ill-founded belief that politicians were the main culprits. To my mind, the popular Hindi/Indian poetry being recited at various platforms by many popular poets deriding politicians and leaders has been causing immense harm to our consciousness over past many decades, without our realizing so. Similarly, at times, we blame the judiciary, the bureaucracy, or the media; conveniently losing sight that the part emanated from the whole, that all these parts we blame emerged from a larger society—from us. We find it very convenient and self pleasing to hear how someone else was being blamed for our sufferings.

No one dares tell us how we err, since it will make us angry, and the speaker/poet/preacher will become unpopular in no time losing all the earned popularity.

The political systems—whether democracy, communism, autocracy, or any other—and the political leaders are also subsets of the whole—the people. India is a democratic country. There is a ruling party, and there are a number of opposition parties. Establishment is supposed to be governed by the ruling party, and opposition parties are supposed to be taking on the ruling party for its wrong-doings. But all opposition parties and opposition leaders of various parties have been absolutely mum all these years when the government of India was historically failing in acting against an ongoing monumental fraud and crime. They can't feign ignorance since, as mentioned earlier, the copies of my book/s telling all about the fraud were mailed by me to a number of leaders from almost all the parties, across states throughout India. Does it not mean failure of existent political system, at least in India? To comprehend the political complexities as these exist, far from what the naive believe, one must see the Hindi movie '*Tashkent Files*'. Anyway, the point here is that it lies established that the continuing fraud has the blessings of all the politicians of India as well. Does that give it (the fraud) the sanctity?

Late Rajinder Puri once told me that nothing will happen until it becomes a political issue since it was necessary in India for anything to become a political issue for something to happen, or it was necessary for something to become a political issue for anything to happen—whatever way you may put it. He has proved to be dead right. The shame of the political subset is also the shame of the whole—of us, the people; whether we are able to appreciate it or not, whether we are able to comprehend it or not. That also goes to show that the weightage we give to various political leaders, all our discussions about them, is not of much consequence. Whether they deliver or not, depends on us, how we make or don't make them deliver. It is for us what we accept and what we don't accept. **Being obsessed with worthless and rogue politicians, even though as a result of media's doing, is our own undoing.**

We need to examine critically whether fraudulent cricket was thrust or forced on the people—the whole—by parts, by someone beyond our control, or whether we, the people, ourselves were responsible for its continuation for years or decades. What did the people/the masses do or didn't do during these years to stop the fraud? The social media can make any information viral and can make it reach millions in no time. Its effect works exponentially, much faster than the way any virus spreads. We daily find confronting ourselves with loads of fake news, propaganda material, or PJs (poor jokes) because of such potency of social media. Wisdom messages float in abundance giving one the impression that everyone was now brimming with the attained wisdom of centuries. What were these people, wise in every respect, doing during those long 7 years after the news of cricket being totally fixed was first broken to the world? They were talking about every other thing on earth and were largely busy in forwarding and spreading fake news, propaganda material and PJs. They were busy showing off their intelligence and boasting of their knowledge. At times, they also shared real wisdom and good humour. But the existence of massive corruption in a sport so religiously followed by it, along with the masses not on social media, hardly bothered the social media. It was akin to hundreds of millions of those on social media being troubled by pick-pocketing, brawls, molestations, etc., but not feeling affected in the least by a crime equivalent to thousands of robberies, murders and rapes committed, and still counting. The highly knowledgeable, intelligent, and the wise were not only happy in being fooled 24 × 7, but took pride in their folly discussing the fake as real with their friends and peers. What an irony! So more than the subsets in the form of media, authorities, the government, the politicians, the activists, and the judiciary, it is this larger set of people—the intellectuals and not so intellectuals belonging to various professions and age groups—that is at the centre of our collective hypocrisy and folly being announced so loudly through the continuing monumental crime through cricket. It amused me no end when I came across that even CEOs of world's top companies were enthusiastic cricket fans ignorant of what a fraud the game had been. **We continued and still continue to be deaf and blind, waiting for Nature to restore our faculties.** When would that happen, only Time knows. A few who sympathised with my efforts didn't matter much, far outnumbered and outmanoeuvred by the mob. And even most of them, including my co-petitioner, lost their interest along the way in the face of the continuing apathy of the billions and deafness of all the institutions including the top executives and the top court of a country.

The man (or woman) next door, let us say in India, whether a commoner or an expert or highly knowledgeable or very intelligent or a genius, is hit by corruption round the clock. He is hit the most by corruption when made to eat adulterated food and made to suffer physically and financially needing medical help. He cribs day and night against corruption, makes inconsequential noises about petty and big instances of corruption and injustice perennially coming to his knowledge. A rape or murder is a topic of discussion for weeks and, at times, results in candle-light marches. Nothing wrong in all that, but Satyendra Dubeys and Shanmugam Manjunaths losing their lives crusading against the same corruption that the man next door so much detests becomes just passing news for him. The known corrupt leaders and those who rise in society through corruption are adored and continue to be heroes and superheroes for him. That is so because hypocrisy inherent in man governs him. Mob mentality governs him throughout his life, whether he knows it or not, accepts it or not. **He goes through the motions of life with a largely conditioned mind, unaware.**

The best minds get conditioned unknowingly and unsuspectingly. To illustrate it, I divulge a recent experience from a WhatsApp Group. One fine day, a very senior member of the group, an octogenarian, presented a very simple puzzle to us '*Akbar Humayun ke bête ka kya tha*?' (What Akbar was of Humayun's son?) It was a question that could easily be answered by any kid who knew of the relation between the two. But, still, none of us who were attempting could answer it. Why? Because this question had been preceded by another question asking about the relation between the two, '*What was Humayun to Akbar?*' So, our minds had been conditioned to think about answer in terms of relationship between the two, and, hence, we failed to answer the obvious that 'Akbar was the ***name*** of Humayun's son'. The WhatsApp Group I am talking of consists of the cream of the society in terms of intelligence and knowledge.

This very interesting incident and simplest of the puzzles manifested a great/deep truth that almost all of us—the sapiens—don't realise (probably, there is a big difference between knowing and realising) throughout our lifetime. If one simple question could have conditioned the minds of those with above average intelligence, just imagine how much we remain conditioned since childhood. Our behaviours/actions/ reactions throughout are the result of how our minds have been conditioned since childhood. Successful preachers/leaders are those who succeed in conditioning the minds of the masses—for good or for bad. In the present-day world, our thinking is conditioned a lot by media/social media (without our realising so), even though we are quite aware of the rogue/fake character of both.

To understand and appreciate the contents of this book, one will have to rise a bit above one's conditioned mind—conditioned over the years through various sermons received, and manoeuvres of the media—as mentioned earlier and above. The readers will have to forget and unlearn the falsehood they have been nurtured with throughout their lives. **They will have to employ what I call zero-based thinking.** That is, we shall have to understand the reality, freeing our mind from the conditioning, and the hypocrisy that has governed our existence and our institutions more than anything else, howsoever intelligent we may consider ourselves.

Sense of proportion is as uncommon as common sense. And a man's comprehension appears to have its limitations. Neither scores of journalists who attended my press conferences in Kolkata or Delhi or elsewhere over the years, nor the men next door, could ever comprehend the vast implications of the gigantic fraud through cricket as it existed, since they continued to take pride in indulging in all other petty matters and issues led by their sense of proportion all these years, or bounded by limitations of comprehension. That would apply to all the illustrious editors as well. I don't know or understand whom they all had been kidding all these years by pretending that the cricket matches being institutionally fixed was only something insignificant on the sides and not a big key issue.

Could they not understand what the continuing institutionally fixed cricket meant? Could the millions of educated and intellectuals not see that it was not just about a sport being corrupt in some isolation? Could they not see that it meant that all the talk about cricket or cricketers by celebrities and experts or anyone else, knowingly or unknowingly, had been something totally bogus and counterfeit for years and years continuously? This is so because all the talk has always implied that competitive cricket had been taking place while the truth had been just the opposite. And such a talk has been ruling the consciousness of billions in the world. How could they not visualise and appreciate that cricket being as thoroughly corrupt as it is, meant that our very existence rotted since this sport was more than a religion for the people of some countries including India? How could they not see that this fraud was being sold to them for decades by none other than the media, and that, therefore, it meant total loss of credibility of media not only in India, but at least in other cricket-playing nations also? Especially, the cricket and sports journalists like Vikrant Gupta, Boria Majumdar, Ayaz Memon, Harsha Bhogle—to name a few—lie thoroughly exposed as first-rate idiots if nothing else. These gentlemen couldn't see and know that the sport they were reporting on for years was thoroughly fixed and corrupt while quite a few ordinary cricket fans and bettors knew that and know that?

How can man next door crib about petty or big wrongs he comes across daily, and yet feel unconcerned about a massive fraud staring him in the face 24 × 7? It speaks volumes for us, the people. Unknowingly and uncomprehendingly, we support a thoroughly corrupt system consisting of all the institutions including government and judiciary and crib when the same system hurts us. We keep deadly quiet when crime equivalent to thousands of murders and rapes is openly taking place, but start screaming when its offshoots result even in slight injury to us. Some of the offshoots like adulterated food, inflated hospital bills, etc., have been mentioned earlier. I doubt if anything could exemplify more the wounds given by a thoroughly corrupt system to the common man, hardly anyone spared, than the pandemic of COVID-19 and its (mis)management by the World Health Organization and many countries including India. The common man, yet, remained unaware of what had in reality been hitting him. That will be dwelt upon briefly later on to bring home the point.

Strangely enough, even the eminent and great journalist as he has been, Mr. Shantanu Guha Ray also displayed amnesia in his few and far writings on the subject after being a co-petitioner with me. I didn't get much cooperation from him in my further pursuit. The writer of the book **'Fixed! Cash and Corruption in Cricket'** had lost much journalistic interest in the subject. I found it quite strange and out of place when he completely shut up on the subject (to the best of my knowledge) after Sanjeev Chawla's explosive revelations as reported. Clearly something had befallen him. Was it fear of the mafia, or sudden loss of interest in the issue altogether, or was it something else? He alone would know.

Inexplicably, we all yearn for a just and fair society. Yet we value the rogues and shun the crusaders as said earlier. That is happening day and night around us. Media that controls our agenda and conscience round the clock is always telling us about which rogue leader said what. Similarly, it becomes the mouthpiece of other rogues who could rise up in the society. Don't we frequently come to know how those in high places, whether in bureaucracy, in government, in industry, in financial institutions, or in other private institutions had indulged in cheating or fraud? Do we ever pause to think how those with such a character had risen to such high positions? Not necessarily rogues, men of straw abound at the helm in almost all spheres. Didn't it mean that the so-called checks and balances in our systems had been a sham? Could anyone rise to a high position without the support of the society one lives in? Doesn't it happen in any social gathering that we tend to crowd or hang around those in position even if known rogues or men/ women of no substance?

We forget a very pertinent saying '*Nip the evil in the bud*', and go about life accepting the evils, many cribbing about those and some even not cribbing. Acceptance of evils leads to their reinforcement, everyone destined to suffer. Are authorities, media, or judiciary to be blamed for continuance of an open massive public crime debasing the humanity as a whole? Or is it public to be blamed for accepting and allowing this crime to continue? Surely public is more to blame. To many, the thrill and excitement from the cooked-up matches was more important than any of the far-reaching implications of the crime and the fraud; to others it was none of their concerns.

In essence, there was nothing in religion, scriptures, morality or constitutions that allowed the common man to coolly accept such a public crime. Then what right could such a man have to crib about any other wrong befalling him?

What about great preachers in India like Sadhguru and Sri Sri Ravi Shankar? What is their relevance if the society teeming with their followers remains so thoroughly degraded as continuing to celebrate a massive fraud and crime—contributing to killing of hundreds across the world including their own countrymen through terror funding— as a source of its entertainment? Don't all their teachings and advices become a source for strengthening of the existing corrupt systems and rotting roots since they not only fail to address these, but also condition people's minds towards other things, away from addressing the rotting roots? One would hardly ever find their followers or those of various other sects bothering to fight degenerative systems because they are taught to purify self and always goad others to search for deficiencies within only, dissuading one to see those outside. 'Look inwards only' remains the dictum of almost all the preachers and spiritual gurus. So, our minds conditioned by such very logical looking doctrines never ever dare to see the decaying institutions and systems, leave alone taking them head on. That is one of the reasons that in recent times one would hardly find any mass uprising in India against even very serious wrongs in the society or by the governments. Consequently, we continue to deteriorate and decay more.

Should not continuance of the international fraud and crime totally unbridled for seeming eternity, even after recently reported explosive revelations by Sanjeev Chawla, be something of utmost concern to anyone who considers self to be educated or a responsible being? Not in India alone, but across the world? Should it not make everyone sit up and wonder what was happening? Should not the governments be hammered? Should not the newspapers and news channels be flooded with letters to editors and communications from angry viewers respectively asking them why they all were quiet on this? Were not these

actions within the competence of us all? Couldn't all of us, the common people, make our concerns viral on social media forcing the authorities to act? No one could stop us if we thought so or wished so. Can there be any justification for our own silence? Only those who don't feel bad about anything, even if adversely affected themselves, may be justified, not anyone else. Undoubtedly, there will hardly be anyone who doesn't feel bad when himself/herself being on the receiving end. How wrong we are in blaming authorities or leaders alone for our ills!

Why did we not do what we must have done? Probably we don't act as we should, because we give priority to self-defeating and extravagant issues or non-issues, like religious animosity, other animosities, political affiliations, historical events, personal lives of those sold to us as celebrities, religious customs and discussions etc. or whatever media or propaganda machinery on social media directs our attention to. We protect our own comfort zone first and foremost, while giving sermons to others, or pointing fingers at them. We give top priority to display our worth on worthless matters—driven by ignorance, conceit and conditioned minds. To cite an example, one will find millions of intellectuals in India worrying and parading their knowledge about elections in USA, **but not at all aware of or troubled by a magnificent crime being telecast live in their drawing rooms day and night. Our haughtiness to stick by our conspicuous folly reigns supreme. Greater the intellect, greater is such haughtiness. Greater the pride in being fooled! Having been bamboozled long enough, we ensure continue being bamboozled, as said by Carl Sagan decades ago.** Unfortunately, we have over the decades made ourselves incapable of or immune to looking for the basics and thinking in the larger interest with a free mind, not knowing how to apply pure and simple common-sense.

Above is in no way to say that there is nothing good or great existing in the human world. This book is to make us all, especially the intellectuals of the world, realize how and why we are far from a happy world, much below our potential, despite our inherent goodness and greatness. There is no dearth of stories of individual capabilities, good deeds, and acts of greatness; these abound.

We all like to give moral education to our children at home and in schools. Have we ever thought what morality the generations growing up in an atmosphere of a massive open public crime and fraud will have? What inspiration they will get and what lessons they will learn? Those worrying a lot about education policies and discussing a lot about these should first and foremost answer these questions to themselves. Those worrying and discussing about deteriorating law and order all around, increase in all sorts of crimes, rioting etc. should answer themselves how foolhardy it is to expect a society to be law abiding when it is being subjected to a splendid open international crime 24 × 7, a number of role-models and dignitaries of the same society being fraudsters and criminals; all the authorities—executive, legislative, and judicial—continually looking the other way!

I find that people around me don't get tired of talking about religion and the Constitution/Law. My simple question to them: Which tenet or scripture or law or act or clause of Constitution of India allows or justifies that people should continue celebrating a massive fraud and no authority should do anything to stall or even attempt to stall it after it remains thoroughly exposed for 7 long years through a scientific proof? If they can't answer it convincingly, then does it not mean that we have already rendered religions and the Constitution as frivolous and it is nothing but hypocrisy of the highest order continuing hailing these still? Is it not rather strange that people don't realise how self-defeating they have been in fighting fanatically among themselves in the name of religion while all the time they were being fooled together across religions by rogue forces that belonged to all religions? If people were to realise this alone after going through this book, the book would have achieved a lot for the humanity.

Should we give much importance to individuals vis-à-vis the society; be it PM Modi or President Trump or even Mahatma Gandhi? To my mind, it is the collective consciousness of the society that matters more and individuals at best reflect that. Though the world I live in follows just the opposite. The people are always interested in talking about, or are bothered about, other people; whether connected with them or not. Many like to worship gods or deities, and they like to worship individuals - men and women just like them. They hardly ever try to go to basics for systemic corrections, for all around happiness. I have named many individuals, a number of known celebrities, journalists, activists; have named or implied to name almost all the illustrious cricketers—present or of recent past—in various contexts in this book, and have talked about even my family and friends. My purpose in no way has been to point fingers at anyone or implicate individuals. All such mentions have been necessary only to make the readers and the posterity realise and comprehend at a much wider horizon as to how we have been evolving as human beings and why and where we have to look for the necessary corrections. In continuation of the enormous crime through cricket despite efforts as brought out in this book—it is stinking degradation of our collective consciousness—that comes to the fore. **And that is too depressing.**

Or is it that rather than being logical and rational beings, as we believe ourselves to be; we, the people at large, are also just numbers? Like number of fish in a pond, like number of sheep in a farmyard? Mere zombies? Despite our technological and scientific advancements, we have still been evolving just like herds? We are not the people anymore, but have allowed ourselves to be the oodles? Men and women easily maneuvered or manipulated? Those who run cricket, and others who all join them in the crime, actively or passively, have amply demonstrated for years that indeed it is so. This is even more depressing.

Must we not introspect truthfully and realise our numerous failings? Can't we set on to mend selves, overcome natural compulsions of looking after immediate personal benefits, and think in our larger interest? Can't we make efforts to overcome hypocrisy and ego? Would we not be serving ourselves better if looking after the greater interest first? Will not part be beautiful if whole is good? Will it not be in our own lasting overall interest? Sure it will be.

I do realize that I have said a lot and hope that I have talked sensibly. Yet, I do apprehend the inefficacy of my efforts, because I am trying to address the minds conditioned over the ages through evolution, religion, preaching, or otherwise; the minds naturally endowed with hypocrisy and conceit or ego as the controlling traits. The combined might of the rest of the world is challenged. Then what has been the motivation?

□

Quest for Revolution

In order to appreciate the whole gamut of this book, it is not only relevant, but necessary to answer 'why did I take this issue as a mission and am pursuing it even today for almost a decade (counting time since I started writing my first book on the subject)?' and 'at what cost?' 'How difficult or easy the journey has been?' To dwell on these and related questions also becomes necessary so that nothing is left unanswered; one can never be sure of being around even next moment, especially with COVID-19 firmly in place.

I shall try to answer the above from my heart, at the same time thinking about or treating self as a third person, as objectively as possible. That at places may demonstrate absence of humility one would generally expect from someone talking about self.

The answer to the first question exists in my earlier books, our petition and various submissions to the Hon'ble Supreme Court of India, especially the latest ones. Marx and Marxism came and went; religions got founded and immortal scriptures written and followed; great literature got created and read around the world; great leaders and preachers walked on the earth with many millions as their followers; activists abounded; but can we call ourselves civilised, has it all made us civilised in essence? Would civilised and cultured people be unashamedly celebrating an open public fraud highly detrimental to them? Are we happy the way we are today? Don't we experience and feel at times that we have been erring in our evolution, without being able to understand or pinpoint what it has been? Is the present state of affairs acceptable? Aren't we found tremendously wanting in dealing with the calamity of coronavirus across countries? **While many of us—most of those who would be reading this—remain well fed and well provided for even in post corona days, controlling or running the world and feeling happy with their bellies full; a much larger number of our fellow beings, not in millions but in billions, still remains underfed and underprivileged. It is easier said than feeling the pinch. It pierces one's heart if one has real sense of compassion.**

Is it because the mother Earth doesn't have enough resources to take care of us all? A clear answer to this is a big 'no'. As mentioned earlier, the loot by the Cricket Mafia itself is sufficient enough to sustain the whole mankind. Untold loot is always going on around us in various other forms also. There is concentration of wealth in some hands, while the vast majority remains deprived. What the world has been refusing to heed to and learn till now, the Nature or Time is making it learn slowly but surely through the dreaded COVID-19. And if man is still too haughty to listen, as he appears to be, Nature will come out with sterner lessons. Let us not worry about that.

The judicial systems, especially in India, remain a big joke with justice continuing to be elusive, highly delayed, and unaffordable for the common man. Doesn't advocates charging fees in lakhs of rupees for one appearance in the High Courts and the Supreme Court in India imply an obvious mockery of our judicial system—of equality before law for the common man? The mankind that should have been united with compassion as *'vasudhaiv kutumbkam'* remains polarised on religious or territorial lines. While all our collective energies as humans are required to combat Nature and Nature alone—as Coronavirus and COVID-19 reminded us very recently—we have been piling arms and ammunition against each other.

I am sure many would agree or would have realised that for years, in India, we have been engaging in heated discussions by the privileged and celebrities of the society on our prime news channels in prime time, evening after evening, as to who or which political party was a bigger rogue, or which leaders or people were bigger rogues? We have allowed and accepted that to be the ultimate for our collective efforts. Not only that, leaders continue to be accused of various sins and crimes for years and years, yet they continue to enjoy all the perks and privileges and also continue to be at the helm. Accusing leaders and people infinitely with nothing ever reaching a logical conclusion has become a way of life for us through our continuous acceptance of something so absurd. That is what we have come to be.

So, there had to be something wrong with our evolution, and corrections were necessary. It is easier said than understood. As I said earlier, we ourselves had to undertake the course correction; no aliens were going to do that for us. I could clearly see how a massive public fraud involving about half the world—involving all those who mattered in that world—was going on merrily. Rightly or wrongly, I thought and foresaw that if it was exposed, the world would act and react giving rise to a chain reaction that would, in due course, result in the course correction necessary for the humanity—one would understand this if one could visualise the massiveness of the fraud in its totality (that is including its continuance despite lying exposed for 7 long years, and taking into account all those involved directly or indirectly). It is towards that end that I have been going on, though nothing has stirred till date. I aimed at setting the overall corrections in motion, discerning that charities or doles here or there could not be any solution for the billions. My sense of proportions has still kept me going.

The fraud lies totally exposed—a miracle in itself (since it was one common man against combined might of half the world from beginning)—but the world has failed to act or react. That is a much greater miracle to my mind. While interacting with me, Shantanu Guha Ray once emailed me that the whole thing was too explosive to result in any action by anyone. He has been proved correct, but I have not understood till date why it should be so when everyone, especially the intellectuals, feels so self-important otherwise in arguing about right and wrong, and on being on the side of the right. Probably, it is good that I have not understood and am still continuing with my efforts. Probably, it is not good not to understand and accept the reality.

What has happened and is happening now is beyond my comprehension; though we maintained in the petition that the fraud itself was beyond normal comprehension. Today, the agents of those controlling and running the fraud themselves are telling loud and clear that cricket was all institutionally fixed (a matter of record as brought out in our petition and my various submissions to the Hon'ble Supreme Court)—it doesn't require any efforts by anyone anymore to bring out the truth—**it is all too open on social media all the time, every moment when a cricket match is being telecast and betting is taking place**—but the media and the authorities still continue to act deaf, dumb, and, blind, and, consequently, the masses remain ignorant of what can now easily and unambiguously be said to be a State-sponsored fraud and crime. Those who are fully aware of the reality—may be a few hundred at best by now—prefer or choose to keep quiet. I am sure most of them must simply be feeling helpless, not knowing what to do. The whole so-called intellectual class is simply unconcerned. **The cricket continues as a fraud perpetrated by the people against themselves.**

It may be interesting and worthwhile to see what my efforts have cost me apart from time, energy and money. What were the big obstacles? When I first told the world that the cricket was institutionally fixed with the involvement of all players, coaches, team managements and cricket experts, I was considered to be crazy and mad, especially by family and friends—everyone thinking and saying how could everyone be involved? How could Tendulkars, Dravids and Kumbles be involved? Today, I stand vindicated with not only institutional fixing of cricket becoming so clear and evident to anyone bothering to open eyes and applying mind a little—Bishen Singh Bedi, a top ex-international cricketer, having said so publicly independent of me though quite belatedly—and with tens and hundreds of agents of the mafia themselves coming in the open and continuing to announce loud and clear day and night for months that cricket was all fixed; but also as a result of our petition having stood vindicated in the Hon'ble Supreme Court of India. Still, for years, I was considered unhinged by family and friends. Ego so governs human mind that even today, the same people won't accept and realise how wrong they had been in not listening to and believing one among themselves and continuing to be governed by fixed ideas, and conditioned and closed minds. Unfortunately, the human race largely continues to be affected, influenced, and run by falsely built reputations, and not by basics and common sense; its evolution having been governed by mob mentality more than by reason. If one could apply mind a little, one would easily see how mob mentality governs human behaviour. And, unfortunately, as we have evolved and as we go, the rogue media, as we have seen its credentials, controls the mob.

It is rightly said that there is nothing new under the sun. There must be parallels in human history, though to be counted on fingers. One such situation that comes to mind was in the 16th century when the world didn't accept the truth of earth revolving around the sun for about 100 long years. Given the advancement since then, especially in communication, 7 years of the 21st century would probably compare with 100 years of the 16th century. **The world with pre-conditioned minds failed or rather refused to see reason then; same way as it is doing now.** That was a much larger scientific issue; this is a very big issue concerning public probity and human degradation. Its relevance is different, but not much less significant. It tells us that collective human folly and bigotry have remained as such despite all our technological advancements.

To believe in common sense and oneself against the rest of the world and continue believing so for months and years without getting much support and yet remaining sane and normal is not easy and is quite a tough job. I am sure many would realise almost impossibility of living in the same world while not only knowing, but also continuing to make all-out efforts to tell it that it was all absurd and crooked. That near impossible/tricky situation hasn't changed for me even today after 7 long years. The irony all these years has been that my deductions and insight were the result of my knowledge about betting and session betting. Yet, the others including my own family and friends and Vinod Rais of the world (in all likelihood, Vinod Rais did it on purpose even though knowing the reality) didn't think twice in dismissing me instantaneously without ever bothering to know and understand what betting or session betting was—the basis of my explosive findings to start with—and applying their minds to what all had been told and explained. That is another absurdity how the human world works/has evolved, or a sure manifestation of how humans continue to exist and grow with closed and shut minds, remaining duly brainwashed.

I don't know how many would realise that fighting the crookedness of the rest of the world single-handed necessitates insulating one from the ways of the world while at the same time surviving in it. Many would laugh, but to my mind, it amounted to something like continuous meditation—to cut off from the world while living in it. Being a pensioner helped me in this regard. Could I write the books I did or continue my fight as I did had I been working in some office governed by the ways of the world? Rightly or wrongly, I always felt that that would have weakened me—my perspective, resolve and delivery. But now, looking back, I find that I have wasted seven long precious years of life, the world having moved on, completely ignoring my efforts, insulating itself from me. The time—I can't get back. The time and energy wasted by me in this mission could have been used in doing some other creative or non-creative work and/or in earning money that the world and my family would have valued, or in satiating various pleasures of life. Years of my life got lost and wasted probably when my faculties were at their best.

The biggest cost I have had to pay is that I have been a pariah among family and friends, and in the society in general, all these years—because to them I had to be absurd, how could the rest of the world be? The pain I felt or had to go through at times was too excruciating; I just blocked my mind and carried on. That is probably the good thing with emotional pain; one can simply decide not to feel it anymore. Probably one can't do that with physical pain. I won't deny that it has all been my own doing, because one has to take responsibility for one's own actions. I should have understood the impossibility of achieving what I had set to. I should have understood the limitations and undesirable but necessary traits of human mind. I should have understood that no one else was going to be much interested in, forget being whole heartedly associated with, the cause I had set to pursue – **no one**. I should have anticipated the brickbats, rather than words of appreciation, from those around me.

Probably, every plus has a minus, and every minus has a plus. While I suffered no end as above, I had the unparalleled satisfaction of successfully calling the bluff of such a humongous international fraud, taking on the world, getting godsend support from time to time. But was it any achievement at all?

There is no dearth of intellectuals in the world who see or would see all I did as my fault or misdoing. Who was I to challenge an out-and-out hardened, foolish world? To continue to be fooled, being hypocrite, and to continue celebrating a fraud was the prerogative of the people. What was my problem? The educated intellectuals would have strong objections to some of my harsh words to the Supreme Court of India, not bothering about and appreciating the context, but they have absolutely no problem with the continuation of such a fraud for ages and with inaction by the 'zero tolerance against corruption' governments and the Hon'ble top Court for years. They have no problem if ICC has been acting as a top criminal body for decades. 'Might is Right' holds, Truth and Righteousness don't matter. They have no respect or regard for my efforts and achievements—probably unparalleled in the history. They have their own level of thinking and sense of proportions as a result of the way they have been taught and brought up. For them, one has to be honoured by the establishment to be of some value; one taking on the crookedness of the establishment and the world at large with untold conviction at great personal risk has no value. The messengers deserve to be shot. The crusaders laying their lives for the larger public good are to be soon forgotten or not even to be known while the rogue leaders are to be garlanded and voted for again and again. This is the accepted world for most of those crowding social media.

I am sure most of these highly intelligent and self-righteous people are incapable of even remotely understanding and imagining what it takes in terms of common sense, intelligence, self-confidence, and guts to do what I have been able to, despite the world happily continuing to celebrate its massive degradation. They are even more incapable of valuing efforts such as mine, since for them fasting and going to places of worship, or singing well has more value. I don't intend to blame them since it's none of their fault as this is how they have been nurtured and their minds conditioned. How would they understand something unparalleled, beyond their comprehension and understanding; unless someone else in the media or from establishment recognises and explains to them? Yet these very people yearn for a just and fair society; criticise every other smallest wrong doing, and cry when injustice or absurdity hits them or their near ones. They are taught to believe the rogue media and establishment more than someone well-meaning among them. Who was I to point a finger if the world had chosen not only to accept, but also to celebrate a fraud? How could it be that all the authorities and the media failed together? How could a common man stand any ground in front of hundreds of celebrities? Who was I to bother about terror funding if Modis and Trumps were comfortable with it? Who was I to bother about tens of millions of bettors being looted and hundreds of millions being fooled 24 × 7 if they were not bothered and the world was not bothered? Were my *whims* to prevail or the majority will—even though defying all religions, all preaching, all laws, all scriptures, and all the norms set by that very majority—was to prevail? I don't know if some of such people even feel or felt jealous (a natural human instinct) of me—just one among them—for having achieved what I could.

From my experience on social media, I am sure many would say, 'but what have you achieved that you are talking so big?' They would ask because they have lost habit of seeing anything on their own, can't see beyond their nose, their mind being clustered and brainwashed by all the muck fed into it and being fed into it by the media all the time. First what I have achieved:

(a) Cricket is an international sport followed by billions and billions the world over, over decades. And I was the one among those billions who could see through what a massive fraud it was despite so much camouflage created by the fraudsters. The intelligentsia of the society laughed at me, to be proved wrong in due course, but unfortunately the false ego of man doesn't allow it to accept his mistakes and correct himself.

(b) Writing detailed books covering all the aspects of such a massive fraud was not an easy task. It required a lot of hard thinking and application of common sense. To get the books published was no less tough, tougher at times. I continued with my efforts through periodical public posts on the Facebook page of 'Bettors Beware'. These books and posts today are an indelible rĕcord of cricket being thoroughly scripted at least during the last decade. No one or no authority ever challenged the contents of my non-fictions.

(c) To understand something is one thing and to stick out one's neck and take on the world is another. Holding Press Conferences single-handed to tell how the might of the world was involved in a colossal fraud was not a common feat.

(d) Yes, continuing believing in self and common sense despite the finding being so unbelievable and despite being ridiculed by those around, especially on social media, was the most difficult part.

(e) To go about my business in a way that the authorities could never counter me, and that I remained unharmed (by God's grace) has been the greatest of my achievements, if one can understand. In India, one can't take on even local SHO (station house officer of a local police station) and remain safe and well, and here I was taking on all law-enforcing agencies, the government, the top court of the country (as was necessitated later on), the media, the mafia—all at the same time—all being comrades (knowingly or unknowingly). **Credit for this also goes to Indian culture and society, all said and done. Probably it**

just couldn't be possible in many other countries.

(f) To arrive at the mathematical and, hence, scientific proof of the fraud was a very remarkable achievement to my mind. The scientific proof presented years ago not only applied to matches in the past that time but also to the matches of the future. **And it has stood the test of time.**

(g) While going public with my mathematical proof, I had realised that though the fraudsters could change scripting and patterns to prove me wrong, they could not change the basics of fixed scoring patterns (as analysed in the mathematical proof) since otherwise they would start losing money to punters in session/ bracket betting. I backed myself that the mathematical proof I brought out would always stand even after fraudsters came to know of it. Time has vindicated me.

(h) It was a result of the efforts put in for years that a water-tight petition could be filed in the Supreme Court of India in 2017.

(i) Filing of the petition with evidence of the continuing fraud in the name of international cricket (no one known to me ever thought it was possible) and vindication of its contents in the Supreme Court of India was no mean achievement—a miracle in fact, as some of my friends said so afterwards.

(j) I didn't allow the all mighty Supreme Court to escape, and continued pursuing within the limited opening available to me; such that though the Hon'ble Court didn't deliver, but it lies totally exposed today.

What I have achieved can be summarised in five words: Impossible, Impossible, Impossible, Impossible, and Impossible. Nothing may look impossible today, but it was impossible for one like me sitting at home to know on my own with total conviction that all cricket matches were fixed like movies/theatre directed by someone (just what Sanjeev Chawla is reported to have said very recently only). To come out with a mathematical proof for the same was probably more impossible. It was impossible for me to expose this fact to the world and still remain unharmed by the mafia reportedly talked of by Sanjeev Chawla. It was impossible to file a watertight petition in the Supreme Court of India and to get vindicated there. And not only to remain sane in the face of fraud still continuing unfettered, but even to pursue such as to make the Supreme Court of India to expose itself thoroughly was no less impossible.

Secondly, the achievements are so extraordinary that any mention about those would look like talking big. The purpose has never been to talk big (one has to keep oneself motivated though), but to make the world aware of a massive fraud so that it could take the necessary corrective actions. I gain nothing by talking big, having wasted years of my life and my energies because of the haughtiness of a highly stupid and hypocrite world—all that is a matter of record. And even if I was talking big or rude or amounting to unbecoming of a gentleman, or was mad, or was a big criminal, should that be an issue or the continuance of a massive fraud with very serious adverse implications for the mankind should be an issue for the people? **Should any errors by me in this book, whether linguistic or otherwise, or any misdemeanours—perceived or in reality—count, or the overall sense of what is meant and**

conveyed should count? Again, it's a matter of common sense and of sense of proportions. Irrespective of whatever I have done, the fraud is too open now; only thing is that the world is acting blind still. It was for the media and the world to act and react after my first Press Conference and first published interview in January 2013. I have been paying the price for the miserable failure of the world all these years. And today the world is paying price for its accumulated sins (as would follow subsequently), though hardly any wiser yet.

I recount the above not to brag but to drive home the point that my extraordinary efforts were towards an extraordinary cause, a cause much beyond normal consciousness of human beings—to bring about a silent, imperceptible revolution that is necessary, is the need of the hour, for the larger human good. Probably, the sense or significance of this will be better understood after one goes through the next chapter. I didn't indulge in idle talk; I acted, I continued acting, and I am acting. If the world remains unconcerned still, it shouldn't be my fault or failing.

My experience tells me that there won't be any dearth of the highly intelligent ones who would feel happy dismissing me as a disruptor and satisfying their own ego so. To my mind, that exactly is what I have never intended. For the simple reason that the world has seen many well pronounced revolutions, but is not any better off. An improved world couldn't be indulging in and celebrating sports that reeked of deceit, fraud, and crime. It couldn't be celebrating something that openly looted millions of people and funded terrorism in a big way – same terrorism that killed people across nations and against which the world leaders cribbed perennially. It couldn't be facing the inexplicable and mysterious crisis of Corona Virus as it is doing today (as we shall see in some detail in next chapter). Through continuing to pursue a crime and fraud as big as Cricket, at total risk and great personal cost, my endeavour has been to make the world come to the required realization, and act and react intrinsically, to carry on necessary deep rooted corrections – beginning an imperceptible revolution as mentioned above.

Here was a monumental international fraud and crime that lied exposed years ago. There was no reason why the world should have not reacted to carry out detailed investigations and bring about the required necessary corrections. Those were bound to have a chain reaction, exposing much more, and leading to a far reaching impact; if carried out with the genuine intentions and in the right spirit. That was imperative, given the volume, the value, reach, and the extent of the persisting crime. Amazingly, nothing of that sort happened; the people – those who mattered - continued with hollow big talks, same selfish and self-defeating ways - hardened over lifetime. They failed to visualize or realize the consequent heavy toll in store for the coming generations.

There are too many allies in this crime who publicly portray themselves as enemies. Any true investigation would have taken hundreds of masks off, mostly off our leaders and role-models. We would have seen how ostensibly political adversaries were partners in cricket crime. A total overhaul in existing regime would have become inevitable. Yes, I didn't take the risks, and make the efforts, as I did, for peanuts. This book is a continuation of my efforts for over a decade now. May be the realization that has evaded the world so far finally dawns on it if and when it goes through the contents herein.

Probably, I could achieve whatever it was worth, because of earlier having done something unprecedented while in

Railway service—having been instrumental in exposing a very big systemic lapse/corruption in the organisation while working in it. In doing so also, I had subjected myself to all possible adversities and actions against me.

It is only incidental that I am alive and writing this with my faculties working and my spirit still up. I could have been bogged down in multiple ways. I could well have been bumped off by the betting mafia after my first press conference in 2013 or could have died a natural death. I could have easily been harassed by the establishment no end. Nothing of the sort having happened doesn't mean that there wasn't any such threat. The threat was very real, more than real as they say. Many cautioned me then and afterwards that I could be bumped off, but now I know that what saved me was the knowledge to the mafia that my efforts didn't matter since the whole establishment and media was with it, and the people, the mere numbers, didn't matter. May also be that I didn't get much support on social media since ordinary mortals were too scared of antagonising the mafia or Dawood Ibrahim by siding with the cause. It could be or could not be so. I could have developed health issues or could have had any other concerns. I could very well have been disheartened long ago; my continuing even today with almost the same spirit after many gruelling years is another impossible happening in retrospect. Probably because Time has ordained so.

The threat to my safety and life being real, as the recent reported revelation by Sanjeev Chawla should leave no doubt about it if there was any; in some of my communications to the Hon'ble Supreme Court, I also raised this issue. But my life was never considered of any value by the authorities or the Hon'ble Court! On the contrary, my well-wishers remained scared all the time that I could invite contempt of the Court (for pursuing the larger good!).

Had I not been living today or would have forgotten the issue, the issue of such a massive public fraud would have died long back even after having been unequivocally exposed publicly with the publication of my book 'Bettors Beware' in 2013. No one from the rest of the world, no cricket journalist or no activist, has found it worthwhile to pursue it, even though cricket continues to be religion above religions for the teeming masses. Is that not a matter of utter shame and, hence, intense contemplation for the world full of intellectuals and responsible beings? Humanity's collective guilt continues to haunt.

Didn't my job end after filing the PIL WP (C) 1163/2017 in the Supreme Court of India, if not after holding Press Conference in Press Club of India, New Delhi in end February 2014, subsequent to publication of the book '**Bettors Beware**'? Did the onus for corrections or pursuing for those, rest on me forever and not on the rest of the world including the establishment, the media, the judiciary, and the intellectuals? Was it not for the rest of the world to take over from thereon? If the Hon'ble Supreme Court of India has failed to deliver causing great disappointment, is that a fault of the petitioners? Unfortunately, the world, as it is, would mostly perceive it as a failure of the petitioners, rather than realising its own shame and shame for the institutions evolved over time that have allowed such a massive fraud to continue and prosper for at least more than a decade. Am I answerable to the Hon'ble Supreme Court of India or that august institution is answerable to me? I would have been answerable if I was being tried before it or I had violated it. But the Hon'ble Supreme Court of India is now answerable for evading responsibility, for dereliction of duty, to me—the taxpayer—their master—the citizen of India—who pays to keep the institution going. The earlier the judges and the officials manning the Supreme Court and others like them understand it, the better it would be for the human civilisation.

My family and friends are nothing but a subset of the world around me, so no wonder that quasi intellectuals also abound among them—though the same has distressed me the most all these years. To be a madman/a conceited being in their eyes was akin to drinking poison silently, while trying to fetch nectar for the humanity. To many among them, it has been my failure if the fraud is continuing as it is; that is, I have not succeeded in achieving anything. Rather, to some among them, even it was wrong on my part to have taken on the system, even if that was on the side of an open and marvellous international crime. To them, the governments and the authorities were invincible; the oodles didn't matter or count. To them, those not in governments must behave like zombies, to carry the commands. That is how we have our minds conditioned—everyone to one's own. The masses, the uneducated, are not bothered. They behave as they do because they remain ignorant of the reality. It's anybody's guess how the masses would have reacted if they knew what a big fraud in the name of cricket was going on. It was the sacred duty of the establishment and the media to make the masses aware. But they failed. They failed on purpose.

I might have exposed this fraud first, and remained the only one to publicly spell it as it exists in its totality till the reported revelation by Sanjeev Chawla to Delhi Police. But, from time to time, it has been exposed in parts and indicated as it exists by sources and forces independent of me during the past 7 years. All such exposés have been brushed under the carpet. None of these has been investigated or pursued to a logical conclusion. Had that been done honestly enough, the truth would have been known to the world long ago independent of me. The exposé by Al Jazeera brought out by me in my rejoinder to the COA's report remains the biggest of such exposés, to my mind, that needed a thorough investigation. But it and any talk about it also disappeared as dramatically as it had appeared—exactly as prophesized by me in my rejoinder to the COA's report.

No one lives forever. So will be the case with me. All the facts and my efforts with my take are here before the readers for them to form their own judgement, to introspect, to think deep and hard, and to find a way forward for the humanity. As far as I am concerned, the world will remain my culprit forever, irrespective of what it does or doesn't do now, for having failed my herculean and unprecedented efforts. It taught me norms, rules, laws, etc., that it never meant. It bombarded my consciousness for years through a media that has no credibility whatsoever and has hypocrisy as its watchword, a media to which all the bad adjectives ever phrased by man would apply. The world that elects liars as its top leaders who lie repeatedly, like PM Modi claiming zero tolerance against corruption, and doing the opposite by hailing one of the key fraudsters, a man having lied under oath, Mahendra Singh Dhoni, through a letter. The world made me believe that there was an institution called the Supreme Court of India that won't fail me because it had '*satyamev jayate*' as its logo. The world that made me falsely believe through its talks and deliberations that there was a large population of educated and intellectuals that would always stand up for the right and the values—is the world that is my culprit. **The world just can't brush off its crowning shame arising from being deaf and blind for years and**

years to an open splendid public fraud and scam.

The above is in no way to forget that it is the world, especially my family and friends, that has sustained me and has kept me going with my idiosyncrasies, when I had been fighting the historical impossible battle. On my part, I shall ever remain culprit of my family, especially my wife who kept me well fed and despite having reservations allowed me to carry on with my pursuits. At whose cost I fought the impossible battle I won with flying colours, yet losing out to a world full of moron and conceited hypocrites who even today pompously go on exhibiting their wisdom on everything, but gleefully accept and celebrate the known and proven gargantuan public fraud. We all come with one life; so did me and my wife. Yes, I do regret losing out to the existing world—a world in immense suffering because of its own doing. The following may sum it up better:

न मैं जमाने से हारा
न जमाना मुझ से हारा
मैं हारा कि जमाना हारा
जमाना हारा कि मैं हारा

(Neither I have lost to the world nor is the world defeated by me. I lose if the world loses out; the world will lose if I get defeated in what I have set to achieve)

□

Nature's Fury, Man's Folly

Unfortunately, all those choosing to continue accepting their collective degradation and degeneration with open arms don't realise what cost they or their descendants will have to pay one day for their folly. The most damaging aspect of a highly degraded human world is that it would not be able to adequately deal with Nature as and when the need arises. I had mentioned so also in the letter documented earlier, to Mr Ranjan Gogoi, the then Chief Justice of India. I reproduce the relevant paragraph here: 'The greater question worrying us all should be *"how can a civilization blatantly continuing to feast on Falsehood deal truthfully with any issues confronting it, especially challenges from Nature?"* ' I had expected a man of the stature of the Hon'ble Chief Justice of India to have wisdom and depth to be able to grasp the import of the contents of my letter and act accordingly. But alas! that was not to be. Probably, arrogance/misplaced ego and wisdom don't stick together.

I never imagined, and I am sure no one could imagine, that these words would prove so prophetic so soon, tragically! However, now it will be difficult for the intelligentsia to charge me that I was being wise afterwards. As I write this, the world is grappling with a new pandemic—COVID-19. The failings of nations and the international organisations in many ways are coming to the fore when innocent lives are being lost and people in tens of thousands the world over are dying painful deaths. Dying or not, infected or not, the whole world is passing through a torturous period, already running into months. No one bothered when the international body ICC (International Cricket Council) and the cricket-playing countries were overseeing a colossal fraud for more than a decade; now many are feeling the pinch of failings of another international body WHO (World Health Organization) since its enormous failings have directly come to door of each and every one. Response of many affected countries also has been quite intriguing. Without going into seemingly unending debate of whether the virus causing COVID-19 originated in nature or a lab, some too obvious but pertinent questions that arise are:

(a) China, the country where it all started, is an important member of WHO. Yet how China dealt with the virus and the affected patients remains largely unknown to the world. No country appears to be interested in finding it out from China or WHO, even though thousands of their citizens have been dying. At the time of writing this, around two hundred thousand infections and 5,000 deaths from the dreaded coronavirus were taking place daily in the world, while both infections and deaths had been negligible for about past 3 months in China.

(b) There were a number of other countries as well where deaths had been nil or minimal. Why WHO and other suffering countries couldn't learn from these countries?

(c) Why should WHO and leading countries of the world have not been seeking clear, logical, and convincing answers to some fundamental questions, the foremost being: '**How come the virus didn't spread in China,**

the country of origin, and yet it spread to the rest of the world?'

(d) What magic did China, the world's largest populated country accounting for about one-fifth of the world population, have to restrict deaths to below 5,000, whereas the number of deaths in the world had crossed half-a-million at the time of drafting these lines, and no end to the count was near in sight?

(e) How come even months after China and some other countries having been successful in combating the deadly virus, WHO and other seriously affected countries continued changing advices as to how the virus spread, what needed to be done to guard against it, etc., continuing to confuse the people in the world? For example, after declaring COVID-19 as pandemic for the world, WHO declared that it mainly spread through touching surfaces covered with droplets containing virus; and months afterwards, after virus having created havoc in Europe and other countries, the world was being told that the virus mainly spread through air—directly from the infected. How bizarre and inexplicable! **Would the blatantly wrong advice for months by WHO not have helped in the initial spread of the virus in many countries, with nothing to stop the inevitable chain reaction thereafter?**

(f) WHO is supposed to be an apolitical international organization set up under United Nations, to serve the interests of the whole world. But the developments on record clearly show that politics governed it and it acted as if under control of China.

(g) Time is the most potent weapon in the hands of the powerful and is very often used, or rather misused, as such. WHO sufficiently delayed announcing to the world that human to human transmission of the virus took place, despite Taiwan having alerted it much earlier in end December, 2019, about the same. This delay by WHO facilitated COVID-19 becoming a global pandemic – putting the humanity to peril. **Probably that has been the worst misuse of power using time as a weapon in recent history.**

(h) If the virus was a biological weapon unleashed on the world, as was being popularly and officially believed by many countries, many world leaders having said so on record, why was this aspect not dealt with top priority it deserved by the world authorities and leaders?

(i) If the virus originated in wet markets of China as was at least initially believed, why the same wet markets are again up and running so soon even when the virus is still causing havoc in the world? Suffering of billions in the world is no concern of China? How and why is the world silent about it despite international treaties like International Health Regulation, 2005 (IHR 2005) being in place?

(j) Why are the worst-affected powerful countries like the USA and India not asking and trying to find answers to fundamental questions in order to save their citizens from untold miseries rather than putting the onus of protecting self from the deadly virus on the poor common man?

And so on. Some of these and similar questions have been

asked by individuals, by distinguished people, by governments and leaders, but just for the sake of it. Nothing is being pursued or meant to be pursued. The questions have been left loosely hung in the air while the common man throughout the world continues to be under torture of the order one comes across in horror films.

WHO is not a group of a few individuals. It is a world body—what it does or doesn't, the whole world, all the member countries are responsible. So, what is happening through WHO amounts to the world ensuring its own torture. Just as through ICC, the world or at least the member countries have been ensuring being subjected to a massive fraud for over a decade. That sums us up, the people, howsoever smart we may consider ourselves to be. To appreciate it, we shall have to see beyond our nose, in larger perspective.

While there is so much trade and tourism amongst countries, a number of international groups and organisations including the United Nations exist, there is no sight of much cooperation among countries in dealing with the common enemy. How strange and inexplicable?

Continuation of cricket as a big-time crime for years showed that we were just big numbers, easily manoeuvred. As victims of COVID-19, men and women of flesh and blood, ordinary or the mighty and powerful, are now becoming just numbers and statistics; not human beings of value. There are no pretensions anymore. No one can be, and is, sure of surviving the pandemic. Man is being shown his place by nature, in case it is nature's doing after all. A more truthful and responsible world would have been better organised to deal with it much more effectively, would have responded quickly to the challenge and taken more timely and truthful actions to contain its spread and consequent loss of human lives and shattering of the world. More than these, only coming times will tell how the psyche of man has been affected. People dying and being buried or cremated without their near and dear ones by their side must have already been a big drain on survivors' emotions and sensitivities. A better cooperation among compassionate and truthful nations would have resulted in quicker and better solutions for all, both in terms of containment and treatment. We forget that the people freely pursuing falsehood won't be disciplined when the need arises. The inherent habit of pursuing false and accepting wrong is bound to damage one's overall character and weaken one's resolve considerably. A culture of total or large-scale distrust emerges that becomes self-defeating for all. It is here that the difference between a civilisation founded on truth and a civilisation founded on falsehood becomes too glaring. But, unfortunately, drowned under conceit, we are still not able to open our eyes and appreciate all this.

Losing the total sight of the key questions, the elite around the world got busy in eluding search of medicines and vaccines. The number of those infected and dying went on increasing. It was bewildering that no country or international organisation thought of giving any priority to address the key questions, answers to which could have saved the world from its calamitous state. The world got busy with statistics of COVID 19, in numbers, in curves, in projections, in peeks into peaks, and what not. It got busy in discussing and worrying about everything, making frantic efforts to deal with the crisis also, except in trying to find key answers. All this time, the hale and hearty—by hundreds of thousands—continued to drop dead around the world. It was too surreal. Like a Horror Show. Did the leaders running the world, million-dollar arms deals still being their priority, anticipate all this? Did they know how the spurious intellectuals and the masses will act and react? Or did they ensure that it all happened so? If someone thought I was talking through my hat, one could have a look at the link https://newsblaze.com/usnews/health/covid-19-no-vaccine-needed-there-is-already-a-cure_166305/. I came across this many days after having drafted above. Quoting Dr. Richard Bartlett, this says that a successful therapy to treat COVID-19 patients existed that had been used in some countries, but was not used in many other countries including the USA where the virus had created and was creating havoc. The author puts the blame on WHO. The write-up is not without some fallacies in it though. As if it was not enough, another much more explosive article was yet to surface telling us how the rogue capitalism controlled the medical world, at the cost of us - the people, the masses - https://healthimpactnews.com/2020/editors-of-the-lancet-and-the-new-england-journal-of-medicine-pharmaceutical-companies-are-so-financially-powerful-they-pressure-us-to-accept-papers/. One need not be a medical professional to understand how all throughout the world were being held to ransom through COVID-19. The unanswered questions and the slowly but surely surfacing revelations confirmed this.

India has been the centre of the global fraud called international cricket. And it is in this country that the battle against this magnificent fraud is being fought for the last 7 years. And it is this country whose media, authorities, and government have displayed unparalleled degradation and hypocrisy in joining hands for allowing the fraud to continue to prosper despite it being brought to their notice time and again over the last many years. It is this country whose top court also has been found wanting. No wonder that chaos has prevailed in this country in dealing with the crisis of COVID-19, at the cost of the common man; the same common man who had happily been celebrating a massive crime and fraud for years thinking why he should bother about darker side of something which was tantalising him. There were also many who were not celebrating being not interested in cricket, but they also remained unconcerned with what was going around them. This self-defeating culture of the country came to the fore. Petty politics prevailed over people's welfare as usual. Books can be written on the COVID-19 crisis and its handling in India, but here let us only see what happened and what all went wrong or defied logic, beyond scope of debates.

The pandemic ensured that the public and the masses were at the mercy of the establishment and the media as never before. What people required to help them was planning and farsightedness of the government and clarity in directives/ directions from the government and the authorities, along with transparency in dissemination of information as to what was happening, what was right and what was wrong. The media was supposed to act on behalf of the public and question the government and the authorities if and when they faltered.

If one was even a little bit objective in one's appreciation, one would straightaway realise that just the opposite happened, at least from March end till June end.

(a) The government and authorities continued changing policies, advices, and directives as men change shirts, a pliable media by their side. That resulted in utter confusion and chaos among the public; the latest at the time of writing these lines being government telling that no vaccine was likely to be ready for public use before 2021, intention to launch a vaccine on 15th August,

2020 having been announced by its top authority on the subject only a few days ago. At the end of 4 months of corona causing havoc in India, one was still not sure of anything about the virus except probably that soap and sanitizer destroyed the virus.

(b) That gave rise to circulation of hundreds of conflicting messages and videos on social media, issued by doctors and others, adding enormously to the confusion and misleading people no end.

(c) A sudden imposition of lockdown, the resulting miseries to millions, and then lifting of the lockdown and afterwards continuing relaxing restrictions just as the spread of infection and number of deaths went on increasing was more than baffling to anyone having the slightest common sense, but the Indian media at large was quite comfortable being by the side of the government.

(d) Lockdown was purportedly imposed to create the necessary testing and medical facilities to meet with the inevitable expected volume of infected patients, but nothing of the sort happened. There was chaos all around, especially in the big metropolitan cities, deaths being under-reported, patients having to run from pillar to post for the necessary medical facilities. The testing continued to be many times less than what was required for the population of India. All this is a matter of record.

(e) After a lot of pomp and show initially and self-patting of backs by the government, authorities, and the Indian media, suddenly 1,300 million Indians were left like orphans to fend for themselves by the governments. And the Indian media had found other issues like India-China stand-off, Vikas Dubey, etc., to keep the masses engaged, relegating corona to the sidelines when it was at its peak causing havoc.

(f) **The deceit by the authorities in India became too conspicuous when none other than the Prime Minister of India publicly congratulated his government saying they had saved lakhs (hundreds of thousands) of lives by timely lockdown and subsequent decisions and actions by them. To claim so, he compared the number of deaths from COVID-19 in India to the corresponding numbers in Europe, USA, or any random country as suited, rather than comparing with China or other neighbouring Asian countries.** I am not aware if anyone in the media or outside even questioned such an utter absurdity. The immunity of Indians to the virus and climate in India could never be compared with those in Europe, USA or any odd country, but could only be compared with neighbouring/other Asian countries. **Moreover, the boasting was done at a time when the ordeal was not yet over, rather was on the increase, poised to go totally out of control.** When the executive heads could make highly irresponsible statements and get away, who was there to question or stop the lesser authorities? To top it all, about the time the book going into print, in mid-August, 2020, India had the highest mortality per million among the surrounding Asian countries; and per day number of infections (> 60000) and deaths (900-1000) in India were the worst or one of the worst in the world.

The above brings out the very serious consequences of

continuing to accept the all-round degeneration for years and years. While thousands were dying, tens of thousands found themselves trapped to pay hospital bills running into lakhs of rupees, well beyond their means. Getting the necessary medical help became a nightmare for thousands in big cities or small towns. The agony and emotional pain of millions of family and friends of those infected probably can't be expressed in words. Many found themselves financially ruined. Even those uninfected and unaffected had been scared to the bones to live in constant mortal fear. Life had become too uncertain for anyone. Above all, the human sensitivity fell away considerably. In short, a chilling horror movie was running for months in the real life. Yet it was all business as usual for the authorities, the governments, the media, and the social media.

The man contracting the disease and/or losing business or job was the culprit. Our upbringing and the sermons we are subjected to throughout our lives, of late, a big number of preachers mushrooming on social media, also made us believe that we ourselves were responsible for our own ordeal, if we contracted the virus. Soon after the ordeal began, every one lost track of the basic questions, and got engaged only in self-preservation and survival. Everyone got busy in adapting to changed life, dancing to the tune of the medical fraternity and the authorities who never knew what they meant or what they were doing. This was evident from the way they went on changing advices/directives/goal posts. The authorities found themselves free to act whatever way they wanted, no one there to question them. Ad-hoc-ism became the order of the day in day-to-day administration, common man being at the receiving end. Approval of medicines, their exorbitant prices, claims of adverse side effects from them, their ineffectiveness in halting the march of *yamaraja*, etc., left many questions unanswered.

No one realised that for a country like India, with its population density, health infrastructure, and indiscipline, coronavirus just couldn't be allowed to enter the country. But the government slept and still then continued patting its back unashamedly in the initial few months till things went totally out of control. Even then the government never accepted how miserably it had failed the people of India, on the contrary, it continued gloating as mentioned above. It also continued diverting attention of people to other issues using the media and its propaganda machinery on social media.

Isn't mankind to blame itself for the situation it finds itself in today? Was it not weakening itself tremendously while acting immune to a massive proven and open international crime for seven long years? If the world had reacted 7 years earlier as it was expected to and it must have, fundamental corrections in human systems would have been necessitated and many would have been in place by now such that probably the world would have not been undergoing the present torture—that of its own doing. But, egotistic fool as man is, people continued celebrating their degradation thinking that why should they bother about the darker side of something that was giving them pleasure and kick; oblivious of the fact that cause and effect mattered, everything under the sun remained interconnected, that they were bound to pay a heavy price for their folly one day. Even today, undergoing so many miseries, we don't appear to have learnt any lessons. Both ICC and WHO are going about with their business as unashamedly as ever. That means the world is going on as it has been, not learning any lessons.

Even though a question is raging in the world whether

COVID-19 has been a natural or a man-made pandemic; in effect, it had to be dealt with as a natural disaster and all above will hold. When the mighty can combine to fool masses through cricket continuously for decades manipulating the human brain/mind and its limitations, one never knows what conspiracy at what level involving whom all is there, if any, behind the pandemic from COVID-19, its spread, and too conspicuous mismanagement. Hopefully, time will reveal the truth in this regard also, and hopefully, application of common sense would help us arrive at the truth sooner than later. It was through application of common sense alone that sitting at home, I could expose the deceit and fraud through international cricket years ago that has now become a foregone conclusion. Its continuation still makes the mankind all the more contemptible.

What we conveniently forgot was that the degradation of the magnitude evident in our cricket couldn't and didn't remain confined to only one pocket. It had to percolate to other pockets also. Has it not been utterly self-deceiving to expect the media having no credibility, and an establishment and judiciary acting blind to a massive fraud, to deliver truthfully in the interest of the people in routine? And when it mattered most? While the culprits like media and establishment continue scratching each other's back, the masses and, unfortunately, also the intellectuals continue being fooled, rather helplessly. More misinformation than information is the order of the day and the masses are being used as guinea pigs, while being given the impression all the time that they were being cared for a lot. The enormous human tragedy is being used by those in power to self-serve to the extent possible. It is too apparent in India where in public calamity and on dead bodies, leaders, both in centre and in states, are doing chest-beating. That was somewhat akin to setting a jungle on fire, and then telling the animals, escaping on their own, what great efforts had been made to save them.

As I give finishing touches to the contents of this book towards end July, 2020 and revise in mid-August, the picture in India as well as rest of the world is becoming gloomier both in statistics and sufferings of people; periodical claims of new scientific research and new medicines to fight the viral disease notwithstanding. The testing and test results for the disease have come under question. Qualified doctors are asking a number of pertinent questions of the authorities that remain unanswered. The statistics continue to be used by the Indian government to fool the public. For example, amidst all round chaos, the increase in recovery rate continues to be harped on and highlighted as an achievement by the Prime Minister of India and his officials, and some state Chief Ministers – something naturally bound to occur with time, if the disease is known to kill only a very limited percentage of those infected. The overall scenario remains creepy with the media and the world continuing to indulge in petty talk and non-issues as ever. The intellectuals have become habituated to their ordeal, forgetting the basic questions that remain unanswered. No one knows for sure how the virus is spreading or not spreading. The life remains as or even more uncertain than it was at the start of the scare months ago, no one even not infected today can be sure of being alive after a fortnight or so. Social media or media still continues to worry more about religion, politics, hollow words of wisdom, or individual egos – all comparatively mundane things!

We shall really help ourselves much if we realize how

we are at the receiving end all the time, being fooled round the clock by media, establishment, and those who matter. The big question is shall we? To do so, we shall have to rise above our petty mindedness, immediate self-interests and self-indulgence; shall have to find a way to free ourselves from the clutches of crooked media, sham preachers, and self-serving leaders. We shall have to shed political, religious, and all other bigotry. We shall have to unlearn a lot that we have been taught. Nothing will be easy. In fact, it will be far from easy.

We, ourselves, will have to strive for a new world order. A new world order where people are not just numbers driven like herds, at the mercy of a few rogues; but they, the vast majority, are men and women of substance, having free spirit, living lives of fulfilment. No special creature from Earth or from Mars will endeavour to do that for us.

The earlier we commence, the better it will be, especially for the younger generation. I do shudder to visualise what young ones must be going through; not only forced into confinements, but also living with a continuous fear of infection from coronavirus. They must think hard, freeing their minds from all sorts of conditioning, to appreciate and perceive what befell them and to chart a much superior world for themselves and their future generations. There won't be any short cuts.

Hiding behind veils for too long
Time came we had to wear the mask
How and where did we go wrong
Time for us all now to honestly ask.

□□□